Cunning Revenge

JANE BLYTHE

Acknowledgments

I'd like to thank everyone who played a part in bringing this story to life. Particularly my mom who is always there to share her thoughts and opinions with me. My wonderful cover designer Letitia who did an amazing job with this stunning cover. My fabulous editor Lisa for all the hard work she puts into polishing my work. My awesome team, Sophie, Robyn, and Clayr, without your help I'd never be able to run my street team. And my fantastic street team members who help share my books with every share, comment, and like!

And of course a big thank you to all of you, my readers! Without you I wouldn't be living my dreams of sharing the stories in my head with the world!

One

January 20th
10:45 P.M.

This lab was a lot more remote than the others on the list they'd been given.

High on a mountain top, deep in the forest, with nothing much surrounding it for miles.

If he was running a secret lab to try to perfect a formula that turned people into super soldiers, then this was exactly the kind of place Voodoo would choose.

There was every chance that they might find real intel there. Possibly even the man he and his team sought, and yet ...

The feeling of death hung in the air.

Before he'd signed up for the experimental drug program eleven years ago, he'd never thought all that much about death. Of course, he'd been special forces before joining the program, but that only meant he'd thought about the fact that one day he might go out on an op and never return. He'd lost people he cared about, killed plenty of people, some with a weapon, some with his own two hands. But he had never considered the actual act of dying.

It has always just been something that happened. Everyone died, everything died. Any living being, be they human, animal, or plant was going to die at some point. It was a given. Something to be feared, sure, for many it was. Something that might be painful or even horrific, would unfortunately be the case for many.

Now, he felt death in a way he hadn't expected. It was weird. His ability to heal was something that wasn't natural. Voodoo had even spoken to Whitney Daley about it and gotten an answer he wasn't expecting.

He was never supposed to be able to heal others the way he could.

According to Whitney, the former child genius who had created the original version of the drug before she was sold by her parents to Dr. Ridge Gardner when she was only ten years old, the variation of the drug he'd been given was supposed to bolster his own ability to heal himself. Which it had, he'd seen himself come back from injuries he shouldn't have, watching as his skin, flesh, and bone all but repaired themselves before his very eyes.

But he could heal others as well. Voodoo had no idea how it worked, or how he did it, and while he'd hoped Whitney might be able to explain it, she hadn't. She promised that when this was all over, when Dr. Gardner, the man who had tortured all of them in his attempts to gain money, power, and respect for himself, had suffered and died, she would take samples of his blood and study it.

Now, as he and his team surveyed the small complex spread out before them, he could sense death hanging heavily in the air. It was hard to explain to anyone else just what it felt like. Dragon could smell death, Blade would be able to hear the moment a person's heart stopped beating, their lungs no longer inflating, and Lion would be able to see that a chest no longer rose and fell from a great distance.

None of them could *feel* it, though.

"What is it?" Steel asked, and Voodoo cast their team leader a glance.

"Death," he said simply.

"You think some of the experiments recently died?" Thunder asked.

"Maybe," he replied, unable to properly explain that the death he was feeling was on a wider scale than just a couple of dead people who were unlucky enough to either be taken by Dr. Gardner or sign up for a program without understanding the magnitude of it.

Just because Dr. Gardner had lost access to the military after they were able to break free of their glass prison after three years being held captive and experimented on, didn't mean he had stopped his work.

If anything, the scientist had doubled down.

Now he might operate in the shadows, hidden labs, and secret experiments, but he wouldn't stop until he achieved everything he wanted.

"There's no way he could know that we found out about this place," Blade said with more confidence than Voodoo could muster. "We only found Whitney and Terry Richards three days ago, only got access to Richards' phone and this location two days ago. All we did was plan things out, get on a plane, and come here. According to Whitney, Richards had cleared his responsibilities so he could spend some time breaking her, readying her to return to her position, so there's no reason to think that Dr. Gardner suspects his head of security is dead."

"Unless we tripped some sort of sensors as we approached," Lion suggested.

Obviously, their enhancements gave them an advantage in every situation. All their bodies were more resistant to temperature changes, either hot or cold, they could go longer without eating or drinking, they could handle operating with little sleep. They healed well, were more tolerant of pain, and with their individual skills, they were a tough opponent to beat.

But they weren't impervious to making mistakes, and there was every chance a sensor they had missed had alerted the people in the secret lab to kill the current batch of experiments rather than allow them to fall into anyone else's hands.

"Only one way to find out," Steel said as he nodded at the building standing before them.

It was dark and silent, and while it was late, it wasn't late enough that everyone would necessarily be in bed asleep. Especially depending on whether the scientists working here were here voluntarily or had been coerced or outright abducted like Whitney had been. Not that there was any reason to believe that anyone other than the young woman who was now safely tucked in Blade's bedroom back at their home had been forced into a position of working for the crazed scientist.

Like the well-oiled machine that they were, the six of them began to move without the need to communicate verbally. It wasn't that they could necessarily read one another's minds and therefore knew that they were all on the same page, it was more that they had been together for so long, lived in such close quarters, learned to depend on nobody but each other, that led to them having a kind of sixth sense when it came to the members of their team.

No one fired at them as they slunk through the trees, and there were no shouts or anything from inside the building.

When Blade gave a quick shake of his head to indicate that he couldn't hear anything, Voodoo assumed that like the previous lab they'd searched, which had wound up exploding around them, almost killing the six of them and Rose Gardner and Cassandra Charleston, a white noise generator was running that messed with Blade's ability to hear.

Dragon's nostrils flared, and from the look in his unusual violet eyes, it was clear that the man could smell the death that Voodoo felt oppressively pressing down around him. Whoever had been there had died. Recently. Meaning the idea that they'd set off a sensor of some sort was a viable possibility.

With all of them wearing night vision goggles, Lion being the only exception, his enhanced vision worked perfectly well in the dark, they didn't need to flip on any lights as Steel picked the lock, and they all stepped inside the quiet building.

If he'd had any doubts, which he hadn't after ten years of living with his abilities, he didn't have to understand them to trust them, Voodoo knew he'd been right.

Death clung to this place like a second skin.

Moving as one, they worked their way past several labs that almost looked as though they had been abandoned in a hurry. As they continued deeper into the large building, they found a living room with a TV still turned on but put on mute, and then a kitchen with the dishwasher still open and some dirty plates piled up beside the sink. There was even a couple left sitting on the large table dominating one wall of the room.

They kept going, all hoping they'd find someone alive, someone who could give them intel that Whitney no longer had access to, had never truly had access to since she was there as what basically amounted to a slave. Of course, they'd all hoped that Dr. Gardner himself might be there, but at the very least they wanted someone who could give them the address of the scientist's home so they could end this—end him—once and for all.

As they kept moving, they found a room lined with glass cages so reminiscent of the one he'd been trapped in for three long years that Voodoo had a visceral reaction to it.

One that passed quickly when he saw them.

Bodies.

Lying on the floor of each of the cells.

People like him, like his team, dead.

Killed right while he and his team were outside.

~

January 20th
10:45 P.M.

Flashing red lights lit the otherwise dark room.

Someone was coming.

That couldn't be a good thing. Nothing in this place was a good thing.

Pain.

It had become normal for her to the point that while Indigo Yates registered it, it felt distant, dull, and almost disconnected from her.

How long had she been there now?

Days?

Weeks?

Couldn't be months. Could it?

Honestly, she wasn't even sure anymore. Kept in a glass cage, no windows, no glimpses at the outdoors, it was hard to mark the passage of time. Other people were there, but the bulletproof glass cages were mostly soundproofed, and besides that, she'd learned pretty quickly that attempting to communicate was only going to wind up with more pain.

Tugging at the collar on her neck as she lay on the table she'd been placed on, she wished that …

She didn't even know anymore.

Wished for an end to her suffering.

Wished for rescue.

Wished for solace.

Wished for someone who would actually care about her.

Maybe the reason she was so good at enduring the pain they kept heaping upon her was because she was an old hat at it. Pain had been part of her life for as long as she could remember. It had filled her childhood as her dad beat on her every chance he had. Some of her foster families had beat on her too. Foster dads, or foster moms, or sometimes even foster siblings.

Her first boyfriend had put his hands on her as well, although rather than hit her, he liked to wrap those long fingers of his around her neck and squeeze until she could no longer draw in air and was sure she was going to die.

It was why when she'd met her husband—*ex*-husband now—the fact that he'd been sweet and gentle had her falling hard and fast. He'd wound up hurting her, too, just not with his fists. Still cheating on her, kicking her out of their home and sending her divorce papers hurt just as badly.

Maybe it was because of a lifetime of pain that she lay where she was for a long moment after she knew she needed to move.

If something was happening, it could be her chance. Chance at what she didn't even know. Living, dying, surviving to see another day, even if that day would be filled with nothing but darkness and horrors.

"Move," she ordered herself. No matter how much Indigo might find the idea of death appealing, after a lifetime of suffering, who wouldn't find the notion of peace appealing, she had to take advantage of this opportunity while it existed.

Surviving childhood abuse of every kind you could think of, then abuse at the hands of a partner, had made her determined and resource-ful. It had deadened her somewhat to the harsher realities of life, and she was now pretty sure that was all that was keeping her alive.

This was supposed to be a chance to rebuild her life. She'd been homeless ever since her husband kicked her out. So when someone came around to the shelters, offering a chance at good money just for signing up to be part of an experimental drug program, why wouldn't she say yes?

How could she have known these people were really sadistic psychopaths, who intended to inject her with a drug that had made her feel like her blood had been set on fire? That they would put a shock collar around her neck and use it to enforce her compliance? That they would keep her in a cage, and refuse to let her out unless it was to experiment on her some more? That the drug filled her with a rage that was hard to contain, while simultaneously urging her to end her own suffering by taking her life?

Or that it somehow gave her an enhanced tolerance for pain that these people seemed to enjoy exploiting.

Now, though, she had to decide if she was going to fight or give up, and even though she badly wanted to give up, she pushed herself up into a sitting position and then looked around.

Around her, she could hear shouts, panic, and even the muffled pops that told her someone was shooting. Whether they were shooting at one another or whoever had set off the red flashing light that indicated that someone was coming, she had no idea.

Didn't care either.

She certainly wasn't going to sit around and wait to find out.

Ignoring the heaviness in her leg, the stiffness in the rest of her body, Indigo drew in a deep breath and then threw herself off the table in the lab.

Agony exploded through her battered body. Whatever had been in that drug she'd been given didn't remove her ability to feel pain, it was more like it dulled it really quickly, so instead of the excruciating agony assaulting her, stealing her ability to think, to breathe, possibly even pushing her into unconsciousness, it slowly seeped out of her system.

Knowing she'd already wasted more time than she should have,

Indigo lifted her head from the cool linoleum floor. There was still shouting going on, more pops that meant more people were dying, but so far, nobody had come in here.

That wouldn't last.

She'd been left because they'd struck her leg with a hammer, breaking the bones in the lower half, and splitting the skin open in the process. In the morning, they'd come back to see how she was doing, and probably give her needle and thread to stitch up the wound. That was a favorite game of theirs, and it wasn't just the obvious horrors of having to stitch yourself up that she hated, it was the fact that she wasn't kept in clean conditions.

Infection was a given, and it was currently ravaging her body from a wound inflicted a couple of days ago.

Nausea had bile burning her throat as she scanned the room, her gaze landing on a supply cupboard she was pretty sure she could squeeze inside. Hiding felt cowardly, but one thing she'd learned as a small child was that pride meant nothing when it came to self-preservation.

So she planted her palms on the floor and dragged herself toward it.

It was every bit the hell she'd been expecting it to be. Pain tore through her, even if it faded faster than it would have a couple of months ago. Her arms were weak and shaky, barely able to keep pulling her onward.

At least the cold floor felt nice against her overheated skin.

When she reached the cabinet, Indigo wasn't sure she had the strength left in her body to endure standing up to reach the handle, but had no other choice.

Well, there was, but lying there and waiting to be found, possibly shot, wasn't on the table.

So once again she planted her palms on the cabinet, not the floor this time, and pushed up. Clamping her teeth together, she held in the howl of pain as she jostled her leg, but still a pitiful whimper escaped.

Vision blurry, sweat dripping down her skin as infection caused fever pushed her temperature up, she somehow managed to grab the handle and open the cabinet. Then she dropped, whimpered again at the pain, and climbed inside, tucking herself into the bottom shelf, which was just big enough to hold her small frame.

No sooner had she pulled the door closed behind her, latching it into place, than she heard footsteps and voices.

"She's not in here," one of the guards said.

"Probably put her back in her cell and shot her," another said, so matter-of-factly that Indigo shivered, and this time it had nothing to do with the fever.

"That's all of them then," the first man said, and she assumed he meant that all the other prisoners, the experiments as they were called, had been killed.

Surely they'd check her cell.

Find it was empty.

Realize she was still alive somewhere in the facility and look for her.

But instead, she heard the pop of a gun and the sound of a body thudding down onto the floor. The sound was close, right outside her hiding place, inside the room. Which meant that one of the guards had just shot the other.

What did that mean?

Were they all going to die?

Was Dr. Gardner so paranoid that the instructions to his employees were to commit suicide rather than risk getting captured?

Indigo got her answer a moment later when another pop and another thud indicated the second guard had also just died.

Did that mean whoever had set off the silent alarm were the good guys? Someone after Dr. Gardner, determined to shut down him and his program?

She could only hope that might be true, but the truth was hope had long since died inside her, and as she curled tighter into a ball, unconsciousness lapping at the edges of her mind, all Indigo expected to come her way was more suffering.

January 20th
11:09 P.M.

"Another two here," Lion called out from a little further down the room.

They were making their way through the building, counting off the dead as they went and snapping photographs of their faces. Not to be morbid, but because they would need to run each person they found here by Whitney to see if she recognized any as previous prisoners, or other scientists or guards she had worked with at the other facilities.

Most of the people on the original list she'd given them when Blade first brought her home with him had yet to be located. Some of the guards had been the men Blade killed when he found them searching for Whitney in the mountains before he brought her home. A couple of others had passed away from illnesses, but the vast majority were still out there.

Or right in here.

Since Whitney had blown up Dr. Gardner's main lab, forcing him to move to another temporary lab, it would make sense that he'd brought all his workers with him. While they were yet to find the doctor himself, Voodoo was sure most of the people now lying dead, scattered about the building, would be recognized by Whitney.

"It's like someone went around executing all of them," Steel muttered as he stood looking into another of the glass-enclosed cages so reminiscent of the one they'd been locked inside, only much smaller.

"Rather have them dead than found," Blade said softly.

Voodoo agreed. It was killing him seeing so many dead bodies. So many lives cut ruthlessly short.

Even before he signed up for the program that had forever changed him and his life, he'd been a healer. As far back as he could remember, he'd always grieved hard for any living thing that died. From animals run over on the road, to birds caught by local cats, to bugs sprayed needlessly with poison because people didn't understand them. He'd been his team's medic before joining up with these guys when they all took part in the experimental drug program.

While he could be as ruthless as his teammates when the situation called for it, death broke off a tiny piece of his soul each time he encountered it.

"Killed everyone, not just their victims," Thunder added as he came to a stop by Lion at a door to another room down the end of the large space they were in.

"Didn't want anyone talking, employees as well," Blade said.

So far, they had counted five dead people—men and women, older and younger, a range of ethnicities—inside the glass cages. The scientists had obviously been rounded up into a single room, likely believing they would be escorted out because there were no signs of a struggle. Instead, the guards must have killed all twelve of them because their bodies lay in a pile.

The guards were likewise dead. Six of them were killed with bullets to the back of the head, like one person had been tasked with making sure nobody walked out of this building alive should it be discovered.

"This one is the only one with a wound to his temple," Steel noted as they all joined Lion and Thunder by what appeared to be an examination room.

"Probably killed his colleague then himself," Thunder said. "Probably the one in charge. Had been given his orders in advance and followed them to the letter."

There were no disagreements from any of them because that was likely exactly what had happened. The scientists didn't appear to have known their fate in advance, maybe the other guards hadn't either, but regardless, this entire op had turned out to be a waste.

Of course, they'd search for intel, maybe find something to bring home to Whitney, who might be able to figure something out based on the vials and formulas covering the walls and stacked in the fridge of one of the rooms they'd been in earlier. But in the end, that wasn't what they wanted.

Wasn't what *any* of them wanted.

They all wanted Dr. Gardner to suffer and die for everything he'd put them all through. The man's little sister Rose, who they'd originally abducted in an attempt to lure Dr. Gardner into a trap, but who had shown them all she was stronger than they'd realized. They'd learned she had been abused her entire childhood by her brother, and she had quickly joined their side and was now dating Steel. Cassandra Charleston, sister of another Prey Security team had won over Dragon from the moment she came to stay with them while her family was in danger. She'd left when she realized they had plans to go after an innocent, but after being dragged unwittingly into the mess by Whitney Daley, she'd found her way back to Dragon, and the two of them were together. Whitney was now with Blade, and they knew that while she had been the one to initially create the original version of the drug, she'd only been ten when she'd been bought by the scientist and kept as his slave for the last twelve years.

Then there were him and his team. Lied to about the program they signed up for, never warned about the side effects, kept prisoner for three years, and experimented on over and over again. Then forced to live the last seven years of their lives in hiding from a man whose name they didn't even know at the time.

Yeah, they all had reason enough to want Dr. Gardner dead and finding one of his labs but not having anyone alive to tell them anything that could lead them to him sucked majorly.

"Maybe we should fly Whitney out here," Steel suggested, and Blade immediately bristled.

"She's been through enough. I don't want her out here, seeing all of this. Bad enough we have to send her photos of people with bullet holes in their heads to see if she can ID them. I don't want her here in person."

"Would be easier than—"

"Wait," Dragon hissed, cutting Thunder off, his nostrils flaring like he'd just caught a scent.

The tension in the room ratcheted up several notches.

When Dragon's gaze began to roam the room they were standing outside of, everyone aimed their weapons at it, catching on that what he'd scented was another person, and they were close.

There was only one place in the room where Voodoo thought anyone might be hiding, and that was the supply cabinet on the other side of the room.

Taking a step toward it, he knew his team would have his back, whoever was in there wasn't getting away. As he moved across the linoleum floor on feet that had long ago learned to step without making a sound, Voodoo noted a few smears of blood on the floor, and as he reached the cabinet, he saw there were smears of blood on it too.

Knowing the others would react instantaneously if the person Dragon had scented turned out to be a threat, he reached out and turned the handle of the cabinet door.

As soon as he did, the door swung open, and a small body tumbled out.

Immediately, he knew it was no threat. It was a woman, long dark hair hung in matted chunks down a pale back, dressed only in a pair of white cotton panties and a simple white cotton bra. Bloody gashes in various stages of healing crisscrossed her legs and lower abdomen, and her leg ...

"Damn," he muttered as he quickly dropped to his knees.

"Voodoo?" Steel asked.

"Not a threat, she's ... one of us," he said, somewhat in awe, because every single other person who had gone through the experimental drug trial didn't survive it, according to Dr. Gardner himself, so there was no need to doubt that intel was correct.

Yet here she was.

A beautiful woman, her heart beating, her lungs inhaling and exhaling, alive, and yet the cuts on her body and the broken leg told him that she had already been given the drugs. Some of the wounds looked several weeks old, so she hadn't just been injected within the last couple of days.

"One of us?" Steel asked, and he felt the others step up behind him as he carefully laid the woman out so he could better examine her.

"Not a guard, not a scientist, so she has to be one of us," he replied as he glared at the shock collar around her neck, then nudged it out of the way so he could press his fingertips to the unconscious woman's throat to check her pulse. It was thready, and her skin was hot to the touch. Didn't take any training to figure out why when he noted three of her wounds were enflamed and oozing pus.

Maybe she hadn't succumbed to the drug's side effects, but without medical treatment, this woman would likely die from infected wounds.

"Her leg," Lion said softly.

"Broken," he said simply.

"Why the hell would they do that to her?" Blade raged.

"Probably something to do with whatever her enhanced skill is," he replied as he began to run his hands up and down her body, avoiding her broken leg, to check for any other injuries he needed to be concerned about.

"We have a problem," Dragon announced.

"What?" Steel demanded.

"Someone just started a fire."

~

January 20th

11:18 P.M.

Something warm tickled inside her.

Weird feeling.

Like a tentacle of something she couldn't describe curling around her injuries and soothing them somehow.

Healing them?

No, that couldn't be right.

Wasn't even possible.

Yet the warmth was pleasant, kind of like how Indigo would imagine it felt to be wrapped up in a sunbeam.

"We have to get out of here," a voice spoke. A male voice, but one she didn't recognize, and she was pretty good at remembering voices.

"Wait. I have to make sure moving her isn't going to do more damage," another man spoke. This one was closer, and as she became more aware of her surroundings, she realized that he was the source of the odd feeling, and he was touching her.

No one touched her.

At least without her express permission, and that was rare. Even her ex-husband had known better than to casually put his hands on her. She wasn't a normal woman. When you lived through almost an entire lifetime of people hurting you, you learned pretty quickly that it was better to be safe than sorry, and she'd learned to accept herself the way she was.

Now someone was touching her.

Someone she didn't know, had never seen, and had no idea of their intentions.

Unacceptable.

Didn't matter that she was weak, that infection had stolen most of her strength, and that her entire body felt heavy, she had to fight.

Had to try to save herself.

Summoning the last of her reserves, Indigo opened her eyes to find not one, not two, but six large men, dressed all in black, gathered around her.

If she had any energy left to panic, she would, but given that she didn't, she just jerked her body out of the hold of the man kneeling at her side. Well, she tried to. But as she tried to pull away, his hold tightened, not enough to hurt, or maybe it was, and she just didn't register it, but she sensed he was doing his best not to hurt her.

"Shh, honey, don't panic, everything is okay now," he said, his voice soothing, calming, comforting in a way she never would have expected.

No one made her feel the way this man did, and she didn't even know who he was.

"We're going to get you out of here," another man spoke, the one she'd heard first. He was standing beside the kneeling man, and he had an air of authority about him that told her he was the one in charge.

Get her out of here?

As in, she was being rescued? Or as in, she was being moved to a new location?

While she had no evidence to support this, something about these men made her feel like they weren't enemies. More, like they were almost friends. But they weren't her friends, she had no idea who they were or why they were there, so she wasn't going to blindly put her faith in them. That would be both stupid and suicidal.

"I'm Voodoo," the kneeling man told her, his voice still soft, unhurried, even though she felt an urgency in the room she couldn't understand. "That's Steel." He nodded at the man she had decided was their leader. "Blade, Thunder, Lion, and Dragon." With each name, he nodded at one of the men, but they were all in black, all wearing night vision goggles, except for one of them, so it was hard to keep a name with a person.

That was when it clicked.

One of the men wasn't wearing night vision goggles.

There was only one reason you would break into a supposedly secure lab facility—and that was what they'd done because they were all armed—and not wear something that would help you to see unless you didn't need its help.

Was it possible?

"Can you tell me your name, honey?" Voodoo asked.

"You have minutes, five of them, then we're out of here," Steel said, his voice harsh, but she didn't feel like that anger was directed at her, so Indigo forced herself not to stiffen.

"Indigo," she whispered. Her throat was dry, and her lips cracked, she was still way too hot, but tentative hope fluttered to life inside her.

She was doing her best to stamp it out because hope had no place in her world. "You ... you're like me," she murmured.

How was that even possible?

As far as she was aware, no one survived the drugs. At least no one had survived them in the months she'd been kept there. People came and went. Usually lasting little more than a few days at the most. Since they all lived in glass cages side by side, she knew they were either consumed with a rage that led to them attacking the guards and getting themselves killed, or they took their own lives. She'd watched in horror as one woman ran her head into the one concrete wall of their cells repeatedly until she died, watched others hang themselves, while some slit their wrists.

But these men were there, alive, functioning, and just like her. Indigo wasn't really sure exactly how she knew, it was deeper than the warmth inside her, or the lack of night vision goggles on the one man, somehow, she just ... knew.

"Yeah, honey, we're like you," Voodoo told her, and when he moved his hands from where they'd been pressed on her legs, she almost cried out at the loss.

Somehow, she kept it in, chewing on her bottom lip to do so. These men might be like her, but she wasn't sure what that meant. They'd broken in there, but she didn't know why. Were they looking for Dr. Gardner? If they were, they'd be disappointed because he wasn't there. He came and went, but he never stayed long. Usually just came and yelled at everyone, complained that his drugs still weren't working, raged about someone called Whitney betraying him, and then left again in a huff.

"How?" she asked. She needed to understand how they lived, even though everyone else didn't. How *she* lived when everyone else didn't.

Something softened in the man's stance, although without being able to see his eyes, it was hard to say what exactly, and Voodoo ran a hand over her dirty, matted hair. "We'll tell you all about it later, but right now, we need to get you out of here. We kind of have a situation."

"A situation?" Maybe some of the guards were still alive. No, that didn't make sense, she remembered one of the guards telling another that everyone was dead before she heard two gunshots.

"Fire," one of the men from near the door, she thought he might have been the one Voodoo introduced as Dragon, told her. "And at least half a dozen men. Could be more. It's hard to tell when the smell of death is so strong."

"They're probably thinking that the fire will flush us out," another of the guys said.

"Must have been nearby, moved in once they thought they had us trapped," someone else said.

"Our five minutes is up," Steel announced.

"It's not, it's only been three," Voodoo countered.

"Then consider those minutes lost. We need to move," Steel ordered.

"No," she said, surprised by the strength in her tone. There was no way she was going to be able to walk on her own, and if more guards were out there, waiting to just pick them off as soon as they left, the men had a better chance of making it out without her. "Leave me."

"Not happening," Voodoo said with a ferocity that surprised her. "We don't leave a team member behind."

"But I'm not a member of your team," she reminded him. They didn't know her, she should mean nothing to them. They were the same, but that didn't make them a team.

"You're one of us," Voodoo said simply, like that explained everything.

Only it didn't to her. Maybe that could be attributed to the fact that her head was pounding, and her body too hot, her skin too tight, and she felt woozy and disconnected. Or maybe it could be attributed to the fact that she'd never had a team. It had always been her against the world, and she wasn't used to anyone, let alone strangers, being willing to put their lives on the line for her.

"Don't want you to die because of me," she whispered, begging him to understand. Her life wasn't worth anything. No one would miss her. She had no family, no friends, no job, and she'd been homeless when she took this opportunity. While she might not fully understand who these men were or how they functioned as they did, it was clear they were a team and they cared about one another.

It was better for her to die than for them.

"No one is dying," Voodoo assured her, but she didn't believe him. "Trust me, I'm a healer, it's who I am, it's what I do. Steel, you guys go, clear the way out, I'll get her ready to move, and we'll meet you outside."

Steel hesitated for barely a second before nodding. And then without another word, the five other men trailed out of the room, leaving her alone with Voodoo.

For once, Indigo wasn't afraid of someone causing her physical pain, but while he didn't know it, Voodoo had the ability to break her in a different way. They were the same, both altered, and he was putting his life on the line to try to save her. No one had ever done that for her before.

CHAPTER

Three

"You should have gone with them, should have left me behind," Indigo said softly from beneath him as her eyes drifted closed.

That she was so quick to dismiss the value of her own life told him that whatever this woman had been through had been rough, made her lose her self-worth.

She'd get it back. He'd insist on it.

Whether she agreed or not, Indigo was one of them, and they didn't leave anyone behind. Didn't matter that they'd known her for less than ten minutes. If she had been genetically enhanced with Dr. Gardner's experimental drugs, then she had just gotten herself a readymade family.

Because that's what he and his team were, a family. They might have been brought together by a drug trial none of them had fully understood, but those bonds that had been forged were for life. Even after Dr. Gardner was eliminated as a threat, and Voodoo had zero doubt that they would eventually catch the man, and his machinations would catch up with him, he couldn't see himself ever moving away from the Gothic mansion they shared.

The men of Delta Team—and now Rose, Cassandra, and Whitney, Indigo as well—were as much his family as the parents who had raised him. Well birthed him and handed him off to a nanny to raise, and then to his own devices once they decided he was old enough to take care of himself.

Hearing Indigo so easily accept that she would be worthless enough not to matter had something stirring to life inside him. Rage, but of a different kind than the one he was used to as a side effect of the drugs he'd been given.

"Stop saying that," he snapped at her, making her body flinch even as her eyes stayed closed. "And don't pass out on me again. I am not leaving you behind, and I am not letting you die."

Slowly—oh so slowly—those eyes of hers opened, beautiful brown orbs, shimmering with unshed tears. "Think it might already be too late," she murmured. "Been sick for a while now. They don't care. Make me keep doing it." One of her hands gestured vaguely at the wounds littering her body before dropping back down to the floor.

"What's your enhancement?" he asked as he rifled through his med kit and found bandages and antibiotic cream.

"Can endure pain. Weird, like it hits me hard but then fades so quickly."

"They made you do this to yourself," he said as he slathered on the cream to the worst of her wounds and then began to wrap them. He couldn't do anything for her broken leg right now, and she'd need more heavy-duty antibiotics once he got her someplace safe, but the cream would at least help for now.

"How did you know?"

"Because Dr. Gardner's sister is with us and he made her do the same thing, only without the experimental drugs in her system," he explained. This woman was one of them, and she was coming back home with them, so that meant she was entitled to every bit of intel they had.

"Didn't know he had a sister. He is angry with someone called Whitney, though. He thinks she betrayed him, and she should be here to help him with the drugs."

"He's right, Whitney did betray him," he told her as he yanked out a spare T-shirt and pants from his pack. It was all he had in there, not really enough to protect her from the elements, although he assumed she had the same ability to better handle hot and cold that he and his team did.

"You know who she is?"

"I'll explain everything later, I promise. Right now, I need to get you out of here. I'm going to sit you up, put this on you," he told her as he slipped an arm around her shoulders.

"Won't hurt much," she assured him. "Never does. What can you do?"

"Healing. I heal people," he replied as he lifted her off the ground and slipped the T-shirt over her shoulders. She winced at first, but quickly relaxed against him as he dressed her.

"The warmth?" she asked.

"Warmth?"

"You don't know how it works?" When he shook his head, she continued. "It felt like warmth curling around inside me. Kind of like getting hugged by a sunbeam."

"Never heard it explained like that." It was an accurate description, though, and kind of what he felt when his body healed itself.

Once he had her dressed, Voodoo pulled his pack back on and then stood. Reaching down to pick her up, he paused, his gaze locked on the shock collar, unwanted memories of how he'd once worn one and it had been used to control him assaulting his mind.

"This has to go," he muttered, scanning the room for something he could use to break it off. Indigo watched him as he found a scalpel and used the metal instrument to twist into the locking mechanism at the back, causing the collar to fall off. Then he was moving again, scooping Indigo into his arms. She whimpered at the movement, but again the tension quickly left her body, and she sagged into him.

"Don't want you to get hurt because of me, Voodoo," she murmured.

"No one is dying today, honey. No one is getting hurt. And no one is going to hurt you ever again," he vowed, surprised by just how seriously he meant it. When he and his team had been in the same position as Indigo had, they'd been together, had each other. Indigo had gone through it alone and that ate at him.

"Don't believe you," she whispered, and a weariness to her tone told him it wasn't just because of what had happened to her at Dr. Gardner's hands.

There was no time to convince her, though. The smell of smoke was strong enough now that he could smell it, and the sound of bullets began to whiz through the air as he tucked Indigo close and headed back out into the hall.

Getting her safely out was his priority number one, then he could work on showing her what it meant to be part of a family. It was a lesson he himself had to learn when he joined the military and, for the first time ever, had people in his life who had his back rather than just attempting to control him and mold him into the image they had of what their child should be like.

Out in the hall, Voodoo found it clear, so he made his way to the opposite side of the building from the one they'd entered to avoid the smoke. He could hear the others firing their weapons, no doubt picking off the guards one by one. Between their training, experience, and their enhanced skills, they weren't an easy opponent to beat, even for people who thought they understood their abilities.

If the men even realized who they were up against.

"Moving out with Indigo," he said into his comms unit, although he knew Blade, with his enhanced hearing, would hear him without it, had probably been half listening to his entire conversation with the woman only half conscious in his arms.

"Take her out the side entrance, they're mostly concentrated at the main door. We've already picked off half of them, but they have some training and are making sure to stay out of range after we took out the first few. We'll keep them distracted here while you get Indigo out," Steel told him.

Adjusting his position, he headed for the small side entrance they'd noted as they surveyed the building. It was quieter there, slightly away from the gunshots, but he knew that as soon as he stepped out of this building, they were in danger. Carrying Indigo put him at a disadvantage. She was in no condition to assist in her own rescue, and even if she was physically healthier, he had no idea if she had any training.

Locating the door, he unlatched it and pushed it open. Nothing seemed to move out there. While he might not have Blade's ability to hear, Dragon's ability to smell, or Lion's to see, he still had several years as a special forces' operator, then a decade working and training with Delta Team, so he had learned to sense the presence of another person.

Sensing nothing, he stepped out into the night. It was an hour's hike back to the vehicle, and to get to it, he'd have to either circle around to the side of the building where the guards were, or he would have to hike out into the forest and then double back. Neither option was appealing when he had a small, trembling woman racked with fever in his arms.

"More coming in, Voodoo," Steel's voice came through the comms.

"Need me to come help?" It was the last thing he wanted to do because it would mean leaving Indigo alone, and she couldn't protect herself, couldn't even hold her head up. But he also couldn't abandon his team.

"Focus on Indigo," Steel replied. "But watch your back. These guys are like cockroaches, they keep coming and coming."

"Noted."

This meant he was on his own, no backup, nothing but a woman who had been willing to sacrifice herself to give him a better chance at living. No way was he allowing anything to happen to her, which meant he would do whatever it took to ensure he got Indigo safely out of these woods.

~

January 21st
    12:34 A.M.

Suspended halfway between awake and asleep.

That's how Indigo felt as she bounced gently against Voodoo's chest with each running step the man took.

If she were anyone else, she would likely be in excruciating pain with her broken leg jostled. It was a fresh break, made just hours before the flashing red light alerted them all that someone was coming, and Voodoo and his team showed up. The cuts littering her body were older, but since some were red and enflamed, filled with infection, they should hurt as well.

Instead, all she felt was the distant echo of pain, too far away for it to affect her.

Too bad it wasn't the same thing with the fever ravaging her system.

The enhancements done to her system allowed her to tolerate heat and cold, go longer without food and water, and function well on little to no sleep. They also made her nearly impervious to pain. If she had to, she could stand on her broken leg right now and walk on it provided it could support her. She wouldn't be slowed down by pain, although those first couple of steps would be hell. It would only be the physical limitations of an injury that would hold her back, although her body healed much faster than it should.

Somewhere around them, far too close for her liking, Indigo heard gunshots. More of Dr. Gardner's guards were fighting against Voodoo's teammates.

What if something happened to one of them? Voodoo should be there with them, helping them, not worrying about getting her to safety. There was no one to care if she lived or died, but he had at least five men who would grieve his loss.

"Put me down," she mumbled, trying to lift her head from his shoulder and finding it much harder than it should be.

"No." Voodoo didn't elaborate, just offered that one word, said with a finality that indicated arguing was pointless.

But it wasn't pointless if it meant this man got to live.

Honestly, Indigo didn't really care if she died. She'd fight. That was ingrained in her from birth, but fighting was exhausting, especially when you were doing it all alone. It would be nice not to have to fight all the time, for everything, even if that meant the only way she found peace was in death.

"Leave me behind," she insisted. "Not too late for you to go back and join your team."

"What part of no don't you get?" he asked as he continued to run with her in his arms like she weighed nothing. He wasn't even winded, and she had no idea how long it had been since she passed out in the lab.

"Not worth risking your life to save mine," she whispered, being completely honest. As she tilted her head a little, she could make out Voodoo's profile in the thin light of the moon. Even with the night vision goggles making it a little disjointed, it was a nice profile with a chiseled jaw and high cheekbones, he was handsome. She liked his lips, too. They looked like they'd be nice to kiss.

The thought caught her by surprise. She usually didn't waste time thinking about kissing men. After all, what man would want to kiss her? Even her own husband used to tell her often how lucky she was that with everything she'd been through as a child, a man like him was still willing to marry her.

Damaged. That's what he always called her. Damaged goods.

People who were damaged goods didn't deserve affection, tenderness, or love.

"Going to pretend you didn't say that, but we'll address that thinking when we get home," he informed her as more gunshots peppered through the night.

Would it be worth reminding him that she didn't have a home? Hadn't ever really, given that the one she thought she was building with her ex turned out to be a sham.

"They're shooting at your friends," she reminded him. It was getting increasingly harder to keep her eyes open, but she knew she needed to convince Voodoo that leaving her and going with his team was the better option for him.

She didn't want his death on her conscience.

Would sacrifice herself in a heartbeat, without a second thought, to save him.

"They won't beat them," Voodoo said with such confidence in his voice that for a moment she almost believed him.

But what if he was wrong?

Even with their enhanced skills, Voodoo's team could still be outnumbered. It didn't matter that she'd only just met these men, wasn't even sure she could put names to faces for all of them, they were like her and that made them allies.

"Don't want anyone to die because of me," she said, pleading with him to understand that she held no value, no significance, she wasn't worth risking everything for. "What if … what if you killed me?"

Abruptly, they halted. The sudden lack of motion was so unexpected that her stomach lurched, and that sickening nausea washed over her like a wave, making her groan.

"What the hell did you just say?" Voodoo demanded, making her tremble.

Not really from fear, more just because he was an intense guy, and when he was focusing all of that intensity on her it was a lot.

"Umm … if I was dead, then you could go back to your team and not feel like you were leaving one of you behind," she said in a rush because while she absolutely believed that what she was saying was the right move, she was pretty sure Voodoo disagreed.

Vehemently.

Although she didn't really understand why. There was only so far the fact that they had both fallen victim to Dr. Gardner's machinations could carry her.

"Going to pretend you didn't say that as well," he said through clenched teeth. Balancing her with one arm, he tipped back the night vision goggles. While the dark meant she couldn't really see his eyes properly, she felt their penetrating gaze.

"Being honest," she said, forcing her teeth not to chatter. "I won't go back to that place. I'd rather die. And I don't want you to die. And I don't want any of your team to die. Killing me seems like the solution to all of those problems."

Instead of answering her, he glared.

Then as quickly as he could, he darted forward a few more steps and bent, setting her down on the ground, before abruptly turning and disappearing.

He'd agreed.

For a second, Indigo stared in shock at the spot she'd last seen Voodoo.

While she still one hundred percent believed that his killing her and going back to his team was the best option, it had seemed there had been zero chance of him agreeing. But now he was gone. He'd left her, but she was still alive. She'd thought that, at least, given that they were the same, he'd give her a mercy killing to prevent her from getting recaptured.

If she could hide out for a few days, she might be strong enough to find her way to the nearest town. No one would believe her if she got to a hospital or a police station, but she'd tell what she knew anyway. The worst that could happen was that Dr. Gardner had connections that got her back in his hands and she'd be punished.

But her life had been one big punishment, always for sins she'd never committed, so what was one more?

Footsteps caught her attention, and she turned her head to see shadowy figures moving through the trees.

Guards.

Not Voodoo's team, because if it were, he wouldn't have left her. Indigo didn't care that he'd left her, but why couldn't he have killed her first? Why would he allow her to go back into that hell he'd only just rescued her from? Maybe he didn't really care that she was like him and decided to leave her behind as a sacrifice so he and his team could escape.

"Got her," a voice shouted, and a beam of light suddenly danced over her, making her shrink into herself.

There was nowhere to hide. Nowhere to escape.

Just because she would heal quicker than any of the men approaching her and could walk on her broken leg if she had to, she wasn't going to be able to get away from them.

"Grab her and let's get out of here, they're still out here some-where," another man said, and he sounded worried about that fact.

He should be. Voodoo and his team would be fierce opponents.

Even though she wished Voodoo had killed her before bailing, she couldn't fault him for it. Self-preservation was a strong motivator, and she was glad he was going to get to live, to go home, maybe to take down Dr. Gardner one day.

A man moved closer, was just reaching for her, when suddenly a volley of shots was fired, and the men surrounding her dropped one by one.

Breathing hard, it took a second for her foggy mind to process what had happened.

It wasn't until a large figure suddenly stalked toward her that it clicked.

Voodoo had never left, he'd simply realized someone was coming, known that as soon as they saw her they would temporarily let down their guard, then picked them all off like sitting ducks.

He hadn't left.

Reaching her, he dropped to his knees at her side, and one of his large hands grasped her face, his thumb and forefinger on either side of her jaw, holding her just tight enough she knew she would have felt a twinge of pain if she were anybody else.

"Don't want to hear another word about leaving you behind or killing you, got it?"

Indigo gulped. How could she argue with an order like that?

"Got it," she murmured, but she was pretty sure she didn't get anything about his man or his determination to save her.

January 21st
6:55 A.M.

The sun was rising.

Not good news for them.

Voodoo had been running through the forest for hours now, trying to avoid the guards that did indeed seem like cockroaches. They were everywhere, and several times he'd had to adjust his direction to avoid them, meaning they were miles away from where he wanted to be.

Unfortunately, the guards swarming the forest had found their vehicle and blown it up, it had been useless by the time the rest of his team got there, walking right into an ambush. If they'd been anyone else, they likely would have been picked off one by one, but instead, Lion had seen them, Blade had heard them, and Dragon had smelled them long before they'd gotten to the ruined vehicle.

Of course, his team wanted to head right for him, but he was the one who could hold them back so long as he was with Indigo, and there was zero percent chance of him leaving her behind despite her many insistences that he do just that. The last thing Voodoo wanted was for his entire team to be recaptured by Dr. Gardner. They knew what would happen if they did, Whitney had told them. The doctor claimed to have a way to undo what he'd done, and that's what he was going to do, then he'd study them and reinject them. Something Whitney didn't believe they could survive and given that the woman was a genius who had created the original version of the drug, he believed her.

That couldn't be allowed to happen, and if necessary, he was prepared to sacrifice himself to make sure the others got away.

Although he'd been wiping out every guard they came across, there would be plenty of time for them to have realized who they were fighting against and called it in to their boss. There was no way Dr. Gardner would pass up an opportunity to try to get them back in his clutches.

Which meant more and more guards would come.

On his own, he could make quick work of getting himself out of the woods, but carrying around an injured woman who was in and out of consciousness slowed him down significantly.

Not that that was changing his mind.

Indigo was an innocent. He might not know yet how she'd wound up in one of Dr. Gardner's labs, but she was one of them, and that made her family. Protecting her was already a done deal, but she needed more than just protection.

She needed healing.

Deciding he'd put enough distance between himself and the last lot of guards he'd seen, Voodoo found a small cave and headed toward it. After killing those first guards when he was pretty sure Indigo had believed he was going to do as she asked and leave her behind, he'd had to stop another three times to kill more of those cockroaches. Each time he used Indigo as bait, and each time it worked like a charm.

Now, though, he needed some time to examine her properly.

Once inside the small cave, Voodoo stooped and set Indigo down on the ground. It was cold and dirty, and he needed to get her into something warmer. Even with the enhanced ability to withstand cold he believed she had, she was sick, and he couldn't take anything for granted.

First things first, though, he had to know if she'd been tagged.

Rifling through his pack, he brought out a scanner and began to run it up and down her body in search of a tracking device that could have been planted on her without her knowledge. He was pretty sure that if she knew she'd been tagged, she would have let him know before they left the facility or along the way. But since she was running a high temperature, he couldn't guarantee she was thinking clearly.

Especially with how determined she was to have him leave her behind. And he wasn't even willing to think about the fact that she'd actually asked him to kill her.

What the hell kind of life had this woman lived that she could decide she'd rather die than go back to it?

A worry for a different day for sure. Right now, he needed to see what he was dealing with medically. He would have loved for there to be time to do a proper examination before now. He didn't like the pasty color of her skin, the sweat dotting her brow despite the freezing winter temperatures, or the way her breathing had worsened over the last few hours.

Sometimes when she woke, she was barely coherent, mumbling over and over again that she didn't want him to die because of her and that he should leave her behind. Voodoo had given up trying to convince her that wasn't happening. All he could do for Indigo now was keep her alive, get her healthy, and then once she'd been debriefed and started to feel safe, dig into her past and find out who had hurt her to the point where she literally chose death over life.

When the scanner didn't indicate any trackers on her, he relaxed a little more. They might still be spotted, but at least he knew that no one was systematically working their way to this location because they knew Indigo was there.

Now that was out of the way, he touched his fingertips to her neck again to check her pulse. It was a hell of a lot faster than he would have liked, and he wasn't happy that he could hear each harsh intake of air with every breath she took.

Pulling the pair of pants he'd dressed her in down her legs, he tried to work carefully, to ease them down without causing her pain, but Indigo didn't even rouse. That was some hell of a pain tolerance the experimental drugs had given her.

Too bad they didn't prevent her from getting this sick.

He couldn't do much for her leg without an X-ray to make sure the bones were in the proper place, so he focused on the cuts littering her skin. From the looks of them, he'd guess some were a few months old, meaning that was likely how long she'd been with Dr. Gardner.

Three in particular concerned him.

They were deep, and the stitches looked like they'd been put in by someone with no experience. Since he assumed Indigo was that person, he could mark off some sort of medical career as her job.

Pus oozed out of all three wounds, and the skin around the edges of the wounds was red and enflamed. There was no way these weren't going to leave horrible scars behind. But as long as he could get the infection out of her body, he doubted Indigo would mind.

Using what he had in his med kit, Voodoo moved from one to the other, cleaning them as thoroughly as he could, wincing every time he was sure he must have hurt her, only to find that the pain didn't even register. Once they were thoroughly washed and all rebandaged, he pulled out an IV bag. He'd add antibiotics to the fluids so he could both rehydrate her and work on making her better at the same time. Voodoo would also add painkillers. It didn't matter that she seemed all but impervious to it, he wasn't risking it when she was weak and vulnerable, and they weren't someplace safe.

Once the IV was set up, delivering the much-needed medication, he rocked back on his heels and looked down at his pretty patient. Now that he had the time to look at her properly, he couldn't help but notice that she was gorgeous. High cheekbones, pouty lips, a slim figure with just the right amount of curves to get his blood heating. While closed at the moment, he knew she had eyes the warmest shade of brown, and given that she'd been more worried about him than herself, he knew she was a good person with a big heart.

"You're safe now, Indy," he murmured as he brushed his knuckles across the overheated skin at her temple. The nickname came easily, and something warm bloomed in his chest as he looked down at the unconscious woman.

Warmth.

That's how she described the feeling of his healing touch. No one had ever really described what it felt like when he touched them, although he knew everyone at Prey was aware of his ability to heal in ways that shouldn't be possible, his team even more so.

"Not going to let anything happen to you," he assured Indigo as he closed his hands around the two worst wounds and held them there.

Did she feel that warmth that she'd described? Did she know she wasn't alone, that he was right there beside her, and that despite her protests, he wasn't going anywhere?

Whether she believed it or not, she was safe now, with him, with his team. They protected their own, and she was one of them. As soon as he had her healed, he was going to find a way to convince her of that fact.

~

January 21st
   3:17 P.M.

Everything was so vivid.

Like God had turned the world up to full brightness.

It hurt her eyes.

"Shh, honey, it's okay, you're okay," a voice spoke from somewhere far away.

Or maybe not far away because she felt something cool brush across her forehead. It was so nice against her overheated skin that she whimpered when it suddenly disappeared.

"Not going anywhere, going to make you well again," the same voice said, and while she got the feeling the words were supposed to be soothing, the tone of voice was more panicked than anything else.

Maybe it said more, but she drifted further away.

Hot.

She was so hot.

It felt like the sun had shifted to take up residence inside her body. It was awful. Indigo would rather feel the full pain of her injuries than this horrible, overheated feeling.

There was no escape from it.

Her body squirmed, seeking solace, but there was none to be found.

Instead, she drifted further away, her thoughts becoming disjointed, unsure if she was awake or asleep.

Snippets of memories filtered through her mind. The lab, the cuts, the hammer shattering her leg, the gunshots, the men.

Voodoo.

He'd carried her for hours through the forest, and he didn't even seem to be winded, her weight nothing compared to his strength. Was that who had been talking to her now? He had an ability to heal, she understood that, but she didn't feel any better for whatever he was doing.

Or he was doing nothing.

Like everyone else.

Using her.

Abusing her.

"You should never have been born, girl. Didn't want a kid, and if I was forced to have one, I wanted a boy. What am I going to do with a girl? Useless. Pathetic. Waste of air. Should have beaten you right out of your mother's body before you were born."

Indigo tried to hold it in, but a whimper escaped anyway. Her daddy didn't like her to make a sound. Sounds bothered him, although she had no idea why. He was always so loud. Screaming and hollering. Yelling about everything.

When he drank, he was even louder.

Meaner too.

"You got anything to say for yourself, girl?" he snarled as he shoved away from the kitchen table.

There was no answer she could give that would stop the inevitable from happening.

If she answered, she was an insolent little brat who talked back when she should keep quiet, and he'd hit her for it.

If she didn't answer, she was an insolent little brat who had no manners and didn't answer a direct question when asked one, and he'd hit her for it.

Even at five, she knew there was no way she could avoid the coming pain.

Worse, there was no way she could hold in her tears as his fists connected with her tiny, fragile body.

"Answer me, girl," her father snarled as his fist connected with her cheek, the force of the blow sending her flying out of her chair and sprawling onto the floor. A moment later, his boot connected with her ribs, and pain splintered through her body, making her scream.

Through teary eyes, Indigo saw her mommy sitting at the table, calmly finishing up her dinner like her husband didn't have their daughter on the floor, assaulting her.

The blows kept coming. His boots and his fists, hitting her over and over again until darkness started to fill her mind.

Didn't matter that she was only five years old, Indigo was old enough, experienced enough, to know that death was coming for her, and she wasn't even sad or scared about it.

"Come on, Indy, stay with me, honey."

More coolness dotted her skin as the voice spoke, but it didn't even come close to easing the heat consuming her from the inside out.

Infection.

Some distant part of her mind was still cognizant enough to remember that.

Remember that the voice was Voodoo's. A man who was supposed to be able to heal people. Only it didn't seem like he was able to heal her.

If she had the strength to do it, she would assure him that she didn't mind, that it was okay, that maybe it was just her time to go, and given that her life hadn't been pleasant, she wasn't all that unhappy about it.

Death couldn't be worse than life, that she knew for certain.

But the reassurances that tried to come out got lost somewhere along the way, and she didn't have the energy left to summon to try to force them out.

Just holding onto a thought was almost more than she could manage.

"Here, drink this."

An arm slipped around her shoulders, lifting her slightly. There was no pain at the movement, just a feeling like her skin was too tight for her body, and she was quite literally burning up.

Water sloshed against her lips, but she choked on it as it tried to dribble down her throat.

"Drink, Indy. You need the water, it'll help cool you down," Voodoo's voice urged, but she didn't know how to tell him that she didn't have enough control left over her body to do as he asked.

How could she swallow water when it was like she'd forgotten how to breathe?

"Come on, honey. Hold on for me. Fight," Voodoo urged, but the thing was, she didn't want to hold on, didn't want to fight anymore.

Didn't he understand she was tired?

Exhausted.

Every single day of her life from birth until now, twenty-nine years in total, had been a struggle just to survive. There was nothing wrong with wanting a break, with reaching the end of her rope and being ready for it all just to be over.

Maybe she should still have some fight left in her, especially now that Voodoo and his team had gotten her out of that hellhole of a lab. But that didn't mean she expected anything better out of her future than she'd gotten in the past. Maybe she wasn't the prisoner of a psychotic and sadistic scientist, but what happened next? It was hard to believe there wasn't someone else, equally as horrible, waiting in the wings to become the new villain of her life.

Damn, she sounded so morose, like she was throwing herself one major pity party.

That wasn't who Indigo Yates was. She was a fighter. She kept going, no matter how bad things were, she never gave up. But everyone had an end to their rope, and maybe she'd just reached hers.

"Time's up," the sun taunted, *its big, round yellow face dancing in front of her.*

Its smile was mocking, like it was enjoying what it was doing to her.

"Please, stop burning me," she whimpered. "Enough."

"Enough? It's never enough, is it?" the sun sneered. "How many times have you already begged for it to be enough? Did your father ever listen? Ever stop? Your mom? Your first boyfriend? He certainly had some fun with you, didn't he, made what your dad did look like child's play."

Unfortunately, that was true.

Her dad hurt her, hit her, kicked her, and raped her when her mom had passed out and could no longer scream. But he would hurt her then leave her for a while. Her first boyfriend had taken great pleasure in playing psychological mind games with her, prolonging his torture and being inventive about it.

"Even your knight in shining armor turned out to be a devil in disguise, didn't he?" the sun asked with a laugh.

Of all the horrible pain the people in her life had inflicted on her, her ex-husband dumping her and telling her that she was never going to be good enough for him might have been the wound that hurt the most.

"Nobody wants you, Indigo. Nobody. Not your mom, who willingly stood by and let your father hurt you, not your dad, who wanted a son not a daughter. Not any of the foster families you lived with, they only wanted a paycheck, didn't they? A punching bag. Your first boyfriend wanted a victim to torment, and your ex-husband only wanted to pretend he was doing his good deed, making the poor, pathetic girl believe she was worth something. But you're not worth anything, are you, Indigo? Do you know why?"

"Why?" she begged, needing an answer, needing to know what was wrong with her and why nobody loved her, why nobody cared.

The sun moved closer.

The heat crescendoed until it felt like she was on fire.

"Because you're nothing. Never should have existed. Nobody loves you, nobody cares about you, and no one wants you. Better off dead, aren't you, Indigo? No one will mourn you when you're gone."

Heat consumed her, and she couldn't take it a single second longer. The sun was right, she couldn't offer a single argument.

"Just do it," she screamed. "Just burn me to a crisp and get it over with."

CHAPTER *Five*

January 21st
8:04 P.M.

She wasn't getting any better.

Why wasn't she getting any better?

Voodoo had brought people back from closer to death than Indigo had been when he found her, and yet as he sat beside her on the floor of the cave, he knew he was watching her slip away.

What was wrong with him?

In the last ten years, he'd come to take for granted the fact that while he accepted he couldn't save everybody, he could save almost everybody. Just a couple of weeks ago, he'd healed almost on the spot after a piece of debris had pierced his abdomen when he and his team were in an explosion while searching for leads on Dr. Gardner's whereabouts. He'd healed his team members more times than he could count and saved innocents on ops. A couple of years ago, he'd even saved the life of Beth Lindon, a close friend of Delta Team's, and married to Bravo Team's leader, Axe, after she was buried alive.

If he could do that, he should be able to do this.

But it didn't matter how many times he pressed his hands to Indigo's infected wounds and willed his body to do what it did, nothing changed.

Not only did the wounds look just as bad as they had almost twenty-four hours ago, when he and his team had found her inside the lab, but her fever was much worse. She'd been delirious, fever dreams making her scream at the sun to just hurry up and kill her, whimpering and crying, tearing at his heart with her sobs about how she was ready to die and no one would care.

He would care.

Didn't matter that he'd known her for a day, he knew all he needed to know. She was one of them and she cared more about others than she did herself. He also knew that once he got her well and back home, he was going to find out from her who he had to kill for making her feel like she was worthless.

Once he got her home.

Because he couldn't accept another possibility.

"Keep fighting, honey," he urged as he blotted at her sweat-dotted brow with a bandage soaked in cold water.

The cave he'd found for them was near a stream, and he'd been backward and forward between the two, making sure he had plenty of water to keep her hydrated and to try to bring down her fever. Already, he'd gone through the IV bags he had in his med kit, so now he was having to work on dealing with her fever the old-fashioned way.

Since he couldn't safely keep moving while carrying a sick woman with him and hope to keep evading each threat that presented itself, Voodoo had already made his peace with the fact that he'd be hiding out in the cave, for as long as it took Indigo to get well enough to move. The broken leg was actually the only part of her he'd been able to heal in any meaningful way, and while he still couldn't be one hundred percent sure that the bones were in the correct place, he was fairly confident he'd been able to line them up while she was unconscious.

She hadn't even roused, although the pain had to be excruciating. Chances were, even his teammates likely would have passed out from having a bone snapped back into place without any sedatives or painkillers to dull the pain.

But for this woman it hadn't even registered. The ability to withstand horrendous amounts of pain would be a major asset in the field, and he could see why Indigo would be valuable to Dr. Gardner. That and the fact that she had actually survived the injection process and not succumbed to the anger and suicidal thoughts.

How had she done it?

They'd always assumed the reason for their surviving was the fact that they'd bonded quickly as a team when they first signed up for the program. Those bonds had strengthened after they were injected, and they'd had each other to lean on, support them, ground them, and as such, they'd been able to push through the rush of emotions and find their footing.

Only Indigo had survived without that kind of support system, and he was wondering if that could be attributed to her already being so used to being on her own that she was able to be her own support system.

Not that he had any way of proving that until she woke up and told him for herself.

"Which you better hurry up and do," he told her unconscious form. If she didn't get better in the next twenty-four hours or so, he might have to rethink his entire strategy and come up with a new plan.

But he wasn't ready to accept that yet.

Wasn't used to feeling this out of control either.

One thing he and his team had been forced to learn pretty quickly after they received the first round of injections was control. They had to keep their emotions on a tight leash or risk not only losing their own lives but taking out the rest of them in an anger-fueled breakdown.

Control he'd learned from his parents, who punished even the smallest of outbursts when he was a child, that had then been honed in special forces training, and then again after entering Dr. Gardner's program, was now slipping.

If he couldn't save Indigo, he didn't know who he was anymore.

Healing people had always been his thing, a product of coming from two doctor parents so obsessed with saving lives they forgot all about the one they created. After the enhancements left him with an unexplainable ability to heal himself and others, one not even Whitney could properly comprehend, it had become his entire identity.

Now it was failing him.

"Won't let you die, honey. Can't. You hear me?"

There was no answer from Indigo, not that Voodoo had been expecting one, but he did hear a sound that had his head snapping up, his gaze shifting from the woman lying beside him to the entrance to the cave.

Someone was out there.

Second-guessing himself wasn't even an option. If he sensed people approaching, then he knew someone was out there. Not his team because they would have alerted him to their presence, which meant it was more guards still combing the forest.

He was confident they didn't know exactly where he was, he hadn't lit a fire because the cold wasn't bothering him, and Indigo had been stuck mostly in fever highs, although the chills had come for her a few times. Her broken pleas to let her in from the cold and that she wouldn't upset him again if he did so he didn't need to punish her again had simultaneously broken his heart and stoked the fires of his rage.

Keeping control of your rage didn't mean it wasn't constantly prowling around waiting for an outlet.

Anything that threatened this woman was something his anger was more than happy to latch onto.

Now he rifled through his pack, pulled out the emergency blanket, and draped it over Indigo. It would exacerbate her fever, but it would help block her from any thermal trackers they might be using. Then he grabbed a thin woolen blanket and draped it over her as well, which would make her less visible if anyone should get close enough to look inside the cave.

Not that he intended to allow that to happen.

Pulling his pack back on, he scooped up his weapon as he stood and slunk out of the cave and into the night.

While he might not have some of his teammates' enhanced skills, he could still make out the sounds of footsteps and adjusted his path accordingly. He was going to need to take them all out quickly and silently because otherwise they'd get off an alert to their colleagues of his and Indigo's location.

Then he'd have no choice but to grab her and run.

Moving closer to the sounds, Voodoo made sure he stayed out of sight, keeping each step he took silent. Grunts and muttered words soon began to filter through to him, and as he took another few steps closer, he saw them. Four men moving together through the forest. From the annoyed scowls on their faces, he assumed they had long since lost interest in this pursuit. Not that they'd give up because he had no doubt that if they didn't produce Indigo, every single one of the guards would be punished.

Between all of them he'd already killed, and the ones he knew his team had taken out, Voodoo was a little surprised that any were left out there. Dr. Gardner must have more contacts than they'd been aware of. Or the man was just buying teams of mercenaries much the same way he'd put out contracts on Cassandra and Rose.

Regardless of whether they were permanent members of the scientist's team or not, they were going to die tonight, and Voodoo couldn't deny that it was bloodlust pumping through his veins as he moved into position. Maybe he couldn't slay his girl's dragons yet, not until he knew who they were, but he could damn sure slay the men out there determined to find her and return her to hell.

~

January 21st
    8:50 P.M.

Hot.

Why was she always so hot?

Sweat was dripping from her body, pooling beneath her, and when Indigo shifted slightly, it suddenly felt too cold against her skin.

Great, chills were coming.

At least she was snuggled into her warm bed, that should help her feel better.

Only ... if she was in bed, why did the mattress feel so hard?

And didn't she ... not have a bed since her husband decided to divorce her for someone better and kick her out of their house?

Another rush of heat flooded her system, followed immediately by a chill that had her shaking. Her bony body bounced off the hard surface that she now realized wasn't a bed, wasn't a park bench, wasn't even one of those bumpy and uncomfortable beds at a shelter she sometimes slept on.

It was stone.

Because she was outside, but outside in the forest, not in a local park. Because she'd been sprung by a team of men who were altered like her. One of them had refused to leave her side, and she knew he'd been there through the raging fever dreams, and the chills that threw her body into a tailspin as it moved too quickly from hot to cold and back to hot.

Throat dry, lips cracked, she shifted a little.

"Voodoo?"

He didn't answer, and panic hit her like a ton of bricks. Had he gone? Got tired of her being too sick to move and decided ditching her was the better option after all?

Indigo wouldn't blame him if he had left her, but still, the thought of him not being there left her almost in a panic. It didn't seem to matter that she'd practically begged him over and over again to walk away and leave her behind. Or that she'd asked him to kill her on more than one occasion.

"Maybe he's not gone," she murmured. Blinking open heavy eyes, she found herself staring at a blanket. Two of them it turned out when she shoved the offending material off her as more heat washed over her in wave after wave, until she wanted to rip off her own skin just to find some relief.

When she glanced around the cave that had been their home for however long it had been since Voodoo and his team found her, she saw it was empty.

Worse, Voodoo's pack was gone as well.

If he was leaving, he would definitely take it with him, but as she looked down at the two blankets, she couldn't help but feel that he wouldn't have taken the trouble to cover her in blankets if he was planning on ditching her.

There'd be no point.

She was too weak to take care of herself. Without someone else there, she'd just wither away and die, so the blankets would be pretty much pointless.

Maybe he'd left, but he was planning on coming back soon?

Gritting her teeth, Indigo planted her palms on the rough floor of the cave and pushed herself up. A horrific shaft of pain tore through her broken leg the second she was standing on it, but it passed quickly and as she used the wall of the cave to help her balance, she realized that the leg felt more stable than she'd been anticipating.

Not fully healed, but not like a relatively fresh break should feel either.

Had Voodoo healed her?

Partially at least?

Whatever he'd done didn't seem to have had a huge impact on the infection and fever wracking her body, but it did seem to have worked on her leg.

Keeping a hand on the wall of the cave, Indigo limped toward the opening. It was dark out, but she wasn't sure how much time had passed since she'd been rescued.

Did it count as being rescued if you were still in just as precarious a position as you'd been in before?

Glancing out into the forest, everything was so still. So quiet.

Was Voodoo out there somewhere?

There was food in his pack, she knew because there were hazy memories of him asking her to try eating something, but she didn't know how much. Didn't know how much water he had with him either, but she knew that most of the fuzzy memories she did have of the last several hours were of him constantly urging her to drink water.

Just as she was about to call out his name, a blur of movement suddenly came rushing toward her.

Unprepared for it as she was, Indigo went to move backward, get away from whoever was running at her, and stumbled, her bad leg giving out. She went down hard, pain stabbing through her wrists as they took the brunt of her fall, but like always, it passed quickly.

Lack of pain didn't equal strength, though.

And then a man was suddenly on her, a hand around her neck, pressing her down into the hard, unforgiving ground. Automatically, her own hands wrapped around the wrist of the man trying to strangle her, attempting to dislodge him, but of course that was ridiculous. No way was she wriggling out of this man's hold. The only way she was getting free was if he let her.

That wasn't happening.

"Well, well, well, lookie what we have here," the man said, a slight chuckle in his voice that set her nerves on edge.

It was a voice she recognized, he was one of the guards who worked in the lab. Since she'd been there for months at least, she knew there were four rotations of guards. They worked approximately twelve-hour shifts from what she could tell, twelve hours on, thirty-six hours off. The guards on shift when Voodoo's team broke in were all dead, and she assumed some of the others were as well, since she knew Voodoo had killed men on their trek through the forest.

What she didn't know was how many more of the guards were out there.

Or where Voodoo was.

"Thought you had gotten away, did you?" he sneered.

Indigo didn't know his name, didn't know any of the guards' names, they were all one and the same as far as she was concerned.

All threats.

All dangerous.

"Boss man wants you back. The Doc won't let you go that easily," he said, his hand loosening a little as he shifted his position so that he was kneeling over her, a knee on either side of her hips, effectively pinning her in place. Even if she wasn't sick and weak, she wouldn't be able to buck him off her.

What was she supposed to do besides pray that Voodoo hadn't left her and would return in time? She had no weapon to use and no way to escape.

Helpless.

Again.

"Always thought you were a pretty little thing," he told her, and he let the fingertips of his free hand trail down her cheek then brush across her lips.

Clamping her lips together to hold in a whimper, Indigo wondered how it was that she'd been getting beaten on since she was a small child, and yet at twenty-nine, she still had no idea how to fight off an attacker.

If she survived, maybe Voodoo could teach her.

"Bet you're real sick of them hurting you by now, huh, pretty one?" the man asked, his fingers prying their way between her lips, sticking them down her throat, and making her gag. "Love it when they gag," he told her, and she could feel his hardening length press against her belly.

It was a good thing she didn't need a vivid imagination to figure out what he was getting at, because she'd never had a good imagination. Never had time to foster one because she was too busy trying to survive.

"Maybe we could make a deal," he drawled. Withdrawing his fingers, he lifted his hips a little, enough that he could unzip and pull his length free. As far as penises were concerned, his was rather pathetic, small and thin, and she doubted he knew how to use it either.

"Not interested," she spat out. This wouldn't be the first man to rape her, wouldn't even be the first dozen, between her father, his friends, foster families, and her first boyfriend, there had been sixteen men in total to touch her without her consent, and over that time, the fear of rape had dulled.

Dulled, but it wasn't something she would accept even if it spared her some physical pain or stole her freedom from her. Her body was not for sale.

Instead of getting mad at her, the man just laughed. "Can make it worth your while, pretty one. Pretty sure I'm going to be the best you've ever had. You could stay out here, make this little cave your home, and the others never have to know that I found you."

Not only was it ludicrous to think he could hide her out there, or that she wouldn't find a way to escape, but that he thought he'd be the best she'd ever had was so ridiculous that she laughed before she could stop herself.

Of course, that infuriated him, and his fist connected with her temple hard enough that she saw stars, even as the pain passed quickly as it always did.

"You want to laugh at me, pretty one? Then choke on this."

Without any more warning, he shoved his pathetically small penis into her mouth, right down her throat, where she did indeed choke on it.

January 21st
9:10 P.M.

Voodoo didn't even attempt to contain his rage as he stepped inside the cave and saw a man shoving his penis down Indigo's throat.

Throwing himself at the man, before his body made contact, the most horrific shriek filled the air.

At first, he thought that the man had done something else to Indy, but when the shrieking continued, he realized that the sound must be coming from the man himself.

Still, it wasn't until he collided with the last remaining guard, knocking him sideways as they both crashed into the floor, that he understood what had happened.

Indigo had taken advantage of the fact that the idiot had stuck himself in her mouth by clamping down her teeth on his erection. Now he could see blood spilling onto the ground from the man beneath him, and the bottom tip of his penis was missing.

Behind him, Indigo made a spitting sound, and he had to assume that it was her spitting out that missing piece.

"Way to go, honey," he cheered as he pressed a knee into the man's groin, making him shriek all over again.

Healer though he may be, bloodlust was hot beneath his skin right now.

He wanted nothing more than to make this man suffer for what he'd done. Still, Voodoo clung to a thread of sanity and knew that while he'd killed all the guards in the immediate area, there were likely more out there somewhere, and screaming like that would attract them.

Pulling out the knife he'd just used to slaughter the men in the forest, he kept his knee shoved into the man's ruined penis, then leaned down to reach into his mouth and cut off his tongue. The screams were immediately muffled, and Voodoo tossed the muscle to join the piece of penis on the floor of the cave.

"Your mother should have taught you how to respect women," he snarled as the man squirmed vainly beneath him. His own parents might not have taken the time to teach him many things, but how to respect others had been one of the few.

As much as he wanted to take his time, make the man pay for what he'd done to Indigo, the anger inside him demanded to be let off its leash. Demanded blood be spilled, and quickly.

Since it was the only thing that would satiate his fury, Voodoo let his fists fly. They pummeled into the man, over and over again, not even registering when the muffled squawks stopped and the other man was no longer moving.

"I think he's dead," a soft voice whispered as a hand landed on his back.

For a second, his rage wanted to shift to this new person, continue to fight until nothing and no one was left around him.

But he also registered the voice, knew that she wasn't a threat, that she was the victim he was fighting for.

Curling his fingers into fists, he hoped he hadn't destroyed his chance of earning Indigo's trust. Just because they were the same, that they'd both suffered and been forever altered by the same person, didn't mean she would blindly hand over her trust to a stranger.

"Sorry. Shouldn't have left you alone," he muttered, unable to muster the courage to turn and face her when he was covered in another person's blood, and he still didn't have one hundred percent control over his anger.

Since he let go the least of all the men on his team, he might have better control of caging his anger, but he had worse control getting that anger back into its cage after he let it out.

"Pretty sure you left because there were more of him out there," she replied.

"Still. He had his ... and after he would have ..."

"Wouldn't be the first time someone has done that to me," she whispered, and the resignation in her voice had him turning to find her sinking back down onto the ground and reaching for the blankets he'd covered her with earlier.

"Tell me," he ordered before he could stop himself. "Who they are and what they did."

Her eyes widened in shock. "Why does it matter?"

"Because I'm going to kill every single one of them."

"You're serious." Her brow furrowed in confusion, making her look adorable.

"Deadly."

Indigo sighed. "It's a pretty depressing story."

"Don't care. Tell me. I want to know," he added a little more gently as he ignored the dead body beside him and instead pulled out his canteen of water, offering it to Indigo so she could wash out her mouth.

Which she proceeded to do, and he couldn't help but grin with pride that even sick and injured, this woman hadn't gone down without a fight. Although that smile slid off his face as he thought of the reason she was likely able to push aside fear and panic to act.

"Pretty typical tragic backstory," Indigo said with a shrug, and he didn't like how she dismissed her own pain and trauma as if it didn't matter, although it definitely fit with the little he'd gathered about her so far from her insistence that he leave her behind.

"Nothing typical about suffering, honey," he told her as he sat by her side.

"Dad was an alcoholic, mean, and abusive. Mom was just glad he was turning his attention to someone else, even if it was her three-year-old. Dad almost killed me when I was five, and CPS got involved. Bounced around the system for a couple of years before being sent back. Things turned sexual when I hit puberty. On the nights he beat my mom too badly that she couldn't cry when he raped her, he turned to me instead. Then realized he could make some money out of it."

Unable to listen to her story without offering some sort of comfort, Voodoo reached out and took her hand, entwining their fingers and squeezing gently. After a moment of silence, Indigo squeezed back.

"CPS removed me again when I was thirteen, and that time it was permanent, but not better. For the next five years, I lived in fourteen foster homes, only three of which didn't involve abuse of some sort, and only one family treated me like a real person who mattered and not a paycheck. I was out on my own at eighteen, and so desperate to be loved that the first guy I willingly gave myself to turned out to be a psychopath who abused me for two years before I got free."

Damn, this woman's life had been hell. All he wanted to do was haul her into his arms and find a way to heal her heart.

"After that, I gave up on being loved and accepted and focused on myself instead. I got through college, got a good job, I'm an accountant. Met a nice guy who worked there. He treated me well, took me on dates, respected me, bought me flowers, and went on vacation with me. When he proposed, I thought that all the bad was behind me. Unfortunately, he turned out to be a different kind of psychopath. When I started pushing to start a family, he became increasingly distant. Eventually, a year ago, he told me that I wasn't the kind of woman he wanted to have as the mother of his kids. I was dirty and tainted because of the things that had been done to me, and he wanted to divorce me. He kicked me out, I lost my job because he'd been at the company longer and was in a more senior position than I was, and I lived on the streets for months before I signed up for the program."

"Program?"

"Dr. Gardner's program. It paid money and offered accommodation while you went through the drug program. Well, it was supposed to anyway. I wasn't aware of many details at the time and didn't care. A roof over my head, a bed to sleep in, food to eat, and I was going to be paid on top of it, that was all I needed to hear to sign up."

"Were all the people there homeless?" That could be a great way of finding new victims to experiment on because often times homeless people were all but invisible.

"I think so. They would advertise outside several shelters, and I'd seen their flyers a few times before I decided to go for it."

"And you can withstand pain, right? That's your enhancement?"

"Yes. Hence the cuts." She waved a hand at her body. "He makes me cut myself open and then stitch those cuts back up. The pain ... I feel it at first, hot and sharp, but then it just ... disappears. I've been here for months now, I think, and he's upping things, seeing how far he can push them. Hence the hammer to the leg."

A growl rumbled through his chest. "When we finally find him, I'm going to take a hammer to his leg, see how he likes it."

"You don't have to be angry on my behalf," she said softly. "I'm guessing you and your friends have all suffered just as much at his hands as I have."

Another growl, and this time he grabbed her face and angled it toward him. The dribbles of blood on her chin, the feverish glint in her eyes, the red staining her cheeks, and her overheated, sweat-dotted skin, all had him in awe of her. After the hell she'd been through she'd still fought, and might even have been able to kill her attacker if he hadn't first if she'd gotten to his weapon after biting him.

"I don't care if you're ready to believe it or not, but you are not alone anymore. You're one of us, I'm not leaving you behind, and I'm not killing you, but I am offering you a family. One who absolutely gets what you've been through and will take out every person who ever puts their hands on you as soon as we have a list of names. All you have to do is find a way to accept it. Accept us."

~

January 22nd
   11:32 A.M.

. . .

"You can put me down for a while," Indigo offered, not for the first time since they'd started trekking through the forest.

According to Voodoo, they were heading for a meeting point that was further away than the original one he and his team had set up before they'd stormed the lab and found everyone dead but her. With the number of guards searching for them, they couldn't afford to stay in the cave any longer.

Apparently, the rest of Voodoo's team—who she had learned now all worked for one of the best security companies in the world, Prey Security, as part of Delta Team—had stuck around. They weren't anywhere close by, but they'd trekked deeper into the forest, further away from the nearby towns, and now she and Voodoo were heading off to meet them.

Maybe it should be daunting to know that soon she was going to be surrounded by six huge men who could do things no ordinary person could, but it wasn't. Indigo was safe in the knowledge that since they were all survivors of Dr. Gardner's program, they had enough of a connection that she knew they would never hurt her.

Besides, they'd had ample opportunity to kill her back at the lab if that was what they'd wanted, and Voodoo had had plenty of time to kill her since.

Instead, he'd spent that time trying to save her. More than that, it seemed to be working.

While Indigo still felt sicker than she ever had before in her life, her head was clearer today, the heat under her skin not nearly so all-consuming, her wounds were still oozing pus, but they seemed a little less red and enflamed.

"Don't think you can walk on a broken leg, honey," Voodoo replied, and he looked down with kind eyes.

Now that it was daylight, he didn't have to wear the night vision goggles, and she felt less like she was talking to some sort of alien and more like she was interacting with a real human being. Which was nice, it made it feel like they were on a little more of an even footing, even as she knew that wasn't really true. Maybe she had some of the same enhancements as he did, but she didn't have his strength, his skills, or his experience.

"Pretty sure I can, and I did when I woke up and found you weren't in the cave," she reminded him. "It doesn't hurt. At all."

"Just because it doesn't hurt when you put weight on it doesn't mean that you aren't causing more damage to it."

"You healed it enough already that I don't think that will be a problem."

"I did what I could to heal it without being able to use an X-ray machine to confirm the bones are in the correct place."

Studying him for a moment, that strong jaw, and high cheekbones, she could read the tension in him as easily as she could read her own emotions. More than that, she felt an almost uncanny ability to just know what he was thinking. It wasn't like she was reading his mind, kind of more like they were on the same wavelength, and as such, she was privy to certain thoughts he was having.

"Why do I get the feeling you don't, in fact, actually need an X-ray machine to ensure the two ends of the broken bones go back together?" she asked.

Voodoo just huffed, but he started walking with her again, and she knew that she was going to have a fight to convince him that she was capable of walking for a while. Indigo wasn't being stubborn—well, maybe she was being a *little* stubborn—she really did think she could walk.

Knowing more guards would be out there somewhere, or if there weren't now there would be soon, made her want to put as much distance between them and the lab as possible.

Memories of what had happened in the cave were still fresh in her mind.

The feel of the penis shoving between her lips.

The taste of blood in her mouth.

The choking sensation as blood and the end of the penis went down her throat.

"You really think you can walk on it for a while? You're not just trying to be a martyr?"

The questions pulled her out of her own head, and she couldn't help but wonder if that feeling of being on the same wavelength went both ways. Was he privy to her thoughts and feelings? Did he feel an echo of them like she did with his? It was so weird, but if he'd been like this for years, then he was probably a whole lot more used to it than she was, so it probably wasn't freaking him out like it was her.

"I'm sure I can," she said firmly. But then to be safe, added, "Maybe we can find like a large stick or something that I can use as a crutch. My leg won't hurt, but it's not particularly strong, and I won't be able to balance on it properly."

Nodding approvingly, like her honest assessment and answer was what he wanted to hear, Voodoo stopped and bent, lowering her to sit on a fallen tree trunk. Then he straightened and began to walk about in their immediate vicinity, searching for an appropriate branch.

"What are you, about five three?"

"Five three," she confirmed. She had no idea what she weighed anymore though. She'd always been skinny, her parents hadn't cared about keeping her well-fed. Foster families hadn't wanted to waste the money given to them specifically for her care on things she needed, and she'd been homeless before joining the program, so she'd lost weight recently.

"What's something you like?" Voodoo asked out of nowhere, and for a moment she startled, unsure how to answer that.

Things she liked had been few and far between. She'd had an old teddy bear when she was young that she'd been obsessed with, but it hadn't been with her when she was taken in by CPS the first time, and when she returned home, she learned her father had burned it in a rage. She'd loved school, although she'd been bullied for being so tiny, usually dirty, and often covered in cuts and bruises. But learning new things, realizing the world was so much bigger than she was, had been exhilarating.

When she'd moved into her first apartment on her own, she'd loved choosing each piece of furniture, indulging her desire for soft, fluffy towels, and high-quality sheets. Being able to cook anything she wanted, never being hungry, having knick-knacks, and pointless items dotted about just because she could. One of her biggest regrets was letting it all go when she moved in with her ex-husband.

Still, one thing filled her mind. It was silly, but if she had to pick one thing, she knew what it was.

"Bubbles," she answered, a small smile on her lips.

"Bubbles?" Voodoo repeated as he obviously found a branch he thought could work and came back to stand in front of her.

Indigo shrugged, very aware that his life had likely been very different from hers when he'd been a kid, and that same flush of embarrassment filled her. "They were cheap, and they're a great way to entertain a toddler. My mom used to buy them for me when she had a few spare dollars, and we'd sit on the front porch while she'd blow them for me, let me chase them. They're some of the only happy memories I have with her. Then, when I was in foster care, most families didn't want to spend much money on me, but they didn't want to lose their fostering privileges, so a few of them would give me a tiny budget for a Christmas or birthday present. Not much you can buy with a couple of dollars, so I always chose bubbles."

No doubt he thought it was silly, but there was something magical about bubbles. They were so pretty, with all their shimmering colors, and the way they floated through the air, so light, and happy, and free, always made her smile. They'd called out to the parts of her that had been beaten out of her by a life that had been nothing but cruel.

"Hey." His thumb and forefinger grasped her chin, tilting her face up so she was meeting his gaze. "Bubbles are beautiful, just like you."

Surprise filled her, and she blushed at the compliment, pretty sure he was just being nice because he felt sorry for her, but she liked that he wanted to try anyway.

"Here, I think this should work. But you tell me if you can't keep going," he said, and she knew it was an order not a suggestion.

Nodding her agreement, she allowed Voodoo to grasp her elbow and pull her to her feet, then push the branch into her hands. Holding onto her as she took it and got her balance, only when he seemed certain that she wasn't going to fall over did he take a step back.

For some crazy reason, she wanted to reach for him, draw him back in.

But she didn't.

He was helping her now because they were the same, being nice to her because he was a good guy, but that was it. Never again was she going to be fooled into thinking someone could actually care about her like she had been with her ex-husband.

So as Voodoo started walking, and she worked out her rhythm as she followed along behind him, Indigo did her best to harden the part of her heart that was desperate and needy for love and affection.

Voodoo was offering her friendship, nothing more, and she had to remember that.

CHAPTER

Seven

January 22nd
3:14 P.M.

This wasn't a good idea.

There was no part of Voodoo that thought Indigo should be walking, but she'd been insistent, and he'd already put her off several times. If he kept trying to control her choices, then he couldn't help but feel as though he were no better than the people he'd just rescued her from.

No better than anyone she'd ever had in her life.

Damn.

Her life had been awful, and he couldn't help but think of Beth Lindon. While Beth had been kept more isolated and then sold when she hit her teens, they'd both lived through similar childhoods, and when they got Indigo back home, he was going to see if Beth wanted to come visit for a while, because he couldn't help but think the two of them would quickly become good friends.

Not that he didn't think Rose, Cassandra, and Whitney would welcome Indigo in with open arms, because he absolutely knew they would. Rose had also grown-up suffering abuse, so he knew those two would form a strong bond, and Whitney had been controlled and forced to work continuously, missing out on her childhood, so they'd bond too. Cassandra might have had a picture-perfect family, with parents who adored her and six brothers who would break anyone who looked at her wrong, with what had happened to her mom, and the ripple effects of it across the Charleston Holloway family, she would also be able to bond with Indigo.

For some reason, it was more important than he would have thought that everyone in his Delta Team family, and that now included all three of those women, accept and welcome Indigo with open arms.

Before even learning about her horrific childhood, he'd wanted her to become part of them, and now that he knew, he would make absolutely sure of it. She deserved a family, deserved to never be alone again, to know that she was worthy and that people would care if she was no longer alive.

"Rest time," he announced as they approached another stream. They weren't walking alongside the river because he knew it would make them easier to spot, and he knew that more guards would be coming. This was as close as Dr. Gardner had ever gotten to him and his team, and he wouldn't pass up this opportunity to get them back. Indigo, too, because she'd also survived the trials.

"We only just took a break," Indigo reminded him, but he didn't miss how harsh her breathing was, or how flushed her cheeks were. She wanted to hold her own, he got that, and prove that she was worth keeping around, he got that, too. But the truth was, her leg was broken, and she was doing more damage to it than was necessary.

"And now we're taking another."

"Thought you wanted to keep moving, put more space between us and whoever else is coming. He won't stop. Dr. Gardner is crazy, delusional. He keeps rambling about needing his own army of super soldiers. You, your team, you *are* that army of super soldiers, and he has to know you're here with me."

Voodoo wasn't denying any of that, but at the same time, Indigo was weak, sick, battling infections that were healing way slower than he would have liked, and walking on a broken leg just to prove to him that she was worth not tossing aside.

She would also tell him to ditch her as soon as she felt like she was a liability.

"I can go further. I'll tell you if I can't," she offered.

"Liar," he muttered, but he started walking again. If she wanted to be stupid and cause herself more damage, then that was up to her. Indigo was an adult, she was capable of making her own decisions and facilitating that seemed important.

For a while they walked in silence.

Each step Indigo took made him cringe. It was the weirdest thing because he knew that she wasn't in any pain. While she'd winced when she took that first step with the makeshift crutch, that was it. He hadn't heard her cry or moan or groan or anything. It wasn't the walking on the broken leg that had him worried, it was the fact that she was still running a high fever, still had wounds oozing pus, and was nowhere close to well.

Actually, strike that.

What had his gut tied in knots was that he hadn't been able to heal her.

Somehow, he'd managed to make her a little better, but Voodoo was pretty sure that had nothing to do with him and his extraordinary abilities. The IV antibiotics and fluids had helped to ease back the infections ravaging her system enough to get her somewhat functional, the antibiotic ointment he'd been slathering on her wounds, and the near obsessive cleaning of them he'd done had all worked to make her a little less sick.

Medicine was helping her, not him.

That hadn't happened to him in a decade.

Of course, they had a well-stocked medical supply closet at the mansion. He had pretty much everything a hospital would have, and he used it whenever his teammates needed it. But more often than not, he didn't need what any doctor would have to use.

Had something happened to him? Did he still have his ability? It wasn't that it didn't work on other people who had received Dr. Gardner's experimental drugs because he'd healed all five of his teammates before. It just didn't seem to work with this particular woman. Had something been changed in the drugs over the intervening ten years that made her immune?

That didn't seem to make sense since Dr. Gardner wanted a team of super soldiers, then he wanted one of them to be able to heal the others.

Once they got back home, he was going to have all seven of them, him, his team, and Indigo, get some blood samples taken so Whitney could analyze them, try to figure out why Indigo couldn't be cured. Figure out if something was wrong with his ability.

Figure out how he did what he did.

For ten years he'd wondered how it worked, and when they'd gotten Whitney, realized she was on their side, he'd thought that those answers were within reach.

Only she had no idea how his healing worked.

Worse, she'd told him that was never supposed to be a side effect of the drugs. That they were supposed to help him heal himself, not other people.

Lost in thought as he was, keeping only a sliver of attention on his surroundings because he knew that they likely wouldn't be alone out there, he wasn't paying as much attention as he should be.

So he wasn't prepared for Indigo to cry out.

Spinning around, Voodoo reached for her, but didn't catch her in time, and she crumpled to the ground, the makeshift crutch falling down beside her.

"Sorry," she whispered, her hands massaging somewhat tentatively at her broken leg.

"Pain?" he asked, concerned that the infection was somehow messing with her system and letting her feel pain she would usually be immune to.

"No. Of course not. It just ... gave out," she said, seeming surprised, although he had no idea why. Her leg was broken, and she didn't seem to be comprehending that.

"Because you shouldn't be walking on it," he rebuked, nudging her hands out of the way so he could take over. "Here, let me take a look."

"Do you think you can heal it more? I don't want to slow us down, and I'm scared more of them are coming." As she spoke, her gaze darted about as though she expected one of those men to come rushing at them at any second.

"No one is close by, I'd know if they were," he assured her. While she nodded, she didn't look convinced. Placing his hands on her leg, he tried to do what he normally did, but from the way Indigo was watching him, it wasn't working.

"I don't feel that warmth this time," she told him.

"It should be working, it always works." He huffed. Concentrating, he tried harder, but since he didn't know how he did what he did, didn't understand the mechanics behind it, he didn't really know how to force it.

Never had to.

This was the first time it hadn't worked.

"I don't understand," he growled. "I don't know what's wrong."

"It's okay, Voodoo." Indigo pressed her hands over his, squeezing lightly.

But when he looked up to meet her gaze, he felt like it was anything but okay. Every time he put his hands on someone, he wanted to heal them, there was never any doubt about that. There had even been times with his team, with the women they had fallen for, where he wanted it even more.

This was on another level, though. He wanted to prove to Indigo that she could count on at least one person, that he would never let her down.

Only he was letting her down. He wasn't healing her, and he didn't know why.

"I'm sorry," he muttered as he shoved to his feet and stalked a few feet away, needing some distance as he tried to handle his emotions, the feelings of failure that he'd dealt with since childhood, but that had dissipated when he realized he had been given an amazing ability.

Voodoo didn't know if his teammates wished they could give back their enhancements, but he had relished his, it was everything he'd ever wanted from the time he realized his parents cared more about saving others than raising him.

Now the one thing that made him special, made him better than his parents, was gone, and the woman who was going to pay the price for that was slowly wriggling her way inside him.

~

January 22nd
    8:58 P.M.

Why had she been complaining for days now about being too hot?

Now, as Indigo lay on the ground inside a new cave, this one smaller, darker, and danker than the last, it was cold that plagued her.

Normally, she was fairly good at maintaining an even body temperature, which she knew was supposed to be one of the enhancements that came with the drugs. She'd spent countless hours being studied in that lab, tested in ways that she couldn't help but feel were supposed to break her.

Mentally, not physically.

Dr. Gardner wanted his super soldiers to be physically strong, but he also wanted to destroy them psychologically so he could rebuild them in the image of what he expected them to be.

So torture was part of her daily routine. Once it became clear that she wasn't going to immediately succumb to the anger or suicidal thoughts, then the crazed scientist really doubled down on those tests. Some days she might be locked in a freezing room, dressed in nothing but the underwear in which she spent all her time dressed in. At first, she'd internally bemoaned the loss of clothing, but over time she'd come to be grateful that at least she had something to give her a modicum of modesty.

One thing she could say about Dr. Gardner was that he saved his sexual depravity for others and left his test subjects alone. Which sucked for those poor souls, but at least it was one mark in her favor.

While locked in that freezing room, one of the scientists would often come in, check her body temperature and her limbs, looking for signs of frostbite. During these tests she was always cuffed to a metal table, they didn't want her to be able to curl in on herself to try to preserve more body heat. Integrity of the experiment was what Dr. Gardner always called it.

During those tests, she'd always felt the cold, she wasn't completely impervious to it, but it had never been all-consuming. Tolerable, that's how she'd describe it. Same way it had been when he'd performed the same tests with heat, or when he'd seen how long she could go without food while still being able to run miles on a treadmill, or how long she could last without water before the effects of dehydration took over.

Tolerable.

Always tolerable.

Until now.

Until she'd gotten sick.

Until heat had ravaged her system to the point where she wanted to give in to the voice that whispered constantly at the back of her mind that it would be better to be dead than to endure.

Until cold seemed to surround her, wrapping around her body, seeping inside it until it took all her effort not to shake convulsively.

Couldn't do that.

Didn't want to worry Voodoo.

The man had been off since earlier in the day when her leg had finally given out on her and she'd been unable to summon enough strength in it to get it to cooperate so she could walk, even with the crutch to take most of her weight.

Indigo didn't quite get what he was so upset about. It seemed that he was upset because he couldn't heal her the way he wanted, but she didn't see how that could be all of it. After all, he barely knew her, although she had shared all her dirty little secrets about her past. Her parents, life in foster care, her first boyfriend, her ex-husband, being homeless, he knew it all and he didn't seem to be disgusted by her.

Still, she couldn't accept that he was truly that upset that someone like her was struggling. Not being disgusted with her and caring about her were definitely different things as far as she was concerned. Voodoo was a nice guy, it was more than clear that he was honorable and compassionate. He hadn't wanted to leave her behind to die or be recaptured, and he was always so gentle with her. Even his eyes when he looked at her were soft and warm.

Which was why she couldn't burden him now.

Maybe he wasn't upset about not being able to fix her, maybe his ability was acting up, and that's what had him all silent and broody.

She missed the chatter of their first few hours walking. It hadn't been incessant, honestly, she'd long ago gotten used to her own company so she wasn't a big talker, but it had been nice to have someone there to speak to. He'd asked her questions about herself, not just her past, but what she liked, favorite foods, hobbies, things that interested her, places she wanted to visit, things she wanted to do, random things that had her considering what her life would be like if she could find the stability she'd always craved.

He hadn't just asked questions, he'd answered them too. At first, she'd been too shy to ask any of her own questions, but the more he talked to her, the more comfortable she got, and then the braver. So she knew probably more about this man than she did any of the people who had been in her life before she was abducted.

A good guy.

That's what Voodoo was, and she didn't want him to be upset, or to blame himself when the inevitable happened.

And that's what it felt like.

Like she was already on a crash course with death, and all she was waiting for now was the collision.

When it came, she hoped Voodoo would accept it, return to his team, move on with his life, and do whatever it took to burn Dr. Gardner and his whole operation to the ground.

If that happened, she would definitely be able to rest in peace.

Honestly, that sounded better by the minute. How nice would it be to be at peace? There had never been a time in her life when peace was part of it. When she'd thought that she'd found those pockets of peace, it had really all been a lie.

Death seemed like the only place to find lasting peace, and she wanted to run toward it.

The only thing holding her back was Voodoo. He was sitting beside her now in this tiny little cave that was barely big enough for two people, and she could feel his eyes on her even if her own were closed.

There seemed to be something he wanted to say to her, but he hadn't spoken, and she didn't have the energy to. All of hers was going into trying not to let it show that she was too cold, that despite her enhanced body's ability to withstand cold temperatures, the infection and fever had messed with it to the point that hypothermia was already claiming her.

Was there anything that she could say to make her death easier on him?

She got that he was upset not to be losing her specifically, but losing another survivor of Dr. Gardner's experiments. There were only Delta Team and her, and they hadn't even known she existed, although she'd heard rumors of a team that the doctor was determined to get back and had been hunting for years.

Guilt was probably mixed in with all of that. He was a healer, and he wanted to save her, but the truth was Indigo wasn't sure that she wanted to be saved. She had no reason to live, no family or friends to get back to, not even a job and a home.

Nothing.

Without a reason to live, she had no reason to hold on. No reason to fight.

Giving up was easier than she would have thought given that she'd spent all her life fighting to just get through another day.

What was the point of fighting, though, if life never got any better?

To fight you had to have a goal, something you were fighting toward, but honestly, she didn't. Nothing in her life was worth fighting for so there was no point in having a life.

She was ready to go, but she didn't think that Voodoo would understand that.

How could someone who had a whole family waiting for him understand what it was like to have no reason to live? She knew from their talk earlier that he no longer had contact with his parents, but that Delta Team was his family now and he was happy with them.

Good. He deserved to be happy.

All of them did.

What had been done to them against their will wasn't fair, and she hoped they would get the revenge they sought and then be able to move on with their lives. Use their skills for good and not the evil Dr. Gardner intended. Find happiness, fall in love, have children, grow old, and be content.

That was what she wanted for him. But it wasn't what was happening for her.

And she was okay with that.

It was time.

Time to let go, time to give into the cold, time to slip away and find her peace.

CHAPTER

Eight

January 23rd

1:41 A.M.

She was slipping away, and he didn't know how to stop it from happening.

Voodoo had never felt so inadequate in his life.

As a child, it had been a regular feeling, one he'd strived to overcome by being the best version of himself that could be. Which meant excelling at everything he did. Perfect grades, best player on the football team, the soccer team, the baseball team, volunteering at a local children's hospice and playing with the dying kids, never ever getting in trouble for anything.

He'd quite literally been the perfect child. There were no calls from the principal about bad behavior, and even at home he did his chores, kept his room clean, and helped out without being asked. As a teen, he'd never done drugs, never drank, didn't even have sex until he finally left home to join the military because he didn't want to disappoint his parents by becoming a teen father.

But no matter how perfect he was, he was never good enough.

His parents never yelled at him. Apparently, they were too intelligent for that because only incompetent, uneducated parents screamed at their kids. They lectured. Long and hard, listing every single thing they found lacking in him and making it clear he was never going to live up to their expectations, and that they weren't going to waste time that could be better spent saving lives on a reject like him.

For so many years he'd wanted to prove them wrong.

It was the biggest reason he'd signed up for the experimental drug program to begin with. He'd thought it was the perfect way to show his parents that he could be a better person than they'd ever given him credit for.

A better person than them.

Every life he had saved, every injury he had healed in the last ten years was like vindication. Proof his parents were wrong about him.

Now, as he sat in a cave, watching the woman lying beside him inch closer to death with each breath she took, he felt like that failure they always claimed he was.

"Come on, Indy, keep fighting," he urged as he swept his fingertips across her brow.

No longer was it hot to the touch, now she was cold. Too cold. Hypothermia was slowly claiming her the same way fever had been the night before.

The problem was, she was no longer fighting.

Instead, she'd given in to the suicidal thoughts that were a side effect of the drugs she'd been given. He knew what those thoughts were like, knew the power they held over you. In those early days, he'd almost given in to those urges countless times, and it was only because his team was always right there and he knew what his death would do to them that had him fighting as hard as he could.

But Indigo didn't think she had anything worth fighting for.

Didn't think she had any worth.

How could he convince her she was wrong when she didn't know him well enough to understand that he would give her a family, a place to belong, friends, people who cared, and anything else she needed to feel safe and accepted?

Trailing his fingers down her cold cheek, Voodoo grasped her chin and tilted her face a little so it was angled toward his. "Indigo." When she didn't respond, he lightly pinched her chin and was rewarded by a moan. "Wake up, Indy."

Eyelashes fluttered against her pale cheeks, and while her eyes didn't open, at least he knew she had heard him.

"Why do you call me Indy?"

"Do you not like it?" If she wasn't a fan of the nickname, he'd come up with something else. It wasn't like he was attached to this one, it had just kind of slipped out, and since it felt right, he'd continued to use it.

"Like it," she slurred, her voice far weaker than he liked. "Never had anyone give me a nickname before."

"Well, you do now, honey." She had that and so much more. All she had to do was ignore the voices whispering in her head that ending her life was the only answer, and give him a chance to prove it to her.

One side of her mouth lifted in a small smile. "Honey. No one ever used endearments with me either."

"I know, sweet Indy. You've only ever had people in your life who didn't care about you, but that's changed now," he urged her to believe him. All he needed was one chance to show her that, but she had to hold on long enough for him to try.

"Too late," she whispered, and she managed to pry her eyes open as she said the words as though she needed him to understand. "Can't ... not strong enough ... nothing to live for ... they're right, this is the best way."

"Those voices *aren't* right," he whisper-yelled. "The best way is to fight, to live. I know you don't believe it, not really, but I swear my team and I consider you family now."

"Don't even know me," she shot back.

"Doesn't matter. I know you're like us. I know you did what we couldn't do and survived on your own. I know that you've been through hell all your life, and all I want to do is wrap you up in a warm, soft cocoon and never let anything hurt you again. I will kill anything that tries."

"Sweet, but—"

"No buts," he cut her off, not even willing to let her entertain any excuses, because if he allowed the whispers in her head to get a foothold, she might not be able to come back from it.

At least now he was pretty sure he knew why he couldn't heal her.

Indigo didn't want to be healed. She was ready to die.

If he couldn't convince her otherwise, then ... he was going to lose her.

"You have a place to belong in this world," he assured her as he palmed her cheek and let his fingertips caress her icy skin.

"I want to believe that, but—"

"What did I say about buts?"

"It's too much." She whimpered, and tears filled her eyes, making them seem warmer somehow, two glowing globes of amber that he felt like he was drowning in.

"You can do this."

"I don't want to fight anymore, it's easier to just ... give up."

Voodoo could tell the admission cost her, because she let her eyes fall closed, but he caressed the soft skin on her temple, coaxing her to open up to him again, and after hesitating for a few more seconds, her eyes opened.

"Maybe giving up is easier, but you're not fighting alone anymore."

"I'm not worth fighting for."

"You're worth more than you realize," he told her gently, wishing for a way to heal a heart and soul so battered and broken they could no longer see their own value.

"I'm sorry," she whispered, a lone tear sliding down her cheek as her eyes fell closed.

"Come on, Indigo, don't do this," Voodoo begged, but she was still beneath him, her breathing shallow, as she refused to keep fighting and let the insidious thoughts in her head win as they convinced her to let go.

If she wasn't going to meet him halfway to fight, then he'd just have to fight for both of them. Indigo was cold, her body temperature dropping so low her system no longer bothered to attempt to get it back up.

Pulling back the blankets he'd covered her with when he found this cave for them to spend the night in, Voodoo began to strip her out of her clothes. If she was hypothermic, then sharing body heat would be the best way to combat that. Once he had her naked, he stripped out of his own clothes, then lay down on the blanket he'd spread out to protect her from the cold ground and tucked the blankets over both of them.

Maneuvering Indigo so she was draped across his body, one of his arms banded around her, their legs tangled together, Voodoo set the fingers of his other hand against the pulse point in her neck.

Even though it thudded sluggishly against him, he held onto that.

As long as he could feel her pulse, she was alive, he hadn't lost her.

Life had beaten Indigo Yates down to the point where she honestly believed that it wasn't possible that anybody could care about her or find anything of value about her. Add in that suicidal thoughts were a product of the experimental drugs Dr. Gardner kept messing with, and it was a miracle she hadn't given up long before now.

"Won't let you give up, honey," he whispered, his lips pressed against the top of her head. "If it takes me until my dying breath, I am going to convince you that you are more than you could ever imagine. I am not going to let you die."

~

January 23rd
7:39 A.M.

"Mmm," Indigo moaned as she burrowed deeper into the warmth surrounding her.

For once, it wasn't too hot, nor was it too cold, and she felt like Goldilocks because everything was just right.

Just perfect.

Which should convince her she was still riding a fever high and being delusional, because when had anything ever been perfect in her life?

But for this moment, she wasn't going to overthink it, wasn't going to worry or doubt, wasn't going to allow her thoughts to spiral, she was just going to ... be.

She had no idea how long she lay there, half-awake but not enough to fully grasp where she was or why she felt so much better, but it was peaceful, calming, comforting. All things that had been missing in her life practically forever, she didn't have any real experience with them, understanding them in theory only.

Even those moments she'd spent with her ex-husband, that she'd thought were full of care, affection, and love, were now tainted because she knew he'd always looked down on her, always been stringing her along, although he'd never been clear about the reason, and to be honest, it didn't really matter.

With a contented sigh, she snuggled closer again, and it wasn't until she turned her head a little that she realized where she was and why she felt so cozy.

A soothing, woodsy scent filled her nostrils. It was all masculine and she knew immediately who it belonged to. Knew where she was, and her cheeks immediately flamed as embarrassment set in.

She was sprawled across Voodoo.

Her face was buried in his neck, his arms were locked around her, and she was draped more on top of him than not with their legs tangled together.

There were absolutely no memories of how she'd gotten like this. The last thing she could recall was Voodoo urging her to keep fighting, that she wasn't alone, and her life was worth living, and the voices in her head shouting at her that he was lying and everyone, herself included, would be better off if she were dead.

After that, she must have passed out, and Voodoo must have realized how low her body temperature had dropped and climbed under the blankets with her to try to warm her up.

Worse than that, she could feel skin on skin and knew that he was naked under there with her.

How utterly mortifying.

"Sorry," she mumbled, immediately lifting her head to find him watching her with kind eyes.

"For what?" he asked, his voice a low, almost lazy rumble, like he'd been asleep and only just woken up.

"For making you get naked in here with me," she replied, although she thought that was pretty obvious.

"Wasn't going to let you die."

"Sorry," she muttered again.

"What for this time?" he asked, but there was a teasing lilt to his voice, and the chest she was lying on shook with a chuckle.

"I let them get to me. The voices. Telling me to end it all. Normally, I'm better at ignoring them, but these last few days they'd been so loud it was getting harder and harder to resist."

A hand coasted up and down her spine. "You're sick. Sick enough that if you were anyone else, you'd be dead by now. Laid up in the hospital at the very least. Instead, you spent hours walking on a broken leg yesterday. Your system was just worn down to the point where you no longer had the mental reserves left to fight against them. Trust me, Indy, I know how insidious they can be, how believable they sound, how hard they work to convince you that not only are you better off dead, but the world will be a better place without you in it."

"You have them too?" she asked. While Voodoo might be used to not being alone in this mess, she'd spent these last several months watching every other person brought into that facility as a test subject succumb to the drug's effects.

"We all do."

"How do you ignore them? Do they get better over time?" She might not know exactly how long it had been since Voodoo and his teammates had been changed, but she knew it was long enough for them to build a life.

"They get quieter over time. Always there but easier to ignore, less powerful, more annoying than anything else. At first, the only way we could all ignore them was because we had each other. We knew what our deaths would do to our teammates, and we used that as motivation when it felt like too much. But you ..."

There was something like awe in his expression as he looked at her, but she was sure that couldn't be true. Nothing about her was awe-inspiring.

"Don't do that," he rebuked, and again she wondered if he was capable of reading her mind.

How else could he know what direction her thoughts had just gone?

"You have an expressive face," he explained. "But you have to know, to truly grasp, what you've survived is incredible. Something I don't think I could have done. Something I don't think any one of my teammates could have either. We survived because we were a team, but you survived because you're strong. Stronger than any one of us."

"That's not, I'm not, it wasn't like—"

"Not good at accepting compliments I see." There was clear amusement in his voice, and it helped her to relax a little.

"Not used to them," she corrected.

"Won't be the same going forward," he said, with such utter confidence that she couldn't even come up with a comeback of any sort. Even though her gut wanted to refute his words, argue with him that nothing ever changed, and her life going forward would be as bad as it had been in her past.

"If you say so," she told him, shifting as she intended to sit up, figure out what the plan was for today, because she felt good enough that she could probably hike for a few hours, but as she moved, her knee brushed against something she hadn't been expecting.

Voodoo had an erection.

A huge one from the minuscule contact she'd made as she touched it, and then immediately jerked backward.

"I'd never force you, Indigo," Voodoo said, and her surprised gaze snapped to his.

"I know that," she assured him. Of that she was absolutely certain. He wasn't anything like the guard who had found her the day before and shoved his penis into her mouth. Besides, if Voodoo tried to do that, he'd get the same treatment the other man had.

"Do you? I don't know what happened to you while you were there." There was a clear question in his words, even if he didn't outright ask it, and she got why. He and his team were all men, she was a woman, and he didn't know if they'd been treated differently.

"No one there touched me like that," she assured him, and because she didn't want things to be awkward between them, she added. "And I know this is just a physiological reaction, it doesn't mean anything, some guys just wake up with one in the—"

A growl cut her off, and the next thing she knew, she'd been flipped onto her back, with one of Voodoo's large hands cradling her head so she didn't bang it on the stone floor of the cave. His large body—his large *naked* body—was pressed against hers, and she felt the heavy weight of his erection pressed between her legs.

For some reason, there was no fear.

No anger.

Nothing but lust.

Oh no. When had she developed a crush on the man who had saved her life?

"If you think this is for any other reason than I just had a gorgeous woman sleeping in my arms, then you're crazy."

Indigo gasped at the sincerity in his tone.

Voodoo thought she was gorgeous?

There was no way that was true.

"Still don't believe me, huh?" Voodoo was above her, his weight balanced on his hands, his face just inches from hers. Then he lowered it down, until there were only millimeters separating them.

The heat of his breath tickled her lips, and she found she wanted him to kiss her.

Which was crazy. After both her exes had turned out to be abusive psychopaths, she'd sworn off men. It was infinitely better to be lonely than hurt.

"This is all you, honey." Rolling his hips, he nudged her with his hard length. "I would never do anything about it without your express permission, but that doesn't mean I'm not wildly attracted to you. Don't ever doubt that." Closing the last of the distance between them, he feathered his lips across hers, and her system went haywire.

Emotions and sensations bombarded her, brief though the contact was, and when Voodoo suddenly straightened, not bothering to cover himself as he started looking for his clothes, it took all her energy not to call him back.

Forming an attachment to anyone was a bad idea, so why did it already feel like a foregone conclusion that she would get attached to this man?

January 23rd
7:52 A.M.

He was preening a little as he gathered his clothes and began to get dressed.

Even more so because Voodoo could feel Indigo's watchful gaze. Maybe pressing her into the ground, letting her feel every inch of just how beautiful he found her, wasn't the most tactful way to explain that he was attracted to her, but he also had a feeling words wouldn't have worked.

All her life, Indigo had suffered at the hands of other people. Over and over again, they'd proven to her that people hurt one another, humiliated them, and used them for their own benefit. If he was going to convince her that he wasn't out to hurt her or use her, then he was going to have to show it with his actions. To her, words were cheap, and actions were the only thing that would prove to her that he was different.

And he *was* different.

The only thing he wanted from her was for her to be happy, at peace, find somewhere to belong, and build herself the life she deserved.

While he wasn't averse to pushing her a little, Voodoo also knew he had to be careful not to push too hard, or he'd push her away. Already, he could tell that even aside from the effects of the drug and the suicidal thoughts that came with it, Indigo had a tendency to get stuck inside her head. Talk herself into things and out of them. Her self-worth had taken a major beating long before she fell into Dr. Gardner's hands, and it would take time for her to work through that.

"I'm going to restock our water supply so I can clean your wounds up before you get dressed. Why don't you take a look through the MREs in my pack and choose what you want to eat for breakfast?"

"MREs?"

"Meals, ready to eat," he explained.

"Do they taste any good?"

"Actually, they taste okay. Regardless, even if they didn't, your body needs fuel, you haven't eaten in days."

"Days," she muttered, and he got the feeling she hadn't been eating much, if anything, much longer than the couple of days since they'd broken her out of the lab.

"I'll be back soon. If you hear anything, you hide, don't come out." Setting his back-up weapon at her side, he saw her glance at it like it was a spider. "Do you know how to shoot?"

"Never even touched a gun before."

"Flick off the safety, then point and shoot," he said, demonstrating before setting the weapon back down. "Aim for the chest, you probably won't get a kill shot but it's the biggest area and therefore the easiest to hit."

Chances were, she wouldn't need to shoot at anyone, but there was no way he was leaving her alone again without a means to defend herself. Not after last time. Voodoo was pretty sure he'd never get the image of that man on top of her, his penis down her throat, out of his head.

Thankfully, it didn't take long to make his way down to the stream, fill up his canteens, and then head back to the cave. After cleaning Indigo up, and getting her fed and watered, he'd make another trip to refill them before they started moving again. Ideally, he'd like to make the meeting point sometime in the next twenty-four to forty-eight hours, so he could meet up with his team and get the hell out of there. The sooner he got Indigo home safe and sound, the better.

"Just me," he called out as he approached the cave, not wanting Indigo to pick up the weapon and fire in a panic. "You find something to eat?"

"Vegetable lasagna," she replied, holding up the pack.

"My favorite."

"Is not. I just know a man who looks like you loves his meat too much for a meal without meat to be a favorite."

Voodoo laughed, because she wasn't wrong in that he loved his meat, but this was actually his favorite. "When I was ten," he told her as he sat down beside her and reached for his med kit. "I had a nanny who was a vegetarian. At the time, I really wanted to learn how to cook because I thought if I could show my parents how self-sufficient I could be, they'd be proud of me. Vegetarian lasagna with this amazing tomato sauce was her favorite and what she taught me. We made everything from scratch, the noodles and the sauce. Took me ages to perfect the recipe, and even to this day, I can't make it quite as good as she did."

"I'm sorry your parents didn't see how wonderful you are," she said softly as he edged the blanket out of the way so he could clean the wounds on her legs.

"Ditto," he told her as he unwound the bandages to find the wounds looking better than he was expecting. It was still weird to know that he wouldn't hurt her by cleaning the skin that was still inflamed and angry-looking but no longer weeping. Even though he knew she wouldn't feel pain, he found himself still being gentle, careful. Maybe it was just because after a lifetime of cruelty, she deserved only sweet things from here on out.

"It would be amazing if you could go back and change the past. Make it better."

Pausing, he looked up to meet her gaze. "It would. But just because the past hasn't been kind to us doesn't mean the future won't be."

Indigo sighed. It was a sad sound, full of so much torment he barely resisted the urge to haul her into his arms. "I wish I could believe that.

But if there's one thing life has taught me so far, it's that just when I think things are improving, that they're going to work out, all of a sudden I'm dragged back into that dark place."

"That won't happen again," he vowed.

"Again, I wish I could believe that, but—"

"No buts. What is it with you and the buts?" he muttered. "You have zero reason to believe things will get better and zero reason to believe anything I say. So don't believe, don't think, just feel."

"Feel?"

"Yes. Feel. Just feel, honey. For a moment, shut down everything else and feel."

Adding more water to the bandage he'd been using as a towel to clean her, Voodoo worked his way up her body. Making sure none of his touches were inappropriate in any way. Not only would he never take advantage of a woman, but he also knew one wrong move would spook Indigo and set back the minimal progress he'd made with her so far.

Gliding the wet material over her skin, he let his hand do more of the work, massaging each place he touched. To maintain her modesty, he shifted his hand under the blanket when he moved to her stomach. Undressing her last night was about saving her life, but now that she was conscious, he wasn't going to invade her privacy without her permission.

As he washed her stomach, his fingers skimmed her soft skin. It was littered in bumps from old wounds, and those partially healed. He felt her flinch each time he brushed over one, and because he never wanted her to be self-conscious he made it a point to caress each one.

"We all have scars, honey," he murmured as he moved the cloth higher, ghosting over her breasts, and noting the way she pressed her thighs together and shifted slightly. "Scars don't make us less beautiful, they make us more beautiful because they're a testament to our strength and determination."

Brushing the damp cloth to her neck, Voodoo brushed it over her pulse points, then let his fingers linger, pressing just hard enough to make her eyes widen, heat, flare with desire.

"You are without a doubt the most stunning woman I have ever laid eyes on. Beautiful inside and out. Your strength is your perseverance, your determination to keep going even when everything inside urges you to give up. Can I kiss you? Properly this time?"

Eyes widening further until they were almost impossible round, her gaze dipped to his lips and then back up to meet his. It was clear she was debating with herself, but when the tip of her tongue darted out to run along her bottom lip, he knew she was going to say yes.

The second she nodded her assent, Voodoo crushed his mouth to hers.

This time, the kiss wasn't brief and undemanding, gone before it even began. This time, he curled a hand around the back of her neck and devoured those pretty, plump lips of hers. He kissed her like she was worthy of only good things and all good things. Her fingers curled into his shirt, holding on to him, as she parted her lips when his tongue demanded it, giving him access without hesitation.

Drowning in the kiss was easy.

Falling headlong into feelings for this woman was a breeze.

But maintaining realistic expectations was almost impossible.

~

January 23rd
   4:13 P.M.

"What did you do for fun when you were a kid?" Indigo asked as the late afternoon shadows began to lengthen, the temperature dropping as the winter afternoon quickly turned to evening. She was back in Voodoo's arms after switching between walking on her own with the help of another makeshift crutch and being carried.

With each passing minute she was feeling better. Now that the infections were beginning to heal and her body wasn't on fire with fever, it was easier to think with a clear head. And with a clearer head, she was better able to push away that nagging at the back of her mind that she shouldn't have let her chance to die slip past her because she might end up wishing she hadn't.

Now that she was being carried again, not focusing all her energy on putting each foot in front of the other, she found that she wanted to know more about the man who had saved her life several times over.

They'd shared several kisses now, although none as passionate as that one back in the cave when he'd been cleaning her up. There had been little touches as well. Nothing overtly sexual, just a soft caress as he helped her stand up or sit down, a lingering stroke of his fingers as he guided her over a broken branch, letting her body slide slowly down his each time he set her on her feet. Brushing hair out of her face, holding her hand, sitting beside her close enough that their bodies touched.

She was falling for this man, and she wanted to not just know more about him, but *everything* about him.

Voodoo groaned, and it was such an exaggerated sound that Indigo couldn't help but giggle. The sound was light and free, and it had been such a long time since she had anything to laugh about that the moment turned almost bittersweet.

Before another wave of despair over something as simple as not laughing for months on end could wash her away, she caught Voodoo's soft gaze watching her with something almost resembling wonder in his eyes.

"What?" she asked, suddenly self-conscious.

"You're beautiful, but when you let go, when you laugh like that, you're absolutely stunning. I want you to have more things to laugh about. *Only* things to laugh about, from here on out."

How could she do anything but fight against all the negative thoughts running rampant in her head when he said sweet things like that to her?

There was always the chance that he was playing her, using her somehow, but honestly, she couldn't come up with a good reason for what he would gain by leading her on. She might be getting stronger, but she wasn't strong enough to make this journey on her own, and if she was on her own, she wouldn't even know where she was going or how to protect herself. And she *wanted* to go with Voodoo, wanted to help him and his team bring down Dr. Gardner, so he had no reason to try to convince her to do it.

"Why did you groan?" she asked, not ready to discuss his compliment. She wasn't used to them and they made her uncomfortable. The only person who had ever given her any was her ex-husband, and he had only been stringing her along, never meant a single one of them.

Voodoo meant them. She knew it. Felt it.

"I'm trying to win you over here, honey, which means trying to make a good impression."

Something warm washed through her, a kind of tingling feeling, similar to what she'd felt when he'd been healing her. She liked the feeling, it gave her hope that maybe he was right. Maybe the fact that her past had been nothing but dark didn't mean there couldn't be light in her future.

"Whatever you tell me will win me over," she whispered shyly. Even if he told her he used to be in a gang and steal cars and rob little old ladies, she knew he wasn't like that anymore, so while she'd be disappointed he'd wasted his youth, she'd be proud he pulled his life together.

"I'll bear that in mind," he told her as he looked down at her and winked, making her blush. "Truth is, I was kind of a geek when I was a kid. I had it in my head that being perfect was the only way to earn my parents' love, so I worked hard in school, played sports, volunteered, learned to cook, and took on more of the household chores. But what I usually did when I had spare time, which wasn't often between all of that, was learn new languages. There was always something about them that intrigued me, so I'd start learning them on my own. Once I got proficient, I moved on to a new one."

"I think that's cool," she gushed. "How many can you speak?"

"Nine. English of course, then Spanish, Chinese, Japanese, Italian, Russian, French, German, and Welsh."

"Wow. I never learned any languages other than English, but maybe … you could teach me some. After. If you still feel the same way. I mean, it's okay if you don't, I just thought—"

Her words were cut off when Voodoo stopped walking, dipped his head, swept the tip of his tongue along her bottom lip, then kissed her until her heart raced and she couldn't breathe.

"Thought that would work better than trying to convince you nothing is going to change the way I feel," he told her, throwing in another wink as he resumed walking again. "I'd love to teach you some languages when we get home."

Home.

The word felt like a mirage to her.

As a small child, she'd always wished she had a home like the other children at her school, or like the children in books she read. Part of her had believed she'd find it when CPS first took her. That notion was long since disillusioned by the second time she entered the system. But she'd clung to the almost mythical idea of home, and wanted it with her first boyfriend, and then again with her husband.

Was it crazy to believe maybe Voodoo could finally give her the home of her dreams?

"Welsh," she said softly, refusing to let hope grow too big inside her, but also refusing to let the dark thoughts take the idea that she'd never have a real home and run with it.

Neutral.

For now, she needed to focus on keeping her emotions neutral. It was okay not to immediately think the worst of Voodoo, but she also wasn't ready to fully commit to thinking the best of him either.

"Welsh it is."

"I was a geek too," she admitted. "But it was mainly numbers, not languages. I think most of the teachers felt a little sorry for me since I was always dirty, super skinny, and often covered in bruises. They'd let me stay inside during recess so I could work since I had no friends, and sometimes one of them would stay with me and share some of their food. It was nice, I liked having some positive adult attention, and it was fun. I got way ahead of my class, and if I'd had the money and opportunity, I would have studied physics at college."

"You can still do that, the whole world is at your feet."

"That's sweet to say, Voodoo, but I don't have a home, much less a job, much less any money to send myself back to school."

"I don't think you truly understand what I'm offering you, honey. The Oswald family, who own Prey, are rich. Billionaire rich. They pay their employees more than well enough to live comfortably. Because of our situation, Eagle also found us a place to live. A remote Gothic mansion. You're one of us now, which makes you part of Prey's family. That means Eagle will do whatever he can to help you get on your feet. Paying for your college and offering you a job is a given. And you have a home with me and my team. If you're not comfortable with someone you don't know paying for your college, then I'll pay. I'd like to anyway, but I don't want you to feel like there are any strings attached."

"Are ... are there strings attached?" she asked somewhat tentatively, not wanting to anger him. She'd seen Voodoo in a rage when he attacked the man who had assaulted her in the cave, and she never wanted to be on the receiving end of that. But she also had to be certain. Voodoo was attracted to her, and he was saying all the right things, only she would never allow anyone's words to suck her in again. She had to be smart about this because she was basically putting her entire future in his hands.

"If I didn't know about your past, I might be offended by that," he said mildly. But then his gaze grew serious as it narrowed in on her. "No strings, honey. Never any strings. I won't lie and say I hope you don't decide to stay with us permanently, that I can woo you into falling for me like I'm falling for you. But there will never be any strings. If you only need help getting on your feet and then want to strike out on your own, we will all do everything we can to make that a reality. All I want is for you to be happy."

When had anyone ever cared about her happiness?

It had never even been on the radar before.

Which made this man the most dangerous she'd ever encountered, because he could break her in ways nobody else ever could.

January 24th
4:38 P.M.

A shift in the air had Voodoo freezing.

Nothing discernible had caught his attention, no sound or sight, it was just a feeling that he and Indigo were no longer alone.

As in tune as she already was with him, something he could only attribute to the fact that both of them had finely honed instincts, even if Indigo didn't know exactly how to use hers, she froze as well.

"Is it them?" she asked, her voice a faint whisper, without any training at all, she seemed to have mastered how to speak without letting her voice carry.

According to Whitney, one of the effects of the drugs was a heightened ability to tap into the more primal part of the brain, those instincts that most people no longer used because mankind had been living in relative safety for too long. All those skills that humans once used to evade predators, that people like him had learned to access as part of their military training, now came easily. Even walking with a broken leg and a crutch, Indigo made a lot less noise than most people would walking normally.

"Yes," he answered without hesitation. It didn't matter that he hadn't seen anything, hadn't heard anything, if his senses said someone was out there, he trusted that.

"What do we do?" she asked, and he was so proud of her for already knowing she was ready and willing to fight.

Still, as much as Indigo was definitely improving, the infections receding, her temperature still elevated but hovering closer to normal, her wounds healing, she was still injured, still weak, and had zero training in how to fight.

This wasn't the kind of thing you could learn in the midst of fighting for your life.

"You're going to hide," he murmured as he reached out and swept her off her feet.

Indigo's lips pressed into a thin line, and he glimpsed the spirit that had gotten her through twenty-nine years of a life that was constantly trying to beat her down. No matter how hard it tried, though, she kept bouncing back up.

"Don't bother arguing," he warned. "I don't know how many of them there are, and we need to kill them quietly, so they don't get a chance to communicate our location with Dr. Gardner and the rest of the guards."

Giving a sharp nod, he knew she agreed, even if she didn't like feeling like a burden. Everyone in her life had made her out to be one, to not be worthy enough of their time, attention, and love.

But not him. He was determined to prove to her the opposite.

"When we get home, we'll get you trained," Voodoo promised as she scanned the area for a place where she could hide. "Then next time you can join in the fun."

Spotting a small tree that was sprouting out of the bottom of a much larger one, he determined there was enough leafy brush to hide her small frame, so he headed toward it. Setting her down, he pushed her back a little so her spine was pressed against the trunk, then arranged the branches around her until she was no longer visible.

Because there was no way in hell he was leaving her without a weapon, just like when he'd left her in the cave to get water for them, he pressed his back-up weapon into her hands.

"Remember how to use it?"

"Take off the safety, aim for the chest. Don't hesitate because if I waste my chance, I might not get another one," she parroted out the instructions he'd given her.

"Only shoot if you absolutely have to," he reminded her. "We don't want them to know we're here."

"I know, because if they do, then they can call in our location."

Convinced that she was as informed and prepared as he could get her in a short space of time, Voodoo still found it difficult to push to his feet. Leaving her behind felt wrong. Not just because she was injured and weak, and not just because she was one of them, not even just because everyone in her life had let her down.

But because she was his.

He knew it, felt it in some deep, dark part of his soul he hadn't even known existed. Voodoo had wondered how Steel had fallen for Rose so quickly, and how Blade had fallen for Whitney even as he thought at the time she was one of the people they were fighting to bring down, but now he knew.

From the first moment he'd dropped to his knees beside her unconscious form as she tumbled out of that supply cabinet, he'd felt it, she was special.

Now he had to leave her behind, knowing there was a chance that he wouldn't ever come back to her. While he always knew that his enhancements gave him an advantage, Voodoo was also careful to never get cocky. Being arrogant led to making mistakes, and he would never make a mistake when his team's lives were depending on him being at the top of his game. Now that it was Indigo relying on him, it was even more important that he not let anything distract him, not even his own superiority.

Assuming these people hunting them knew who he was and that he was out there was the smart thing to do. It was the only logical conclusion given the sheer amount of men Dr. Gardner was throwing at this area. There had been time for that first lot of guards shooting at them as they exited the lab to figure out that his team had been there and call it in.

It didn't take him long to locate the people he'd sensed. There were eight of them, not great odds when he had a vulnerable woman with him to protect. Killing them all wasn't difficult, it was getting it done before anyone noticed something was wrong.

Still, whatever the odds, Voodoo would make sure he got it done.

With Indigo's life hanging in the balance, there was no other option.

No one was getting their hands on her again, that was the vow he'd made to her and he wasn't going to be another person in her life to fail her.

Following the men for a bit, he watched to see how they worked, how they moved. They were fairly thorough in checking their surroundings, although not thorough enough since none of them seemed aware of his presence.

Separating them was a given. It was the easiest way to take out a few without the others realizing it. Once he started, though, he was going to have to work his way through the group quickly. Just one left alive long enough to spot Indigo, or see him, or find one of his colleagues' dead bodies, would be all it took to bring in a swarm of guards, more than he could take out.

Noticing a deer up ahead, Voodoo decided that was the perfect ruse to get things started.

Stooping down, he grabbed a rock, then tossed it gently toward the animal. He didn't want to hurt or scare it, he just needed a sound in that direction that would draw the men's attention but provide a realistic reason that something other than him had made the sound.

The deer looked at the rock as it landed beside him, fussed a little, but didn't take off running, and he thanked his lucky stars as he watched the men stop, whisper between one another, and then break off into pairs.

Luck was definitely on his side tonight.

As he watched from the shadows, he saw two of the men, weapons drawn, approach the area, walk close enough to his position that they could have easily spotted him if they were looking. But they weren't, their attention was focused on where the sound had come from, and he watched as they spotted the deer and immediately relaxed.

Amateurs.

It was almost child's play to sweep in behind them, come up behind the first man, and slice through his neck. The second turned right as he was about to strike, but it was already too late. He was too close, and the man didn't have any time to react besides realizing he was about to die before Voodoo was on him, burying his knife deep in the man's neck, severing his carotid artery, and ending his life even if it would take a moment for him to bleed out.

Since there was no time to waste, the men would check in with one another sooner rather than later, Voodoo left the two men behind and took off in the direction he'd seen some of the others split up.

He wanted them dead.

Now.

Wanted to know that Indigo was safe, wanted her back in his arms where he could watch over her, then wanted her back at the mansion where he knew there were no threats waiting for her.

Another two of the men were down when it happened.

A scream.

A gunshot.

His heart in his throat as he realized that his girl had been spotted and there were still four threats out there.

January 24th
5:06 P.M.

Those voices whispering in her head that she was worthless, better off dead, that no one would miss her, and that she should just hurry up and end it all had been shoved into a box and locked away.

Most of what they said was largely true, and yet for once in her life, Indigo found that there really was someone by her side who actually saw something in her that they liked.

Of course, there was every chance that Voodoo was lying to her, manipulating her, trying to gain something from her, and would turn out to be every bit as awful as both of her exes were.

Yet she didn't believe that.

Maybe she was wrong, but maybe she was right. Maybe Voodoo wanted to help her find her footing after this, maybe he wanted to offer her a home and a family. Maybe he was attracted to her and wanted more than friendship when she was ready to take that step.

That was what she was clinging to as she gripped the gun in her hands, holding it so tightly her fingers ached.

That was why when she saw two figures moving toward her she didn't hesitate.

Just waited to see if they would spot her, prepared to do whatever it took to protect herself and Voodoo.

At first, Indigo thought they were going to move right on past her without even knowing she was there. She was sure Voodoo had done a good job of hiding her, and since it was difficult to see out of her little hidden shelter, she assumed it was also difficult to see in.

But like it usually did, luck turned its nose up at her.

Right as the two men were walking past, there was a gust of wind. It seemed to come out of nowhere, although there had been signs of a storm brewing as they'd walked this morning.

This particular gust of wind blew the branches covering her at the same moment that one of the men happened to be looking right in her direction. If he'd been facing the other way, he might have missed her, but she saw the exact second it registered just what he'd stumbled upon, and she did exactly what Voodoo had told her to do.

Aiming the weapon, she fired at the man's chest.

It worked.

He went down, but the sound of the gun echoing through the forest seemed to fill her ears, her mind, momentarily stunning her.

This wasn't the first time she'd heard gunshots, but it was the first time she'd caused them, and she was pretty sure she'd just killed a man.

There was no regret, per se. Indigo was well aware of the stakes. She knew she was fighting not just for her own life but Voodoo's as well because she was pretty sure he wasn't going anywhere any time soon. If killing a man was the only way to give them a chance, then she'd do it time and time again.

"Well, lookie here," the other man said, seemingly unperturbed by the fact that she'd just shot, likely killed, his friend. He merely stepped over the body and moved slowly closer, watching her warily, but also like he still believed he absolutely held the upper hand.

Which he likely did.

He was armed, too, and he was a whole lot more competent when he came to using said weapon, where she was in shock just over the sound of the gun firing.

Maybe that was because Voodoo had warned her about how they wanted to avoid tipping off the others that they were there, and gunshots would do that. She didn't know how many men had been in this group, or how many Voodoo had already killed, but there was every chance that one of them had already called in this position to Dr. Gardner and more guards were flooding to this area.

Nothing she could do about that now, though.

What was done was done, and all they could do now was deal with the fallout.

"Found the little pain princess all hidden away. Boss is real unhappy that you've caused this much hassle," the guard told her. She didn't recognize him, so he didn't work at the facility where she'd been held.

Although she was sure there were other sites.

Who knew how many people like her, like Voodoo and his team, had been experimented on, tortured, caged, and eventually lost their lives to the scientist's drugs.

"Boss is already annoyed with all the trouble his team has caused these last few months, then his sister joining in, and the Baby Genius turning on him. The last thing he needed was you pulling a little disappearing act," the man continued. "He's going to be *real* happy to have you back. Especially since you met them. He's hoping you're going to be able to lead him right to them. They out here right now?"

Panic stuttered in her chest as the man looked around as though he expected to see Voodoo and his team come striding out of the forest.

Didn't he know enough to realize that if that were the case, he'd be a dead man walking?

Knowing she might not get another chance, as the man was distracted looking about, she fired the weapon she still clutched in her hands.

This man dropped the same way the other man had, and Indigo shivered at the realization that she'd killed two people now. Stolen two lives, even though she knew there had been no other choice, no other way.

Hiding was no longer an option. Not only would Voodoo know that she'd fired his weapon and likely be heading this way, but any other remaining men would also have heard it and be converging on this area.

Which meant she had to move.

Pushing to her feet, Indigo said a quick prayer that her leg could handle what she needed it to do and then took her first step. Between her own enhanced ability to heal thanks to the drugs, and Voodoo's what could only be described as magical powers to heal, her leg didn't buckle beneath her.

Didn't mean the bones had fully fused together, or that she wasn't causing more damage by walking on it, but at least it was somewhat functional. There was no time to grab her crutch, she had to get out of there. She had no idea how close Voodoo was, or how close the nearest guards were.

Running felt like pushing her luck too far, especially since luck never seemed to be on her side, but still, Indigo moved as fast as she could manage. There was no pain from using her broken leg, but she was so very aware with each step she took that it could still give out at any second. It was still broken even if she could use it as though it wasn't.

Stumbling along, she had no idea where she was going, or where she should be going, just moved blindly through the forest. With each uneven step she took, she kept expecting shouts, gunshots, capture.

But she didn't stop.

Couldn't.

Voodoo was counting on her.

Just because she had no idea where she was going didn't mean Voodoo wouldn't be able to find her. She had full confidence that he'd be able to track her, and she knew in some deep place inside her soul that he would come for her. That nothing could keep him away. Maybe she wasn't ready to examine the full scope of what that meant, but she still knew that he would come.

Always come.

So she moved, crashing into tree trunks, almost tripping over roots and rocks, her chest tight as her body exerted itself in ways it hadn't for months. Facts were, she wasn't physically up to a hike like this, wouldn't be even if she wasn't battling infections.

Because she was rushing blindly, Indigo didn't see the decline until it was too late to do anything about it.

Her foot stepped out, but there was no ground beneath it.

Unable to maintain her balance, she fell.

Awkwardly, dangerously, rolling and flipping, tumbling like a ragdoll down the side of the hill. Thankfully, it wasn't excessively steep, and she managed to avoid hitting much on the way down, but by the time she rolled to a stop, the world seemed to be spinning around her, and she was breathing hard, struggling to find her bearings.

"Got her," a voice shouted, and her eyes snapped in the direction to find six men running toward her.

By some miracle, the weapon was still in her hand, and she lifted it, fired it.

She had no idea if she hit anything, but she heard some shouts and assumed she'd at least inflicted some damage.

Not enough, though.

Hands grabbed at her, rough and strong, pulling her up, yanking her arms behind her back, and securing them there.

They'd caught her. Escaping wasn't an option, but they only had her, not Voodoo, and she wanted to keep it that way.

"Don't come after me," she screamed into the forest, hoping Voodoo was near enough to hear her. "Do whatever it takes to destroy him. Bring his entire operation crumbling down. Don't let him get away with what he's done to us," she yelled.

She might have screamed more to Voodoo, begged and pleaded with him not to put himself in danger for her, but something sharp pricked her neck, and then the world shimmered away into nothingness.

January 24th
5:22 P.M.

"Don't come after me. Do whatever it takes to destroy him. Bring his entire operation crumbling down. Don't let him get away with what he's done to us."

The words sent a chill through Voodoo as he approached the top of a small hill, right above where he could hear Indigo's shouted warnings.

He absolutely would go after her.

Destroying Dr. Gardner had been everything he'd dreamed about for a decade, but what good did revenge do if he sacrificed the woman who stirred up a hornet's nest of feelings inside him to get it?

Indigo came first.

Always.

There was no doubt in his mind that it was the right call, just like there was no doubt in his mind that his team would back up that decision. Steel had Rose, Dragon had Cassandra, Blade had Whitney, and now he had Indigo. These four women had already changed their lives in amazing ways, in ways he hadn't even thought were possible.

Watching it happen to his teammates, his friends, the men he considered brothers, was one thing, but experiencing it himself brought a whole new level of understanding. For ten years, they'd lived in darkness, existing only without truly living, consumed by a need to make Dr. Gardner pay. The way they'd caged the rage the drugs had set alight inside them was by promising it that in due time it would get what it craved.

Now he was making that anger take a step back, removing the carrot he'd been dangling in front of it, telling it that the little ray of sunshine that was Indigo Yates was more important and it was going to have to take a backseat.

Without allowing the tiny little changes she'd already set in motion to grow, flourish, then revenge would become pointless. Clinging to the past would keep him angry and bitter. Dr. Gardner deserved to die, and he would, he and his team wouldn't rest until he'd paid for his sins. But it couldn't be his priority, it couldn't be his reason for existing.

The truth was, he finally wanted more.

Seeing what Indigo had survived, how she'd kept fighting even as the voices in her head pushed hard at her to give in and end it all, had been the wake-up call he needed. The final push to make him acknowledge that he wanted the same kind of future Steel, Dragon, and Blade did when they'd chosen the women who captured their hearts over everything else.

As he watched men approach Indigo, she fired off a volley of shots. Most went wide, but a couple hit their targets. It didn't do anything to change the inevitable, though. More cars were driving toward them, already called in by the remaining guards, too many men for him to be able to easily take out on his own.

Especially with Indigo in the midst of it all.

Which meant he had no choice but to watch as one of the men stuck a syringe into Indigo's neck. Almost immediately, she swayed and then dropped, her body caught by another of the men who hoisted her up like she was a sack of potatoes.

The men were whispering amongst themselves, glancing around, knowing he was out there somewhere, but they didn't know enough to know whether it was just him or his entire team, which one of the team was there, and what enhanced skills they had to be worried about.

Unfortunately, twenty men was too many for him to eliminate before the inevitable happened, but he'd seen the vehicles, memorized the license plates, and memorized as many of the faces as he could as well. He'd kill whoever remained behind, and then he'd track Indigo, join up with his team, rescue her, and bring the entire organization tumbling down, just like she'd told him to.

Nothing would stop him from finding and saving Indigo. She'd just sacrificed herself for him.

She had sacrificed herself for *him*.

It should be the other way around.

He would burn the world to the ground for her, but she'd stolen the match before he could light it, and then run off with it so he didn't get burned in the process.

Piling back into the cars, half of the men left with Indigo, likely anticipating that they might meet an ambush along the way. They wouldn't, but as soon as he met up with his team, they'd track Indigo and kill every single one of them.

But for now, he was going to take great pleasure in killing the men who'd stayed behind.

They thought they were there to find him and capture him, too bad they didn't know they'd poked the beast by daring to touch Indigo, and all they were going to find was suffering and death.

First things first, with Indigo and the vehicles now out of sight, he didn't hesitate to make a big move. There was no point in trying to be stealthy when they already had the location and his girl.

Now he was just going all out to eliminate and destroy. He'd keep one man alive to interrogate, but the rest of them were about to meet their makers.

Before the men could disperse into the forest, making this much harder than it had to be, Voodoo lifted his weapon, aimed, and sprayed bullets at the clump of men.

Screams of pain immediately filled the air, and they were like music to his ears.

Bullets were fired back at him, but he didn't stop, emptying his magazine as he moved his weapon back and forth, firing on the group with a relentlessness that left them with little options. They couldn't find cover, they couldn't accurately return fire, they couldn't do anything but pray the bullets evaded them.

By the time he was done, Voodoo was breathing hard, but there were no more bullets coming at him, no more screams, just moans and groans of dying men as they lay bleeding out on the forest floor.

Anger sated for the moment, he made his way down the hill. Voodoo had no idea if Indigo had injured herself in the fall she must have taken to end up at the bottom of the hill, unfortunately close to a small road. While he'd been avoiding roads, they needed to cross this one to get to the place he was going to meet up with his team.

Indigo herself might not even know if she had any injuries, given her ability to not feel pain, but he didn't doubt that as soon as she was back in Dr. Gardner's clutches, she would be tortured all over again. The scientist wanted to push her to her limits, find out if she had any, or if there was nothing she couldn't handle.

Maybe these men had once participated in hurting Indigo, maybe they hadn't. They were going to pay for what had been done to her regardless of the role they had played. They were part of it, and that meant they deserved to suffer.

At the bottom of the small hill, he approached the ten men lying on the ground. Four were obviously dead, he could tell from the amount of blood, and the way their bodies lay. Another two lay still, but he could see chests rising and falling. Three were writhing in pain, and one was trying to reach for his weapon.

Pulling out his knife, Voodoo tossed it at that man, burying the blade in his neck, ending his life, because he didn't have time to waste fighting. He wanted more screams, wanted to know he'd gone a small way in righting the wrongs that had been done to Indigo, but he wanted her back more.

Retrieving his knife, he grinned at the three men clutching at wounds. He ended the lives of the two unconscious men, meaning seven were now dead, and three still alive but no longer presenting any threats.

"Who wants to buy themselves a pass to live?" he asked as he wiped the blood off his knife. None of the three men said anything, and he took a step toward them as he shrugged. "Guess you want me to choose."

Killing the one closest to him, he felt no guilt over adding another death to his tally. Life was precious to him, but not the lives of people who oppressed, hurt, and killed like it was their right to do so. Was it his right to decide that these men paid with their lives for their sins? Maybe if Indigo wasn't involved, he'd say it wasn't, but they'd gone after his girl, which meant any morals he had were taken off the table.

"Eenie, meenie, miney, moe," he said, moving his knife backward and forward between the two remaining men. Despite the pain he knew they were in, they were stubborn ones, and neither was begging and pleading for their life.

Picking one at random, he leaned down and sliced his neck open, enjoying the sight of blood flowing freely, life leeching away. It was satisfying in a way that killing had never been for him before. But everything was different when it involved his girl.

"Guess everything is on you now. I want answers about where they took her, I want a location for your boss," he told the man.

Defeat crossed the other man's features, and for a second, Voodoo thought he was going to get the answers he needed for him and his team to finally end things once and for all.

But then the man gained a surge of strength and shoved himself off the ground.

"Rather die now than be punished for being a traitor," he screamed as he lunged his broken and bleeding body toward Voodoo.

Knowing that the man had put him in a no-win position didn't mean he wasn't frustrated to have to fling his knife once again, ending another life that obviously held vital intel. Not that he'd let this stop him. He was getting Indigo back and then destroying Dr. Gardner and his entire operation. Nothing else was acceptable.

~

January 24th
   8:19 P.M.

. . .

It was the weirdest sensation to have a headache without feeling pain.

Her head didn't technically hurt, and yet it made a kind of pulsing motion that told Indigo something was wrong, even if she couldn't fully comprehend what. It was unsettling, and she didn't like it, but it did nudge her out of the sleepy cocoon she'd been nestled in.

For a second, she expected to feel Voodoo's hard body pressed up against hers, his strong arms wrapped around her, making her feel like she was in a little bubble of safety.

But there was no warm puff of air against her head, no chest rising and falling with each measured breath, no gentle caress as his fingers traced circles against her skin. Nothing at all to indicate that Voodoo was beside her like he was supposed to be.

Because he wasn't there.

Something cool and smooth was beneath her, hard but in a different way than the stone in the cave had been, cold in a different way too.

Even before her brain could catch up to what was going on, her body knew that it was bad, that she was in a whole world of trouble.

As badly as she wanted to keep her eyes closed, allowing the thudding between her temples to lull her back into a hazy sleep, Indigo knew she couldn't do that.

Voodoo was out there.

Unless the men who had captured her had killed him, which she highly doubted, then he would be out there looking for her. He'd come. The certainty she felt about that surprised her because she was so used to having no one to depend on, so sure that no person alive could be relied upon.

Maybe she still believed that to some extent, but not when it came to Voodoo.

It wasn't his words that had convinced her he would never leave her behind, wasn't even his actions. It was that she could sense his honesty when he spoke, when he looked at her, when he shot her one of those smiles that set her whole body alight.

"I know you're awake," the voice from her nightmares spoke from somewhere close by.

Here.

Right beside her.

The man Voodoo and his team had been seeking to destroy for a decade was so close she didn't even think, just flung herself sideways, in the direction the voice was speaking from, as her eyes popped open.

While she would have killed him without a second thought, felt no remorse about it, just like she didn't feel bad for killing the two men in the forest, unfortunately, Indigo couldn't get anywhere near the deranged scientist.

He was indeed sitting on a chair, just a handful of feet away from her, but she was lying on a metal table, the kind that a coroner used when performing autopsies. Her wrists and ankles were cuffed to the legs of the table, making it impossible for her to do more than rock sideways a little.

The smirk on Dr. Gardner's face was more annoying than having the man who had destroyed her life, Voodoo's life, and the lives of so many others so close and yet being unable to do anything about it.

"They'll kill you," she rasped, her voice scratchy and insubstantial because whatever drugs she'd been given were still in her system, but she did her best to convey the depths of her hatred with her eyes.

Dr. Gardner just chuckled. "Actually, my dear, I think you've just given me the key to finally getting them back."

"You'll never get them back. They'll kill you and everyone near you before they let that happen." Although she said the words, believed them, there was a tiny element of doubt. What if Dr. Gardner had too many men on his side? What if those men found Voodoo before he met back up with his team?

"I don't think so," Dr. Gardner said, that obnoxious smile of his only growing wider. "I have something they want."

"Something they want?" The drugs must be making her slow because the only thing Voodoo and the others wanted from the scientist was his suffering and death.

Standing, he crossed the short distance between them and stared down at her with eyes that were so devoid of human emotions that it wasn't just unsettling, it was like being in a horror movie and staring into the evil eyes of the possessed villain. This man might be flesh and blood, but Indigo didn't really believe he could be described as human.

He was missing a soul, and in the end, she felt like it was a soul that separated them from the rest of the animal kingdom.

"You," he said simply. "They're out there somewhere close by. They rescued you, they aren't going to leave you behind because you're one of them."

Even though she hadn't been having any doubts about Voodoo never throwing her to the wolves, hearing the man who had created them reinforce her belief that he'd find a way to come for her bolstered her confidence.

There was no way she was going to allow herself to be used as bait.

No way in hell.

The guys were coming for her, but they weren't walking into a trap for her.

"Before we dangle you out in front of them, we need to make sure they know what will happen to you if they don't swoop in to play savior," Dr. Gardner continued. "They think that they've won. They took my sister, they have my best scientist, and they want to take you as well, my only other living experiment. That isn't going to happen. Once I have them back in their cages where they belong, I'll make them tell me where my sister is, where Whitney is, and then I'll have everyone back under my control like it's supposed to be," he finished on a roar, already slipping back into the madness that consumed him more often than not.

Arguing with the man was pointless. He never listened, and he ran his operation like he was a god and this was his kingdom. Everyone jumped to do his bidding because if they didn't, they'd be punished for it. The last thing any of the guards wanted was to find themselves on the wrong side of the cages. Indigo had seen Dr. Gardner do it before, inject one of his guards with the drugs, the man lasted less than forty-eight hours before he ate through the skin on his wrists to cut open the arteries so he could bleed out.

That kind of fear-dominated environment was hard to overcome. It meant the guards were one hundred percent loyal to their boss and could never be swayed or bought. They wouldn't risk their own lives for someone who was already a prisoner. It also meant that the guards and the scientists fed off the cruelty of their boss. They enjoyed inflicting suffering and watching as the people unfortunate enough to be injected with the drugs lost their minds to the anger and suicidal thoughts.

Now as a man with a particularly savage smile stepped toward the table she was cuffed to, Indigo knew that she was about to endure something sadistic.

But the thing was, she *would* endure it.

Whatever it took to buy enough time for Voodoo to meet up with his team, and for her to come up with a plan, so that what Dr. Gardner thought was him luring the men he was desperate to get back into a trap could really be Delta Team finally getting their hands on the man who had destroyed their lives.

She had no idea how exactly it was that Dr. Gardner planned to dangle her out in front of Voodoo and the others, but it sounded like it meant she would be moved at some point. She also had to assume that wherever they were now wasn't all that far away from where she'd been caught, so that meant Voodoo wasn't too far away either.

Holding onto that thought, allowing it to seep comfort and strength down into her soul, Indigo watched as the man flicked open a lighter and lit a cigarette.

The stench of the cigarette leeched into her nose as he held it above her so she could see the burning orange end, before he roughly grabbed one of her breasts and held the tip to her nipple.

Other than an initial burst of pain, it was just the smell of burned flesh that made her nauseous. That and the knowledge that the man was ruining her breasts, making them ugly, and she couldn't help but feel like an ugly body only matched the unworthy inside that had everyone in her life walking away.

Voodoo won't walk away.

It took all her strength, but she clung to that new little voice as the man grabbed her other breast and pressed the burning cigarette to the nipple. She hoped it was right, because she was opening herself up to the possibility that she and Voodoo might one day be more than friends. If he walked away from her because of physical damage to the parts of her body that were supposed to be the most attractive, she wasn't sure she'd survive.

Twelve

January 24th
10:56 P.M.

Hopefully, he was getting closer.

For hours now, Voodoo had been tracking Indigo through the forest.

It wasn't as easy as it would seem to be, especially on his own. There was no Lion with his amazing eyesight to see miles ahead of them and give them a heads-up on anything he spotted. No Dragon who could pick up a scent just like a dog could and follow it almost indefinitely, so long as too much time hadn't passed. No Blade either to hear things nobody else could and point them in the direction of where the closest group of people was.

Doing this on his own wasn't what he was used to. For ten years, he and his team had been each other's everything. They always had each other's backs, they supported one another even if that support was just their presence and didn't include words. This would be a hell of a lot easier if he'd gotten a response from his comms unit. But he hadn't heard anything since they'd split up, and he wasn't sure if it was because either his unit or theirs had been damaged, or if there was something jamming the signals.

Without them, he found it harder than he would have guessed to track the vehicles that had taken Indigo through the woods. Not that he was giving up. He'd killed all the men left behind, stripped them of their weapons, and then gone through any electronics they had on them to try to gather more intel. He'd kept anything else he thought might be useful, including the least blood splattered uniform, never knowing when something like that might come in handy.

Following the small road had been the easy part, and he'd done it for miles, keeping hidden in case more vehicles came out looking for the men he'd killed. Not that he'd ever seen any. More than likely, those left behind had been expendable. Whoever was funding Dr. Gardner and his research seemed to have a bottomless pit of money. What it would cost to run the labs, then the money he kept throwing at mercenaries willing to attempt to get the contracts on Rose and Cassandra's heads, plus hiring this many guards, meant the financial backer likely wasn't worried about a few extra deaths when they could always just go and hire more.

As he walked, Voodoo did his best to keep his emotions locked down tight. If he didn't, concern for Indigo would override everything else.

Common sense would be lost to fear.

Training would be lost to fear.

Years of experience would be lost to fear.

And the anger raging inside him, screaming to be let out, to be given a target, would find a crack in his armor and slither free.

If it got free after being caged for so many years ... he didn't even know what would happen.

Over the years, he'd seen his teammates slip every now and then. Dragon, in particular, had always been the one to struggle the most to keep his rage in check. Several times the man had lost control, as recently as a week or so ago when Blade first brought Whitney home.

Of all of them, he'd always been the one who had struggled the least. Of course, that anger had always been there for him, just as it was for the others, but his healer instincts always seemed to balance it out. Not that he thought his brothers enjoyed killing, they didn't, it was just part of the world they'd chosen when they joined the military, but they didn't find it as objectionable as he did. They were better able to compartmentalize.

For so long, he'd thought that was a weakness on his part.

That he was lacking somehow. Not as good as the others.

But then he'd come to realize that what made him different than the others was actually his strength. He balanced the team and was a calming force for all of them.

Now he was the one who needed a calming force. It was *his* girl who had been kidnapped by Dr. Gardner's men, it was *his* girl who was in danger. It was *his* failings that had led to that happening.

His team was coming, he didn't need a comms unit to know that, but they might not make it before he lost control.

At the moment, pretty much the only thing keeping his fury somewhat contained was the fact that he didn't have an outlet for it.

Caught up in his head as he was, Voodoo almost didn't see it.

Just up ahead, hidden amongst the trees, was a vehicle.

It was black, and since it was dark out, he might have walked right past it as he battled to keep his anger caged and not allow his terror over Indigo cloud his instincts. Which they quite obviously were.

Palming one of the weapons from the dead men that he'd slung over his shoulders, it was a little awkward walking with all ten of them, but he'd rather have more firepower than less, he slipped behind a tree and watched.

While his instincts might be urging him to act, run, jump in, to do something, he knew he had to play this smart. Smart meant taking his time, assessing, and making a plan before he acted. The more time Indigo spent with these people, the more he risked her being hurt, but in the end, her life was more important. If taking his time meant getting her out alive, he had to do it, even if he hated it.

As he watched, he saw two men standing nearby. Even without his night vision goggles, he could spot them because they were both smoking, and the little red glows caught his attention.

If he could get into that vehicle, then he could use a GPS to find his way to wherever Indigo was being held. Voodoo was holding out hope that it wasn't too far away. He felt sure if Dr. Gardner knew they were out there, and he was positive that the scientist did know Delta Team was there, then he wouldn't leave the area without trying to lure them into a trap.

A trap with Indigo as the bait. As much as Dr. Gardner needed her alive, he needed Delta Team more. They held greater value because they were already a highly trained special ops team, and thus of more use to him.

Deciding on a plan, Voodoo began to move. He wanted these two men dead without any bloodshed, wanted to be able to use their uniforms without needing to worry about someone spotting blood and things blowing up around him, if he could make inroads into wherever Indigo was.

So he snuck around the men, waited until their soft voices told him they were deep in a conversation they shouldn't be having when they knew that he and his team were out there somewhere, then made his move.

Snapping a neck wasn't necessarily as easy as it was portrayed in movies, but if you knew what you were doing, then it wasn't particularly difficult either.

Of course, as soon as he pounced, grabbed the closest man, broke his neck, and let the body drop at his feet, the other man was already shouting in shock and fumbling for his weapon.

Guess he'd never learned the basics of never parting with your weapon while in the field.

Trying to keep him alive to interrogate would only be a waste of time. These men were afraid enough of Dr. Gardner that they wouldn't talk, would only find a way to get him to kill them anyway like the man had earlier. So he merely slammed his foot into the man's chest, sending him sprawling backward with a yelp.

His rage wanted to make the man suffer, wanted to rip him apart limb by limb, demanded screams to satiate it, but he didn't give in.

Time was of the essence.

Playing things smart and wasting time pandering to his own desires were two different things, and he wouldn't indulge the second.

So he leaned down, snapped the other man's neck, and then moved on to stage two of his plan. Dragging the body along with him, he hoisted him up into the passenger seat, trying to balance him so it wasn't obvious at first glance that he was dead. Voodoo had no idea if there was a checkpoint to enter whatever compound Indigo was held at, and if there was, he didn't want anyone catching on that he wasn't the other dead man.

After that, he stripped off the guard's uniform, it was slightly different than what he was wearing, and again, he wouldn't take any chances.

Well, any unnecessary chances.

Because this was taking one pretty damn huge chance.

Worth it though.

More than worth it.

Once he was in the vehicle, he turned on the engine and powered up the GPS system, praying it would lead him straight to where his girl was waiting for him.

Luck was definitely on his side, because a location only a few miles away was programmed into the system.

That had to be it, had to be where his girl was being held. Indigo was close, so damn close he could feel it, but there were still a mountain of obstacles standing between him and his girl, and he wasn't sure he'd be able to overcome them and get her back.

But he'd rather die trying—rather risk being captured again—than give up on her.

~

January 25th
12:00 A.M.

Something was happening.

There was a charge in the air that hadn't been there before, and Indigo assumed it either had to do with her and the plan to use her as bait, or it had to do with Voodoo and the guys.

Please don't let them be caught.

As much as Voodoo had given her a reason to keep fighting, a reason to want to live, she wasn't so selfish that she wouldn't give her life in a heartbeat to save his.

In a sense, nothing had changed since he and his team first found her hiding in that supply closet, broken, bleeding, ravaged by infection, even though it felt in some ways like everything had changed.

She was still just her, alone in the world, no family, no friends, no job, no home, no one to miss her if she was gone, or care that something had happened to her. And Voodoo was still Voodoo. He had his team, people who had become his family, brothers in every way that mattered. They would miss him if he were gone, care that he'd been lost, and he had a job where he saved lives.

It was only fair that if a choice had to be made, it should be her who paid the ultimate price. Maybe Voodoo would miss her, but that was all. Even his team hadn't spent more than a handful of minutes in her presence, so while they might be sad to have lost another person who had been tainted by Dr. Gardner's drugs, they wouldn't miss her.

Indigo was prepared to fight harder than she ever had in her life. She would give it everything she had in the hope that they all might make it out alive, and she had a chance to explore this thing between her and Voodoo. But if the worst happened, she'd sacrifice herself to save him.

Now she watched as people buzzed about her room. Since she'd only been in this one room, unconscious when she was brought in, she didn't know how big this place was, if it was a new lab or just a hiding place, or how many people were in it.

So far, she'd personally seen only four men, but she had to believe there were more. Dr. Gardner rarely travelled anywhere without an entire entourage of guards. Voodoo and his team might have spent the last decade with a target on their backs, but the scientist knew he had, too. He knew that those men had a reason to hate him and could come after him at any time. He also knew better than anyone else just how dangerous they were, after all, he was the one who had created them.

"Let's go," the man who had taken such pleasure in burning her earlier, leaving behind a trail of small, round marks on her skin as he burned her over and over again, said as he strode into the room, three more men with him.

They were the same ones she'd already seen several times, but no others. Maybe there really were only the four of them there with Dr. Gardner.

"Go where?" she asked. While her skin felt a little uncomfortably tight where she knew it was burned it didn't hurt, and while she still wasn't back to one hundred percent strength, lucky to be anywhere near fifty, her head was clear enough to plan.

Before, when she'd been held, she'd never stood up for herself, never caused trouble, never done anything other than be their perfect little test subject. But now she wasn't just fighting for herself, she was fighting for Voodoo as well, so she had to be assertive, strong, and determined.

"None of your business, bait," the man taunted as he unhooked her cuffs from the table and hauled her upright.

Even though she wanted to run, after all, she was prey not predator, Indigo didn't waste the effort. There was no way she was getting away right now, and if she wanted a chance, then she had to be patient, wait for the perfect opportunity.

She wasn't going to let Voodoo down.

So to that end, she didn't try to run or fight as her arms were yanked behind her back, her wrists cuffed together. With the burning man on one side of her and another man on the other, she was marched out of the room. Carried more than marched, but she allowed them to think she was weaker than she was and take more of her weight while she looked around.

It seemed like they weren't in another lab. This building was tiny, just three rooms, one of them the one she'd been in, the one she was walked into, and a third where she could hear Dr. Gardner ranting about something.

It didn't matter what, she was glad he was still around. It meant if she could meet up with Voodoo somehow and let him know, they could find his team—if he hadn't already—and then end this once and for all.

"Is that really all we have?" the burning man asked as she was led outside.

"Yeah. Guess they got all the others," someone else said with a shiver, not one of the men she recognized so there were at least a couple of others there. Still, obviously not enough to go up against Voodoo and the others if their tones were anything to go by.

Beneath her bare feet, the ground was freezing, and since they'd stripped her naked when they brought her there, that cold curled around her body, seeping inside it, attempting to muddy her thoughts by dropping her temperature too low.

Not going to happen.

It couldn't.

While it would help if she knew what the exact plan was, and how they were going to use her as bait, Indigo decided she could at least gather intel that would help, and maybe something she found out could be useful.

"We need more," a third voice piped up.

"Boss doesn't want to wait. Said he's waited long enough, and he wants back what's his," burning man replied as he dragged her over to a waiting vehicle, opened the back door, and all but tossed her inside.

"It's going to get us all killed. More men will be here tomorrow, enough to take them down," protested the man who had shivered and seemed the most afraid of Voodoo and his teammates.

"Boss wants what he wants," burning man said with a shrug, then slammed the car door closed and climbed in the front.

"Easy for him to say," scaredy cat complained as he climbed into the passenger's seat. "He's not the one out there actually putting his life on the line. He wants them back for his purposes, because he wants to continue his studies, but we're the ones those freaks of his are going to kill."

Anger ignited inside her at the insult to Voodoo.

It was one thing to treat her like she was nothing, she was used to it. She'd always been nothing. But Voodoo was the opposite. Voodoo was everything. He'd fought for her harder than she'd fought for herself. He'd treated her with kindness, gentleness, and respect, he'd never made her feel less than, and more than that, he'd made her feel beautiful and wanted.

Fighting for herself might be hard, but fighting for him was easy.

"Careful there," burning man said, his tone mocking, "we got one of those freaks in the back there."

The other man turned to look at her, a sneer overriding the fear that had been there previously. "This one is a little kitten compared to the lions that are out there, aren't you, kitty?"

It was a little unnerving that her instincts told her to hiss and snap at him, bring out her claws, and show him that just because she wasn't big and strong like Voodoo and his teammates didn't mean she was weak and pathetic. Maybe she couldn't fight, but she could endure a whole hell of a lot more pain than this pathetic man could.

Which gave her the beginnings of an idea.

Voodoo had told her a bit about how Dr. Gardner's sister had come into their lives, and while she couldn't say she agreed with what they had planned to do to Rose, having been on the same side of the scientist's experiments as they were, she got the why behind it. He'd told her about Rose joining their side, about the trap they'd laid, about how it went wrong when the car crashed, and Dr. Gardner got away.

What if she could do something similar this time?

Only with the outcome they all wanted.

She was bait, and from the way the men were talking, Voodoo and or his team were still out there somewhere killing Dr. Gardner's men. If she could crash the car, she might kill or at least injure these men enough that they couldn't come after her, but injured or not, her body would tolerate the pain much better, giving her a chance to get away.

Two more cars pulled in behind them as they started driving, but the man in the passenger seat kept watching her, that sneer on his face.

"Here, kitty, kitty, kitty," he crooned. "Maybe you can come up here and put that pretty little mouth of yours to good use."

While she felt the same anger and suicidal thoughts as the rest of the experiments, given her past, it was the suicidal thoughts she experienced more often, because being degraded and abused was her normal.

Now though, unadulterated rage took hold inside her, although she did her best to keep her expression defeated, or at least neutral.

First, he insulted Voodoo, and now he wanted to assault her. Would he still feel the same way if he knew what she'd done to the last man who stuck his penis where it wasn't wanted?

Laughing amongst themselves, it was clear neither man viewed her as a threat, but as they drove, talking about what they'd like to do to her if given a chance, she watched the side of the road like a hawk. It was dark, but she knew there were declines everywhere like the one she'd fallen down earlier.

When she noticed that the trees were falling away, indicating a drop, Indigo let the anger fuel her. With her hands behind her back, she couldn't use them, but she had her mouth, and she'd much rather use it to help her escape than pleasure one of her captors.

Surging forward, she sank her teeth into burning man's neck, making him shriek. Since she refused to let go, he had no choice but to remove his hands from the steering wheel to try to get her off, causing the car to swerve wildly.

Then they were zooming down an embankment.

Only then did Indigo release her grip and drop down between her seat and the driver's one as she braced for impact.

January 25th
12:01 A.M.

This had actually worked.

His crazy idea to pretend to be one of the guards had gotten him access to a small facility where he knew for a fact they were keeping Indigo.

The reason Voodoo knew this was because not long after he'd climbed into the vehicle with the dead body of one of the guards he'd killed propped up beside him, an order had come over the radio.

It was calling in any and all men still alive to fall back to base because it was time to implement the plan. While there had been no details on what exactly the plan was, Voodoo was pretty sure he could make an accurate guess.

Dr. Gardner had Indigo back.

Dr. Gardner knew that some or all of the team were out there somewhere in the forest.

Using Indigo as bait to try to lure them all into a trap would make the most sense. That way, the scientist would have all his living test subjects back under his control. They knew from Whitney what the long-term plan for himself and his team was. The doctor was going to undo what he'd done, study them, then do it all over again, which Whitney didn't believe they could survive. If she was wrong and they did, then Dr. Gardner would once again want to use them as his own personal kill team.

What was the long-term plan for Indigo?

Of course, she could be trained, but he doubted she would ever have the same skills that he and his team did. They had originally entered the military voluntarily, they'd chosen that path for themselves, even if they could never have expected where it would lead. But Indigo had been surrounded by violence her entire life. Wanting to learn how to defend herself didn't mean that she wanted to become a killer like the rest of them. Nor did he want that for her.

In the end, it didn't matter what the insane scientist with delusions of grandeur wanted, because he wasn't going to get it.

Not only was Dr. Gardner never going to get his hands on him and his team, but they were going to get Indigo back. He'd promised her a future that could be anything she wanted it to be—although he'd been clear about what he hoped she would choose—and he wasn't going to break that promise.

So he'd followed the GPS instructions to the small building, hanging back because he wanted to see how many other people had still been out there. Knowing how many men he and his team would be fighting against would make a huge difference in how they approached this.

Wouldn't change the outcome, though.

Especially when a mere two other vehicles approached with two men in each. That made four, plus there seemed to be another six hanging around the outside of the building. Ten against the six of them would be easy. Hell, he could take all ten on his own. Not until he knew Indigo's position, but as soon as he did, he was making his move.

Arriving at the small camp, he'd nodded a greeting to the others, then grabbed one of the cigarettes from the pack in the center console of the vehicle and stood alone pretending he was smoking it while chatting to his friend inside the car.

That was a very one-sided conversation since the other guy was dead.

But it had allowed him to watch, stiffening when the door to the building opened and three figures moved out.

Three people, the one in the middle was much smaller than the other two.

His Indigo.

She was naked, and even though he was a good dozen yards away from her, he could see red welts dotting her chest.

Anger burned brightly inside him, and Voodoo had taken a step toward them before he even realized what he was doing.

Dead.

They needed to die for daring to touch his beautiful, sweet girl. She'd been through so much, suffered so much torment from the time she was just a small girl. It didn't matter to him that she wouldn't be in any pain right now, it only mattered that someone had caused more wounds to her already damaged body.

Before he could do something stupid that would get her hurt all over again, maybe killed, Voodoo caught himself, reined in his rage, and managed to keep it in check by promising it that soon it would be set free.

"Is that really all we have?" one of the men holding Indigo said as he looked around at the small gathering.

"Yeah. Guess they got all the others," another replied, and Voodoo could hear the fear in the man's voice.

Good. He should be afraid.

Nothing was going to stop him and his team from destroying every single one of them.

"We need more," a third man said, also sounding nervous. Seemed all these guards had been briefed on just how dangerous he and his team were.

"Boss doesn't want to wait. Said he's waited long enough, and he wants back what's his," the first man said as he pulled Indigo along with him as he headed for a vehicle and all but threw her inside it.

"It's going to get us all killed. More men will be here tomorrow, enough to take them down," the second man said, and Voodoo was happy to hear that Dr. Gardner's impatience was going to work against him and for Delta Team.

"Boss wants what he wants," the first guy said as he slammed the car door closed and rounded the car, heading for the driver's seat.

Not wanting anyone else to try to get into his vehicle with him, that would ruin his little charade, and Voodoo knew it was only because there were so few of them that hadn't already happened, he quickly tossed the cigarette, stomped it out, then jumped into his vehicle and started the engine. Following along behind the vehicle that Indigo was in before anyone else could try to join him, he saw a man throw up his hands, like he was trying to call him back, but he pretended not to see and kept going.

Thankfully, no one made a big deal out of it, and the rest of the men must have piled into one of the other vehicles, because only one more pulled out behind him.

Good odds.

Only two men were in the vehicle with Indigo, none with him, and if all the vehicles were the same as this SUV, then there were no more than five in the one behind him. That left possibly another five back at the building, likely meant to hang back and then come in as backup once they thought they'd lured him and his team into a trap.

Tonight, the only trap that was going to be set was his own.

Grabbing his radio, Voodoo slowed his vehicle, allowing the one with Indigo in it to move on ahead, while the one behind him was forced to also slow since there wasn't space on the narrow road to go around him.

"Think I saw something," he muttered, making sure his voice wasn't distinguishable in case they could recognize him from it.

When he came to a stop, he jumped out of the vehicle and took off into the forest, pretending he was following something.

A moment later, he heard pounding feet, and he knew the others had fallen for his ruse.

Leading them deeper into the forest, he waited until he knew they were lost to the chase, completely unaware they were chasing after nothing, then he stopped, turned, and much like he'd done earlier when Indigo was abducted, he sprayed bullets into the forest.

Bodies dropped one by one, before they even registered what was going on, before they had a chance to fire back.

Confident in his ability to hit what he aimed at, Voodoo didn't bother confirming his kills, he merely took off at a dead run back to his vehicle. The need to get to Indigo, to have her back in his arms was overwhelming, and he couldn't deny it any longer.

Driving faster this time around, he sped off into the night, praying for Thunder's usual good luck at driving at high speeds while never crashing.

It was only because he was carefully watching the road to make sure he stayed on it, that he saw it.

Skid marks.

Like a vehicle had recently gone over the edge of the embankment.

Slamming on the brakes, Voodoo was out of the car without even thinking. Running toward where he knew deep in his gut Indigo's car had just crashed. He approached with far less caution than he should have. If anyone had been alive in that car, they could have easily shot and killed him.

He might be able to heal himself, but he couldn't raise anyone, not even himself, from the dead.

In the passenger seat of the vehicle was a man who was clearly dead, he hadn't been wearing a seatbelt, and he'd been thrown into the windshield. No one else was in the vehicle, though. No driver, and more importantly, no Indigo.

Movement behind him caught his attention just in time, and he spun around, weapon raised, ready to kill whoever was coming.

January 25th
12:30 A.M.

Was she going the right way?

Did it even matter?

It wasn't like Indigo was running to a certain location, she was just running.

Doing her best to escape, to fight, to live. To make plans for the future, entertain hopes and dreams, and build a life that was secure, that couldn't be washed away in the storms that seemed to continuously rain down upon her.

Nothing and no one was going to take this chance from her.

Voodoo was out there somewhere, and all she had to do was find him and everything would be okay.

She had no idea how he'd become so important to her so quickly. No idea how he'd managed to convince her that he was worthy of her trust, her faith, when she hadn't even known she still possessed the ability to entertain those notions.

But the whys and hows weren't important. All that mattered was that she believed Voodoo was out there, knew he wouldn't leave her behind, that he'd be doing his best to get himself to her. Might even be somewhere close by right at this very second.

Believing in him could be the biggest mistake of her life, after all, she had no experience with people ever being there for her. It was such a risk, her entire life was on the line, Voodoo her only meaningful chance at escape, and even if he did save her now, it didn't mean he wouldn't let her down in the future.

Yet ... in some deep place of her soul, she knew that wouldn't happen. Voodoo was the real deal, she'd felt safer with him than she ever had before. With her first ex, she was so young, so desperate for love and affection that she knew she'd ignored dozens of red flags. With her second ex, she'd always been aware of how very different their lives had been, how much better he was than her, and she'd always tried to be on her best behavior, not wanting to let him down, which meant she'd never gotten to just be herself.

That wasn't an issue when she was with Voodoo. He didn't expect anything from her, didn't look down at her, didn't think less of her because she'd been abused so badly. All he saw was her, and when she was around him, she felt protected in a way she'd craved all her life.

Voodoo was safety, he was hope, he was life ... maybe one day he could even be love.

Which is why she wasn't going to give up. Why she was going to keep fighting, give this everything she had.

As she ran, Indigo barely felt the rocks, sticks, and roots digging into the soles of her bare feet. Since she didn't register pain, all she felt was the pressure of each item that jabbed into her skin. That and the cold. Not fully recovered from the infections that had been close to stealing her life, she still couldn't seem to get her body to properly tolerate temperature extremes the way it was supposed to.

Wasn't just her feet that were cold, her entire body shivered even as she refused to slow down, wanting to put as much distance between herself and the crashed car as she could.

Her plan had worked.

Burning man had lost control of the car when she'd bitten him, and they'd careened down the embankment before slamming into a tree.

Because she didn't feel pain, Indigo wasn't sure if she'd been injured in the crash, and there hadn't been time to pause and take stock to check herself for injuries. She did know the impact had broken the plastic zip ties binding her wrists, leaving her free to focus on running.

The man in the passenger seat, the one who called her kitty, and who kept droning on about how much he would love to sexually assault her, hadn't been wearing a seatbelt. His body had been flung forward, his skull colliding with the windscreen as the car impacted the tree. There was no way he could survive an injury like that, so she knew he was dead.

But burning man had been groaning when she shoved open her door and climbed out. Because she'd been in between the back and front seats, in that little space on the floor of the car, as they hit, she was pretty sure she wasn't hurt. If she was, she didn't think she'd be able to run like she was.

And she was running like the devil himself was on her heels, because in a way that was exactly her situation.

Maybe Dr. Gardner wasn't the devil, maybe burning man wasn't either, but they were pretty darn close. Close enough that she was as scared of them as she would be of the devil.

If burning man caught her …

Maybe thinking about that wasn't such a good idea right now.

So Indigo tried not to think of anything as she ran. Just pictured Voodoo's handsome face, the tenderness in his eyes as he gazed at her, the heat as he kissed her, the promise of more when she was ready in each touch, each caress, each brush of his fingers on her skin.

All she had to do was survive, and all of that could be hers.

Between the dark, the shaky feeling in her broken leg each time her foot struck the ground, and the heaving in her chest as her lungs begged her to take a break and allow them time to rest, she was struggling. The drugs she'd been given gave enhancements to all of her senses, so her sight might be better than the average person, but it wasn't good enough to see normally in the dark.

To that end, it had always been only a matter of time before she hit something.

Turned out to be a broken tree branch. She ran right into it, bounced off it, and went down hard. A brief flare of pain quickly dissipated into nothing, and she rolled onto her back, struggling to drag enough air into her lungs.

Realistically speaking, how much longer could she keep running?

There was no way to know how badly injured burning man was. Sticking around and checking him over certainly hadn't been in her plan, she'd just escaped and run, but he'd been alive, and she had to believe he might be following her.

Was she just supposed to keep running until she collapsed? Until she was physically incapable of taking another step?

Rolling back onto her stomach, she managed to get to all fours before she swayed, the weight of standing too much. It would be so much easier to just curl up in a ball, let nature take its course, let whatever was going to happen just happen.

No.

That's the voices in your head urging you to give in.

You can't listen to them. Can't let them win.

Out there somewhere is Voodoo, all you have to do is get to him and everything will be okay.

That was enough to get her back on her feet, and Indigo resumed running.

For a while at least.

Slowly, her falls got more frequent, and it was harder to get back up each time she went down.

The forest seemed to get thicker.

Darker.

Quieter.

Until all of a sudden, it wasn't quiet anymore.

"Keep doing what you're doing, *bait*," a voice sneered. It wasn't close, but she immediately recognized it as belonging to burning man. Somehow, he must be following whatever trail she was leaving behind, because what were the chances that he would randomly wind up in the same part of the forest that she was in?

Stopping, hand pressed against the closest tree trunk to keep herself upright, Indigo did her best to keep her harsh breathing as quiet as possible. How far away was he? Could he hear her? Did he know where she was or only that she was somewhere nearby?

"Your stupid little car prank didn't change anything. They're out there, and they'll track you, you'll lead them straight into a trap," burning man taunted.

That was the last thing she wanted to do.

Finding Voodoo meant everything to her, but it was also selfish. He was better off on his own, she was a major liability, and she didn't bring much to the table to even that out. Her ability to not feel pain only benefited her, not anyone else. It wouldn't help protect Voodoo and his team, nor would it help them fight against Dr. Gardner.

No.

Don't listen to him.

Voodoo and the rest of Delta Team are going to destroy Dr. Gardner and anyone who stands on his side.

Taking off in the opposite direction from where she thought burning man was, Indigo refused to allow his words to affect her.

She refused to allow anything negative to affect her.

Voodoo had told her that just because her past had been dark didn't mean her future couldn't be light, and that's what she was going to hold onto.

Keep moving.

Don't give in to the voices in her head.

Find Voodoo.

Destroy them all.

That was her plan, she just had to find a way to make it happen before exhaustion, weakness, the environment, and the man chasing her caught up with her.

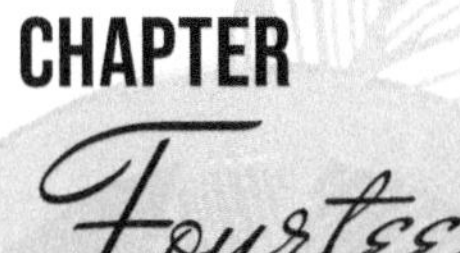

January 25th
12:31 A.M.

"Whoa, you really gonna shoot us, bro?"

Voodoo froze, his finger halfway to pulling the trigger and firing off shots at the people he'd heard approaching.

"Would be pretty rude," Blade continued, "considering we left our women at home and have been hanging around in the forest for the last four days without them."

"Without sex," Steel muttered, making Blade laugh as the five members of his team stepped out from amongst the trees, and Voodoo finally let out a breath and relaxed a little.

"Don't want to get shot, don't sneak up on people," he muttered, but really, he'd never been so glad to see these guys in his life.

"Indigo cause that?" Thunder asked, waving a hand at the crashed car with the dead body in the passenger seat and two open doors.

"Guess she took some inspiration from Rose," he replied, proud of his girl for fighting back, doing what she had to do to try to save herself, unaware he was in the car behind her as she'd been driven away from the facility.

"She did good," Lion said, and everyone else nodded their agreement.

"They're enacting some sort of plan," Voodoo explained. "I believe the goal is to use Indigo as bait to get the rest of us, since they know we're out here."

"How did you find the car?" Steel asked.

"Borrowed one of theirs and followed it," he replied, pointing out his, which he'd left at the top of the embankment when he realized a car had gone over the edge and assumed it was likely the one Indigo was in.

"Do you know where they're based?" Steel asked his next question.

"About twenty or so miles back that way," he said, pointing in the direction of the small building where Indigo had been kept after they'd taken her.

Where she'd been tortured.

Where her beautiful skin had been marred, and more wounds inflicted on her beautiful body and mind.

"How many of them are there?" Steel asked, and the constant stream of questions helped to keep him grounded. Gave him something to focus on other than the raging terror inside him.

"Not sure how many originally, but I killed twelve of them when they found us and got to Indigo before I could. I killed another two while I was tracking her and stole their vehicle. That's how I found the place they were hiding out. There were another twelve of them there that I could see, but five stayed behind, five followed after me in another vehicle, they're all dead. And two were in this car with Indy."

Turning his attention back to the mangled car, Voodoo prayed all over again that Indigo hadn't suffered any life-threatening injuries in the crash.

As amazing as it seemed not to be able to truly feel pain, it wasn't just a blessing, it could be a curse as well. Without pain, she was unable to recognize potential injuries, particularly when she was on her own and afraid for her life.

Each step she took as she ran seeking safety could be taking her one step closer to death instead.

"We'll find her, man," Dragon assured him, and when he turned to look at his friend, he saw the absolute determination in those unusual violet eyes of Dragon's. "I can scent her, she doesn't smell like she's close to death."

"But she's not the only one out there," he said, his gaze moving once again out to the forest behind him.

Even without the open driver's side door, he would know that someone was after her, following her, possibly closing in on her even as they stood there. The car hadn't driven itself, and he'd watched as that man had carelessly thrown Indigo into the back of the vehicle before it drove off.

"The driver is injured," Blade said confidently, and Voodoo wasn't sure if that confidence came from common sense or something he could hear in the man's breathing.

The crash couldn't have happened all that long before he came upon it. He had been no more than a handful of minutes behind the vehicle, and it hadn't taken him more than ten to lead those in the other car out into the forest and kill them. At most, he would guess the car had crashed fifteen minutes before he got there, and his team had been mere minutes behind him.

Fifteen minutes wasn't a huge head start, especially now that he had Thunder with him, but it was still more space than he wanted between him and his girl.

"There's blood on the seat," Lion said, and Voodoo turned to see that his friend had stuck his head inside the wrecked car.

"Course there is, they crashed," he said simply, pointing to the tree the car was wrapped around.

"No, this blood is slightly darker, it happened before the accident, and see the position," Lion gestured, and Voodoo sighed but moved in to check it out.

"It's kind of dripping down the back of the seat," he said.

"Right. Not where you'd expect to see it when he was thrown forward at impact. Even if he then slumped backward, his seatbelt keeping him against the seat, you wouldn't expect to see blood there," Lion said.

"There's blood in the back too," Dragon said, his nostrils flaring.

"Indigo was thrown into the back, behind the driver's seat," Voodoo said slowly. "I thought she might have caused the crash, taking inspiration from Rose."

"Guess your girl decided to get a little payback in the process," Lion told him.

"Her hands were bound behind her," he said, then chuckled. "I'm thinking she bit him. Probably wouldn't let go from the amount of blood we can see, then when she realized she got what she wanted, she let go and huddled down there to minimize her own chances of getting hurt."

Proud didn't even begin to describe what he felt for Indigo in this moment.

Despite how life had beaten her down repeatedly, despite the dark voices, side effects from the drugs they'd all been given whispering in the back of her mind that she was better off dead, she'd fought hard to live.

"How did you see where they put her?" Steel asked.

"After I killed two of the guards and borrowed their vehicle, I used the GPS to track down where they'd come from. It's a small building, and I was going to wait until you guys showed up because I didn't want to risk Indigo being killed if I started a fight I wasn't equipped to win. No one gave me a second glance, I think because they're all scared of us. That guy." Voodoo gestured to the dead man in the passenger seat. "Wanted to wait for more guards to arrive. Apparently, they'll be here tomorrow, but Dr. Gardner won't wait. They're terrified we're going to kill them all. Terrified of Dr. Gardner as well. When they kidnapped Indy earlier, I tried interrogating one of them, but he would rather be dead than give up intel so I think we can assume that's true for any others still around."

Dragon suddenly stiffened, his nostrils flaring wildly. A murderous expression overtook his features.

"What is it?" Steel demanded, and they all watched Dragon expectantly.

"Him," Dragon said simply.

There was only one *him* Voodoo could see his friend caring about. "Dr. Gardner? He's here?"

"I can smell him," Dragon replied.

"Must be back at the building. I should have made a move while I was there. I didn't expect him to be here since he seems to have been hiding out ever since the incident with Rose." If they'd lost their chance at getting the crazed scientist, Voodoo would always carry that burden.

"You couldn't have known he'd be here," Steel assured him.

While he knew it was true, that didn't make him feel any better. The man they'd been hunting for a decade had been right inside the building he'd stood looking at for a solid hour or so before Indigo had been dragged out. Chances were, he could have taken out twelve men. More than twelve if there had been other guards inside protecting the doctor, which there likely were. They probably wouldn't have killed Indigo anyway. They wanted all seven of them alive, they were worth more that way.

"Don't beat yourself up over it," Steel said firmly. "What's done is done, and this time he's not getting away. He wants to try to lure us into a trap, let him try, he's not going to win."

"Do we go after Indigo first, or Dr. Gardner?" Voodoo asked, knowing what his answer would be, but he could hardly demand his team pick a woman they didn't know over a man they'd all wanted dead for the last decade.

"You really have to ask?" Steel demanded, clearly offended. The other four men looked offended, too, and Voodoo relaxed a little as he realized they were all on the same page.

"Indigo first," he said.

"Right," Steel agreed. "We go rescue your girl, and then we finally get our revenge on the man who played God with all of our lives and make him suffer."

Sounded like the perfect plan. Now they just had to hope nothing went wrong.

~

January 25th
    12:45 A.M.

. . .

Keep going.

Keep going.

Keep going.

Was Indigo saying those words out loud, or just inside her head?

Between the thundering of her pulse, and the harsh sound of her breaths sawing in and out of her chest, she didn't really know.

All she knew was that it was getting harder and harder to do.

As badly as she wanted to keep going, sooner rather than later, her body was going to give up on her. Already she wasn't sure how she was still on her feet, still moving, even if she was going a whole lot slower than she had been at first.

Now she no longer felt the cold, and she highly doubted that had anything to do with her enhanced ability to tolerate extreme temperatures.

If she took the time to look down at her naked body, she was sure she would find it littered with marks from her run through the forest, scratches and bruises dotting her skin, but she had no time and no interest in seeing how badly she was banged up. If she couldn't feel them, they didn't exist, that was her philosophy right about now, and she thought it was a pretty good one.

"I know you're out here somewhere, bait," burning man's voice floated to her through the dark.

Each time he called out to her, reminding her of his presence as if she'd be able to forget, his position from her was different. Sometimes he was closer, so close she was sure that if she slowed down and turned her head, she'd be able to see him emerging through the trees to catch her. Other times he was further away, giving her hope that if she just kept going, she could get away from him for good.

At least she knew he wasn't following a specific trail she was leaving behind. He might have seen which way she ran when she climbed out of the car, but he didn't know exactly where she was, and Indigo was pretty sure that was the only thing keeping her safe.

If he knew how to better track her, she'd already be back in his clutches.

Back in Dr. Gardner's clutches.

She so badly wanted to find Voodoo, not just because she'd be safe with him, but because she wanted him to know that the revenge he sought was within his grasp.

Since burning man wasn't taunting her with the knowledge that using her as bait had worked, and Voodoo and his teammates had been captured, she knew they were all still safe.

Safe but out there somewhere.

Pausing for a moment, she leaned up against the closest tree to catch her breath, needing a brief respite more than she needed to keep putting distance between her and the burning man. Exhaustion pressed heavily down upon her, and it would be so easy to give in to it.

All she had to do was stop.

Stop running.

Stop fighting.

Stop trying to live.

Find a small space that would make her feel safe, curl up inside it, let her eyes fall closed, and wait for the inevitable.

An enhanced ability to endure harsh conditions didn't mean that she was impervious to them. Like she'd almost succumbed to hypothermia earlier, it would come for her again, especially when she was in this weakened state.

Closing her eyes would be the equivalent of a death sentence. So she started moving again. No longer really running, but as close as she could get to it.

Dying wasn't an option. She couldn't do that to Voodoo. Already, he'd risked so much for her. He'd stayed out there with her, moving slower, at her speed, rather than just rushing on to join his team. If he could put his life on the line for her even though they'd only just met, then she couldn't give up now.

Must keep going.

Must find Voodoo.

Voodoo is safe, he'll take care of you. Not just protect you but make sure you're okay, clean your skin, dress you in something warm, hold you in his arms, maybe even kiss you.

Despite her exhaustion, the thought of Voodoo kissing her made Indigo smile and gave her a small burst of energy that spurred her on for another few minutes.

When she burst out of the trees, well *lurched* out of the trees was probably a better way to describe how she was moving right now, she found herself at the base of a steep incline, in front of a river. It was rushing too fast for her to consider crossing, although, despite the risk of her body's temperature dropping even further, she might have tried it if she thought it was feasible that she wouldn't get washed away.

Staggering over to it, she dropped to her knees at its side, barely feeling the pressure of whatever debris covered the ground digging into her skin as she held her hands together like a bowl and scooped up some water to drink.

It felt like swallowing ice as it slid down her throat, but it was water, and her body craved it, so she scooped up another handful, and then another, and another.

Satisfied for the moment, she leaned back against her heels and weighed her options. Crossing the river would make it harder for the burning man to follow her, and might lead her closer to civilization again, too. She had no idea how far away she was from the closest road, the closest building, the closest person.

Even if she could find somewhere to get help for herself, leaving the forest meant leaving Voodoo. He was looking for her here, and she had no way of contacting him, no idea how to even begin.

No. Wait.

She *did* have a way of contacting him. If she could find a way to get to a person and then a phone, she could find the number for Prey Security and call them. They'd know how to get in touch with Voodoo. They'd find a way to let him know the revenge he sought was close enough for him to reach out and grab hold of it.

A sound somewhere behind her had Indigo scrambling sideways, realizing she'd made a major tactical mistake in stopping and then getting lost in thought when she knew she was being hunted.

Spinning around, expecting to see the burning man sneering at her as he strode through the trees toward her, instead, she saw no one.

The forest was empty. No one was walking toward her.

Must have imagined the whole thing.

Great, now her mind was giving out on her just like her body was.

Readying herself to shove to her feet, the non-event still a wake-up call, she gathered her reserves of strength. Staying in one place, even for a few minutes, was foolish. Her body would give out on her eventually, but she wasn't quite there yet. As long as she was able to, she was going to keep walking, and when the inevitable happened, she'd just have to hope and pray that burning man passed her by without ever realizing she was there.

Wearily, she managed to stand, and was about to start moving again, probably walking this time, she wasn't sure she had enough energy to run, when she heard it again.

A sound.

A person.

She'd bet anything on that.

Too exposed by the river, she had to decide if she was going to try crossing it or if she was going to keep moving. The ground in front of her went sharply up to form almost a cliff running along the edge of the river. Getting up there would be next to impossible, but she couldn't go back either because back meant heading toward Dr. Gardner and the remaining guards.

Forward it was.

A flash of movement at the top of the cliff had her jerking backward, falling flat on her bottom, terror clawing at her.

It's okay. He's up there, and you're down here. He can't get to you. Not easily anyway, you have time to get away.

The reminder was all she needed, and she scrambled back to her feet right as the figure on top of the hill called out her name.

"Indigo, wait."

He knew her name. Called her by it, not bait, or kitty, or some other term meant to demean her. But she didn't recognize the voice.

How did this person know who she was, but she didn't know them?

"It's Thunder," the man called out. "Do you remember me? I'm one of Voodoo's teammates."

Thunder. Yeah, she remembered that one of Voodoo's teammates was named Thunder. But the guards would know their names, too. This could be a trick, a way to make her think she was safe so she'd willingly go with this person because she thought he was safe.

Those minutes she'd spent with Voodoo's team were blurry at best.

Infection had been ravaging her system, she'd been barely conscious, and she'd never gotten a good look at any of the other men's faces because they'd all been wearing night vision goggles.

She had no way of knowing if this man really was Thunder or if he was trying to trap her. If she made a mistake and trusted him when she shouldn't, she'd be captured again, but if he was safe and she ran away from him, she could wind up captured again.

What a choice.

January 25th
12:55 A.M.

"I'm going to lose her, she doesn't trust me," Thunder's voice came through the comms unit and set Voodoo's heartrate into overdrive.

Sending Thunder on ahead hadn't been his first choice. Splitting up again put them all at a disadvantage, especially when they knew that not only was Dr. Gardner so close, but that more men were being brought in to hunt them.

But there hadn't seemed to be any other choice.

They knew that Indigo wasn't alone out there, that she was being followed, although they had no idea of the condition of the man who had been driving the car and if he was injured to the point that he was no longer a threat. Voodoo hadn't wanted to waste time trying to find him, Indigo was the priority, and he wanted Lion, Dragon, and Blade to use their skills to locate her.

Since Thunder's skill was speed, without any actual physical advantages that could help him track Indigo, they were making this awkward.

Dragon directing Thunder based on what he could smell, Blade directing him based on what he could hear, Lion's enhanced sight not as much a use to them with so many trees around.

It had seemed like such a long shot that this way of locating her would work, and yet it had. Thunder had found her, but from the sounds of things, his girl was ready to bolt, unsure who she could trust.

Not completely unsure, though.

There was one person Indigo was absolutely certain was safe.

Him.

Maybe he wasn't there right now, but there had to be something he could give Thunder to tell her so she would know he was who he said he was and that she could trust him.

Wracking his brain as he ran, Voodoo tried to come up with something that would convince Indigo that Thunder was with him. It couldn't just be something about her past because there was every reason to believe that Dr. Gardner would have done a deep dive into her background to ensure nobody was going to look for her. After all, that had to be why he'd shifted to experimenting on homeless people. Their anonymity provided a safety net that snatching people off the streets or advertising in more mainstream places where people with friends and family looking out for them wouldn't.

It hit him all of a sudden. "Bubbles," he blurted out. "Tell her that Voodoo said her favorite thing that made her smile was bubbles. Her mom used to get her some when she was small because they were cheap and she'd chase them around in the front yard. Then, when she was in foster care, some of the families would only allow her a small amount of money for gifts, and she'd choose bubbles for herself."

Waiting to see if that was enough to reassure Indigo had to be the tensest minute of his life.

"Not far to go," Blade assured him.

"Less than a mile," Dragon added.

A mile was still a long way, though, and for the first time ever, he wished he'd been given Thunder's speed instead of his ability to heal. Healing hadn't saved Indigo. All that had saved Indigo was her own decision to keep fighting. If she hadn't made that choice, he would have lost her to infection or hypothermia days ago.

Keep fighting, honey. Please. I'm coming, but I need you to keep fighting.

"Got her," Thunder's voice through the comms almost brought him to his knees as relief hit him hard.

"It worked? She believes you? Knows you're with me?" he asked, needing a little additional reassurance until he could get there and haul her into his arms.

"Yeah, when I told her what you said about the bubbles, she believed that I was Thunder and that you were talking to me. I told her you were coming, and she started crying." There was amusement in Thunder's voice as he said that, and Voodoo knew it wasn't that the man thought it was funny, but that he was amused that things had progressed so quickly between him and Indigo and that now another one of them had fallen hard and fast for a woman.

"Tell her I'll be there in less than two minutes," he ordered. "Is she okay? How badly is she hurt?" He wanted to be prepared for what he would find when he got there. Indigo had made it a fair distance from the wrecked car, especially since she was moving on a broken leg, but that didn't mean she wasn't badly injured.

"I'm not with her," Thunder said, and Voodoo jerked to a stop.

"What the hell does that mean? You said you found her, that she didn't trust you, but that the bubbles convinced her. What do you mean you're not with her?"

"Relax, dude," Thunder said in a voice that was so annoyingly calm, Voodoo curled his fingers into fists.

"Don't tell me to relax," he snapped as he started running again. There was no way he was relaxing until he had Indigo safe and sound in his arms.

"We wound up taking different routes to get to the same place. I'm standing right above her, but there's a drop of probably thirty feet or so between us. She's down the bottom by the river, I'm way up here. The way you guys are coming, you're going to join me, not her."

"Damn," Voodoo muttered. He'd wanted to be able to hold his girl, but this meant it would take them a while to find a way to get down to Indigo. Especially since they couldn't all leave her at once, one of them would need to keep watch so they could pick off any guards that might find her.

"We'll figure it out," Steel assured him. "Let's just get you to her first."

Nodding his agreement, he was less than a minute out now until they'd reach Thunder, and Voodoo pushed his body harder, making it go faster.

Maybe thirty seconds later, they came out of the tree line to find Thunder standing there, looking down at Indigo below him. She was so close he could almost feel the phantom brush of her in his arms.

Skidding to a stop, he looked down and spotted her. Her thin body was on her knees, looking up at the top of the cliff like it was the only thing keeping her upright.

"Voodoo," she sobbed his name when she spotted him, and he wasn't too macho to admit that his eyes blurred with tears at finally having eyes on her again.

"Right here, honey, I'm right here," he murmured, dropping down to his own knees as he locked his gaze on her, unable to look away for fear that she would disappear in the blink of an eye.

"I knew you wouldn't leave," she called up to him. There was so much faith, so much trust in those simple words that a sob of his own lodged in his throat.

She trusted him.

There was no better gift Indigo could give him than her trust. After everything she'd been through, every person who had let her down time and time again, he knew she had been convinced that she would never hand over her trust to another living person ever again.

Yet she had.

Him. She'd chosen to hand that trust over to him, and Voodoo vowed in this moment that he would never make her regret that decision. He would never let her down, never give her less than she deserved.

"Never, honey. Never. I would never leave you behind. I was tracking you the whole time. Was there when they put you in that car, drove off behind you, killed as many of them as I could before I met up with these guys, and we started tracking you."

"Burning man is out here somewhere. He was close last time I heard him," she told him.

"Who's burning man?" he asked, assuming it was the driver, but he needed to know if someone else was tracking her as well.

"He did this to me." She waved a hand at the marks on her chest. He couldn't make them out from his location, but he remembered seeing them earlier. "Burned me. I don't know his name. But, Voodoo," she said anxiously, pushing up to her feet, "he was there. Dr. Gardner. I saw him. He told me they were going to use me as bait to get all of you back. He's at that building, the one they took me to. You have to go and get him. I'm ... I'm okay. I can wait here. I'll be okay. You need to get to him before he can leave, get away again."

The way she said it shattered his heart. Indigo one hundred percent believed that knowing Dr. Gardner was nearby would cause him and his team to leave her behind, go and kill the scientist first, and then come back for her, even knowing that someone was nearby hunting her.

"We know, honey," he told her. "And we'll get him, but not before we have you with us where we know you'll be safe."

"But—"

"No, Indy. No buts. You first, then him," he said firmly.

Maybe he felt it more than saw it, because with the distance between them and the eerie green light of the night vision goggles, it was harder to read her expressions, but he knew it was joy, relief, disbelief, gratefulness, and something deeper, something closer to love, that crossed her face.

But then from one heartbeat to the next, things changed.

Indigo's eyes widened as her gaze shifted to something that only she could see.

Then she screamed, a bullet cracked through the night, and he had no idea if it hit her or not because she stumbled backward, falling into the river behind her, the water quickly washing her away.

January 25th

1:11 A.M.

Cold.

Wet.

Hard to breathe.

The water tossed her about like she was nothing, not worthy of being considered anything more than another stick, or rock, or debris that fell into its clutches. It didn't care that she was a person, a human being, and honestly, for all her life, she'd never considered herself to be of any more importance than a stick or a rock.

But she was more important.

She was a human being. She deserved to be treated as such.

Voodoo's voice echoed in her mind, screaming her name as burning man had emerged from the trees, obviously guided to her by the sound of their voices, long since gone but still just as loud inside her head.

If she died, he would grieve her, and that mattered.

That made her matter.

So she fought, forced her arms to spin, fighting through the fast-moving water, doing her best to get herself to the bank. The others would come for her, but there was no way they could get to her quickly. They'd been up on top of that cliff, and she'd been down the bottom. It wasn't like they could just jump down to get to her. They'd have to circle around, find the same path that had led her down to the river instead of up to the cliffs. That would take them time, more time than she wanted to admit, and the river didn't care about that. It just dragged her along with it, uncaring of the fact that it was taking her away from safety and toward the unknown.

The only good thing was that it was also taking her away from burning man.

Be thankful for small mercies.

It took her far longer than she would have liked to reach the bank. The water fought her at every turn, trying to drag her under. It managed to at least half a dozen times. Each time her head went beneath the surface, those voices in her head whispered to her how much easier it would be to let go, allow the water to finish her off.

Each time she found herself starting to agree, Voodoo's voice would sound in his head.

That terror when she fell into the water was all for her, and she knew she couldn't give up, couldn't give in. Had to keep fighting. Someone would miss her if she wasn't alive anymore. Someone would grieve her if she died.

Those thoughts were so new for her, but they filled her with the strength she needed to find her way to the land.

By the time her feet touched the bottom, and her weary arms reached out to grab hold of some of the trees growing close to the edge, she was close to complete exhaustion. It was only a miracle, sheer determination to live, that had kept her going in the water when she'd already been close to collapse before Thunder found her.

Hands reached for her, helped her, and she was glad Voodoo had gotten to her faster than she'd thought.

They pulled her out and laid her down on the ground.

The world felt so distant. Maybe she'd survived because she wanted to live, but now she felt unconsciousness drifting in. She couldn't fight against it any longer. Didn't want to. Voodoo was safe. He'd protect her, she didn't need to worry so long as he was there.

"Get her in the truck," a voice said, and even though she'd already been falling into the darkness that tugged at the edges of her mind, a thread of awareness pulled her back.

That voice.

It wasn't Voodoo's.

Wasn't Thunder's either.

And she was pretty sure it didn't belong to Steel, Dragon, Blade, or Lion.

Eyes popping open, she saw six large shapes hovering around her. They were dressed all in black, but Voodoo and his team were in black, and the guards were in black, everyone was in black. Everyone but her who wasn't in anything at all.

Someone grabbed her, lifting her off the ground. They felt wrong, smelled wrong. This wasn't someone she could trust. It was one of them.

"No," she said, trying weakly to push him away.

Of course, it didn't work. The man didn't even waste time talking to her, didn't bother to look down at her, merely carried her away from the water, and toward what did indeed turn out to be a truck.

Seemed she'd washed up on the side of a road.

Not any road, but the road the new guards who had been coming in must have been driving along. That had to be who these people were because she didn't recognize any of their voices, and they were all chattering amongst one another as she was carried to the back of a truck.

"She really feels no pain?" one of them asked as the man holding her physically threw her into the back of the truck.

Indigo oomphed as she landed, the air knocked out of her lungs, but she felt no pain. Her body just absorbed the impact and dealt with it, but the lack of energy she had worried her. Her ability to withstand large amounts of pain wouldn't save her life, the only thing that might was finding a way to fight, a way to escape.

"Apparently so," the man who had thrown her said, although he sounded bored by the entire thing.

"Let's try it out," one piped up.

"We're just supposed to transport her if we find her," another said.

"You're not curious to see?" one asked. "Because I am. I want to see if she really can endure pain like she doesn't even feel it."

"Whatever, if you want to do it, just do it. Then we need to get moving," the man who had carried her, who seemed to be in charge, said, still sounding bored.

"What should we do?" someone asked.

"Kick her? Hit her? Knife? Gun?" someone started rattling off suggestions, each one sounding worse than the one before.

If they weren't careful, they could still kill her. Just because she wouldn't feel anything more than an initial sharp rush of pain didn't mean she wouldn't still suffer from the injury. Her body healed at an accelerated rate, but the very fact that she'd been dying from infections when Voodoo and the others found her proved that an injury could still quite easily take her out.

"What about the stun gun?" someone suggested, and from the rush of agreements, she could see that idea was going to be the winner.

One of the men climbed up into the back of the truck with her, and

Indigo shifted so she was huddled in the corner. Trust her bad luck to have her swim to shore right where these men were waiting for her. They had to have seen her floundering in the water, maybe followed her, probably would have come in after her if she hadn't managed to get herself out.

But if she'd stayed in the water, she still would have stood a chance.

A chance at escaping, a chance at living, a chance at getting back to Voodoo, a chance at ... everything he'd been offering her. A home, a family, a job, one day even his love.

Now it was all slipping through her fingers.

What could have been disappearing with each breath she took.

All the hopes and dreams she had tentatively been allowing to form were now gone. Or they would be pretty soon. But honestly, she would rather have died in the river than be trapped there, a toy to be played with, and discarded eventually.

Reaching her, the man with the stun gun grinned at her with excitement in his eyes. She wanted to tell him that if he thought it was so interesting to be experimented on, have your body changed in ways you never agreed to, then he was free to tell Dr. Gardner he was next in line to be injected.

But she didn't.

Couldn't.

Her voice seemed to have left her, and all she could do was curl into a ball, trying to make herself as small a target as possible.

Not that it mattered. The man leaned down, touched the stun gun to her side, and activated it. One sharp stab of pain, kind of like being set on fire, rushed through her body, then it was just nothing.

Nothing as in no pain, but the electrical current still passed through her, and her muscles jerked accordingly.

"Didn't even scream," the man said, looking over his shoulder at his friends.

"Do it again," someone called out.

"Yeah, maybe it was just a fluke," another added.

So the man shocked her again. Then again. Then again.

Her body spasmed convulsively each time. She was flat on her back now, writhing as there was no relief from the shocks. But there was no pain. No physical pain anyway. Just a deep ache in her chest that was fear that Voodoo was lost to her forever, everything she'd never allowed herself to hope for, and yet had been unable to resist wanting the second she met him.

He'd changed everything, changed her, and now all she could do was hope that he never wound up trapped and imprisoned, an experiment locked in a cage.

January 25th
1:20 A.M.

Watching Indigo fall into that river, uncertain if she'd been shot, was one of the worst moments of his life. And he'd seen and experienced a lot of horrific things in the fifteen or so years since he'd joined the military.

How could any of them compare to this, though?

His girl, already so weak and vulnerable, once again been battered by life. When the hell was the universe going to give her a break?

When was it going to give her back to him?

She'd been so close, he'd been minutes away from having her where he wanted her, safe in his hold, and yet ultimately, he'd been too far away. Now it was further away again. The river carried her away from him and given that his teammates had grabbed him before he could risk jumping down to the bottom of the cliffs so he could fling himself into the river and go after Indigo, it was going to take even longer to get her back.

He would have jumped.

Would have risked everything to try to get to her as quickly as he could.

If Steel and Dragon hadn't grabbed him like they'd known exactly what he was planning to do, he would have done it. Really, it wasn't even anything he had consciously planned, he'd just been driven by the need to get to Indigo, and it overrode everything else, including common sense.

Now they were making their way down to the river. Voodoo was so painfully aware that for each step they took, the river could drag Indigo the equivalent of two or more steps further downstream.

Every few seconds he glanced at Dragon. The man could smell everything, including death, and he was hoping that if the worst happened, his friend would at least be able to prepare him for it.

Dragon nodded, and Voodoo took that to mean that Indigo was still breathing, still doing what she did and surviving.

Whoever had fired that shot at Indigo must have immediately disappeared back into the trees, because they'd never seen who it was. It had to be the burning man, though, who else could it be? They knew he was out there, and that he'd been following Indigo the entire time.

Finding their way down to where Indigo had been was quicker than he could have hoped for, if the burning man hadn't shown up and shot at her, it would have taken him less than ten minutes to get to her. Instead, she was gone, and he was still chasing after her.

Not that he'd ever stop.

No matter how far he had to go or how long it took, Voodoo would never give up on Indigo. He'd track her all night, all day, all year if that was what he had to do to get her back.

"Someone up ahead," Blade warned them, his voice quiet, a hint of sound heard only by the six of them.

Dragon nodded in agreement, and Lion pointed to something so far only he could see.

"I smell blood," Dragon added. "It's the same man who was driving the car Indigo caused to crash."

That was what they were expecting, but there were still at least five other men who had been with Dr. Gardner, and they had no way of knowing if any of them were aware that he'd killed some of the men, that the car had crashed, or that Indigo was free again. Without anything to prove otherwise, they had to play things worst-case scenario and assume that those men were also out there somewhere by now.

"Sixty or so yards that way," Lion said, adjusting their course ever so slightly.

As they approached the man who had burned his beautiful, precious girl, Voodoo felt his adrenaline amp up. While he might be running on fumes after days of hiking through the forest, protecting Indigo, worrying over her, trying to heal her, killing over and over again, when taking lives was something he avoided whenever he could, this was one target he was going to enjoy torturing, enjoy killing.

The sounds of footsteps grew loud enough for all of them to hear, the sound of ragged breathing, the metallic scent of blood strong enough to reach all their noses.

And then Voodoo saw him.

A shadowy figure stumbling through the forest, seemingly oblivious to the fact that not only were they following him, but they were seconds away from catching him.

Because they all understood what Indigo had become to him, none of his teammates attempted to step in, allowing him to do what he needed to do.

Throwing himself at the burning man, Voodoo tackled him to the ground. The other man screamed at the contact, and then began to thrash, attempting to buck him off.

Not happening.

At this second, the burning man was the epicenter of the rage exploding out of him. He wanted to see the man bleed, wanted to feast on his screams, all thoughts of healing or saving gone. This man didn't deserve to be healed, didn't deserve to be saved. From the moment he had decided to burn Indigo's delicate flesh, he had sealed his fate.

Slamming a fist into the man's jaw, he grinned when he felt the bone shatter, teeth go flying everywhere. It wasn't enough, but it was a start.

"I don't think I need to ask if you know who I am," Voodoo drawled as he pressed a knee into the man's throat to pin him in place, taking care to ensure he didn't press too hard and cut off his air supply. Not only did he want to prolong this, but he wanted every drop of intel this man had. No forcing his hand and making him kill too quickly this time around.

Wide, terrified eyes stared up at him. Guess the burning man wasn't such a tough guy when he didn't have a tiny woman to play with. Now he was the helpless little plaything, and Voodoo was going to make sure his last minutes on earth were as horrible as he could make them.

"How many men are back there with Dr. Gardner?" he asked.

Despite his fear, the man remained silent. Broken jaw or not, burning man was capable of talking, and silence wasn't going to cut it.

Not wanting to waste time Indigo didn't have, Voodoo pulled out his knife and held it above the man's eye. "How many men are back there?" he repeated his question.

Burning man whimpered but didn't offer an answer, so Voodoo dug his fingers into the man's eye socket, causing him to howl in pain and thrash about. That didn't stop him from slicing the blade of his knife through the muscles and nerves attaching his eye to his body.

Once he had it free, he held it up before the sobbing, screaming man, allowing him to see it with his remaining eye, then squashed the eyeball in his fist, tossing away the ruined tissue.

"Hard way or easy way. I have questions, and I want answers. I want to make you suffer, but I want Indigo back more. So you answer my questions, tell us what we want to know, and you get to save yourself a bit of suffering before I slit your neck." Normally, talk like this would make him a little queasy. His healing instincts so innate to who he was as a person that even his years in the military, his training and experience, and the drugs that had been given to him couldn't eradicate it.

Now those words flowed easily, he was ready and willing, more than that, he was excited about inflicting pain on this despicable excuse for a man.

"S-seven," the man stammered through his broken jaw. "Seven men back there with him."

"And how many more are coming in the next wave?" he asked. When the burning man hesitated briefly, Voodoo swiped the sharp blade of his knife through the man's nose, severing it and throwing it aside. Burning man choked on the blood now flowing down his throat, but Voodoo merely pressed a little firmer against his neck. "I see why you're so addicted to your knife," he said over his shoulder to Blade, who was grinning in amusement at the ruined face of the man they were interrogating.

"Right? Nothing beats a knife. A gun is so impersonal, but a knife lets you get a whole lot more creative," Blade agreed cheerfully.

"How many more are coming in?" Voodoo asked again. As much as he was enjoying giving his anger an outlet before it could consume him from the inside out, he wanted to find Indigo before she disappeared for good. It wasn't just the river he was afraid of. An undetermined number of people were out there now or would be sometime over the next day, and each and every one of them was a threat to his girl.

"A dozen," burning man wheezed. "You've killed so many of his men, Dr. Gardner is having trouble finding more. Word is getting out that anyone who takes a job for him winds up dead, so most of the mercs will no longer take the jobs he offers."

Perfect.

Bit by bit, they were putting more and more dents in the doctor's operation. Without Whitney to work on the drug anymore, with all of his labs located and destroyed and no longer operational, with his only other living experiment now free, and with no one left willing to take on a death sentence no matter how much money he threw at them, there wasn't much more Dr. Gardner could do to remain out of their clutches.

"When are they arriving?" he asked. Just because the word had been another twenty-four hours didn't mean things couldn't change. He wanted to know how much time he had to find his girl and get her someplace safe before they went for Dr. Gardner.

Burning man's one remaining eye met his, and despite the pain and terror still present in it, there was something else there too.

Something that set his teeth on edge and had the hairs on the back of his neck standing up.

"You're already too late," burning man said, then spat blood at him. "They're already here, and they already have her."

January 25th
  2:02 A.M.

It seemed never-ending.

There was no way to properly position herself in the back of the truck and not get tossed all about as it sped along roads that took her further away from Voodoo, from safety, from a life she shouldn't be brave enough to want but craved with every fiber of her soul.

In reality, they probably hadn't been driving all that long, but to Indigo, alone in the back of a truck, bouncing about, naked and cold, her wet hair still sticking to her back as the long strands couldn't find enough warmth to dry, it felt like an eternity.

After playing with the stun gun for a while, the guys whooping and hollering in amusement as her body reacted to the electrical current without causing her any pain, they'd slammed the door closed behind her and taken off. She'd wanted to try to make a run for it before the door closed, but she hadn't had the energy to move, let alone stand up and run.

At first, when the truck started moving, she'd been bounced all over the place, her muscles too weak to do anything to protect herself. Just because she didn't feel them didn't mean there weren't more bruises layered over older ones in a seemingly endless patchwork map that told the story of what her body had endured.

As they drove along, knowing what waited for her on the other side, another cage, more tests, more experiments, a life of captivity for however long it lasted, it was hard not to wish she hadn't been different. That she was the same as all the other people she'd seen come and go in the months she'd been in Dr. Gardner's care. That she hadn't been able to handle the anger and the suicidal thoughts, given in to them, and ended her suffering long ago.

There were so many points along the way where she could have given in and not wound up back in this position. But as badly as she wished she wasn't there right now, it was hard to wish she was dead.

Oh, she wanted to be, there was definitely a huge chunk of her mind that knew it was better than what was coming. But how could she fully wish to die when Voodoo was still out there? So long as he wasn't captured, too, there was hope.

Hope was the one thing she'd promised herself after her ex-husband served her with divorce papers and kicked her out, that she would never again allow herself to feel. She'd been happy with that plan, knew it was for the best, knew she could endure more of life's suffering if she didn't believe anything would ever change.

But Voodoo had changed that. He'd brought hope into her life, and she hadn't realized until right now, trembling with cold and attempting to brace herself in a corner of a truck, just what a powerful thing hope could be.

Sure, it didn't change her circumstances, and it wouldn't provide her with a magic wand to find a way out of this truck and away from these men. But it did give her a purpose, a goal, something to fight toward. Watch, listen, assess, try to find any weaknesses, and then exploit them.

Maybe that wasn't much of a plan, but it was better than just sitting there and waiting for the inevitable to happen. If it happened then it happened, she couldn't stop it, but she wasn't going to give in, wasn't going to give up. Voodoo thought she was strong, that what she had endured alone, he had only survived because he had a team at his back. Indigo didn't want to let him down, she wanted to be the version of herself that he saw when he looked at her.

And she did have a team at her back now.

Maybe they weren't physically there, but they would come for her. All of them, not just Voodoo. Of course, she'd known that he wouldn't give up on her, but she'd thought there was only so far the fact that they'd all been experimented on by the same delusional man could carry her when it came to the rest of his team.

Only all of them had been there. They'd decided as a team not to go after Dr. Gardner first, even though they'd known before she told them that he was close by. They'd prioritized her over something they had been wanting and working toward for the last ten years.

If that didn't tell her everything she needed to know then nothing would.

So fighting was the only option. Anything else would be disrespectful.

Eventually, the truck slowed to a stop, and she heard the men climb out of the front, slamming their doors behind them and chattering amongst themselves like they didn't have a naked and abused woman trapped in the back of their truck. Like they weren't transporting her to a hell they understood, even if they never truly could comprehend what it was like to be on the other side of the cage.

Thankfully, it was still nighttime when they opened that back door, so she wasn't blinded by sudden light. It was clear from the way they moved, their relaxed attitudes, and the fact that they didn't have their weapons aimed and ready to shoot, that they didn't view her as any sort of threat. If it had been Voodoo or any of the other men on his team back there, she was positive they would have approached with an entirely different outlook.

But it was only her, she was small and weak, always a victim, so they didn't think they needed to worry about her.

Maybe she was weak, and maybe she'd been a victim her entire life, but she didn't want that for herself any longer. She wanted to be different, to live instead of just survive. She wanted to dig deep and find the anger that had almost fizzled out inside her and draw on it, let it strengthen her, prove to everyone, including herself, that she was more than everyone saw, more than a tragic past of abuse.

For now, though, her best bet was to play up being the weak and pathetic little victim, allow them to keep seeing her as nothing, and wait for her opportunity. It would be silly to try to make a run for it, she could barely stand up, and they would shoot her if she tried and then laugh about how she wouldn't feel any pain from the injury.

"Come on, little one, let's get you settled in your new home," one of the men said as he jumped up into the back of the truck and came to collect her.

Throwing her over his shoulder, he climbed back down out of the truck and carried her toward another one. The second truck was much larger, one of those huge ones that transported things across the country. As normal as it looked from the outside, as they climbed into it, she could see that inside someone had fitted it out as a makeshift lab.

"Boss thinks no one will be able to find him if he doesn't stay still," the man carrying her explained as though she cared in the least about what Dr. Gardner thought or did. She wanted him dead every bit as much as Voodoo and the others did.

Inside the truck, one long wall had been transformed into a row of three glass cages. The space inside each cage was small, consisting of a toilet and a faucet along the back walls, and then two single cots. No chairs or tables, nothing in them to keep them entertained, no TVs, or books, or paper and pens. Why would you bother to spend time and energy on entertaining something you considered to be nothing more than an animal?

Along the other wall of the truck was a row of desks lined with the same lab equipment she was used to seeing at the other facility. There was a narrow walkway between the cages and the desks, enough that someone could easily walk up and down, and since there were no bars or windows on the cages, there would be no reason to fear one of the caged animals grabbing hold.

"Might have to ask one of them to share a bed with you," the man carrying her joked as he took her down to the last cage. "Bet one of them could be easily persuaded," he added, slapping her bare backside hard and then balancing her so he could unlock the door.

Inside the room, he dumped her on the bed, shot her a wink, and then walked back out again, locking her inside. The glass would be virtually impenetrable, reinforced and bulletproof, there was no way she would be able to break through it to escape. There was no door handle on the inside or lock that she could even attempt to pick, not that she knew how to do that. No doubt this place was soundproof, so not even screaming for help would garner any attention.

Trapped.

No amount of clinging to hope, assessing, listening, and gathering intel, looking for ways to escape, was going to change that.

Her fate was sealed, and Indigo found herself right back where she'd been at the beginning when Voodoo found her in that supply closet. Coming after her would only wind up with him sharing this cell with her.

He needed to let her go.

To focus on finding Dr. Gardner and hoping that taking him out of the equation would cause his little lab empire to crumble. But even that wasn't a guarantee. Someone else could continue it on, or one of the guards could decide she was a fun little plaything and keep her for himself.

Unfortunately for her, hope was a double-edged sword, and on the other side of hope was hopeless.

Which was exactly how she felt right now, as everything she allowed herself to want shimmered completely out of reach.

January 25th
2:47 A.M.

Voodoo snarled and knocked over the table, sending it crashing to the ground.

Nobody intervened, letting him have this moment, this tantrum, to let out his rage before it consumed him. Not sated for long after slicing the blade of his knife through burning man's neck, it was now pulsing through his body with each beat of his heart. He felt it like it was a living being inside him, urging him to destroy everything in his path.

Even his teammates.

They weren't a threat, his brain registered that, they weren't even doing anything to prevent him from finding Indigo, his brain registered that, too, but they were there, and they had to be destroyed.

Everything had to be destroyed.

The entire world must be burned to the ground because it had stolen his girl from him.

"You've got this," Dragon murmured, his voice low and soothing, not at all how Dragon usually sounded. Dragon was the angry one, the one who indulged his fury more than the rest of them. Now things had changed. Dragon had found a balm for that rage, had found a refuge in the storm that was their lives, had found the peace that eluded all of them for so long.

For that alone, Dragon should be punished.

It wasn't fair that Cassandra was safe back at their home. Dragon didn't have to worry about anyone experimenting on the woman he loved, didn't have to worry about anyone inflicting injuries on her that she wouldn't feel but could kill her, nonetheless.

"Don't give in to it, Voodoo," Steel ordered, his voice hard and unyielding, and Voodoo turned his red-coated vision on his team leader.

Steel had no right to order him to control himself when his girl was also safe and sound at home. Rose was safe, Cassandra was safe, Whitney was safe, the only one who wasn't safe was Indigo.

"I got them," Lion suddenly announced, and Voodoo was legitimately sure that the announcement was the only reason he didn't fling himself at the members of his team, men he considered brothers, and do his best to tear them limb from limb.

This wasn't him.

He didn't give in to his rage.

But then again, he didn't live with the woman he loved in constant danger.

"Got them?" he growled, spinning around to find Lion standing in the doorway. After learning that Indigo had already been recaptured, Voodoo had killed burning man. Then they'd backtracked to the vehicle and driven back to the building where Indigo had been held and tortured in the hopes that Dr. Gardner might still be there.

Instead, they'd found the place empty. The metal table where Indigo had been bound and burned still sat in the middle of the room, abandoned, but was the scene of more of her suffering, nonetheless. He hadn't needed Dragon's scent to know what had happened in that room. It was the only thing that made sense given that one of the rooms had the beginning of a lab being set up in it, and the other had a table and chairs.

Now Lion said he had a lead, and Voodoo prayed his friend was right, because he was dangerously close to losing his mind.

"They left in a hurry," Lion explained, not bothering to mention the overturned table, or the fact that Voodoo had been seconds away from attacking his teammates. "So they didn't do a good clear out. They left behind a computer system. They thought they'd wiped it down, but they hadn't. I got access to their system, and another system just went online."

"What does that mean?" Blade asked.

"It means that I can track their location," Lion replied with a grin.

"Where are they?" Voodoo snarled, feeling in this moment very much more like an animal than a human killing machine Dr. Gardner had been attempting to create.

"About twenty miles away," Lion replied.

Twenty miles.

May as well be a hundred. A thousand. A million.

If she wasn't with him, then Indigo was too far away.

"They're still down by the river," Lion continued, but Voodoo had already lost interest in this little talk, all he cared about was getting to Indigo, and destroying anything that got in his way.

"Let's go," he snapped, already stalking from the room.

The others followed, thankfully without any disagreement, or any talk of working on a plan. Voodoo didn't care about a plan, he'd attack whatever stood between him and his girl when they got there.

In the vehicle, the others talked, probably coming up with one of those plans he wasn't interested in, but he blocked out all of their voices. Despite the fury cloaking everything, trying to take control of him, urging him to do things he usually would never even consider, a tiny piece of his brain was still capable of rational thought.

It urged him to calm down, get back in control. Reminded him that clear heads were what would rescue Indigo, get her back alive and in one piece. If he gave in to the anger fully, there might be no coming back, and where would that leave Indigo? Even if he didn't mess up her rescue, he couldn't be what she needed if he wasn't in control of himself. The last thing she deserved was another person in her life ruled only by anger, that wasn't safe to be around, that was a threat to her physical, psychological, and emotional well-being.

"You doing okay?" Dragon asked quietly.

Forcing air into his lungs, forcing back the rage, forcing himself to find himself again before it was too late, he clung to what little control he could manage. "Yeah," he ground out. It was partially true. Maybe he wasn't really doing okay, but he hadn't fully given in yet, so he had to count that as a win.

The more deep breaths he took, the easier it got. The rage receded a little, enough to clear his head, enough to think, enough to know that this was the only way to save Indigo. If it wasn't for that one thought, Voodoo knew he would already be gone. Once he gave all the way in to the rage, his team would have no choice but to kill him to ensure their own safety. He'd seen it happen before when they were being held hostage. After someone let that fury take over, there was literally no coming back from it, they became the beast their creator had designed.

"Back with us?" Steel asked.

"Yeah," he said again, calmer this time as more of his control returned.

"Good, because we're almost there," Thunder said from the driver's seat, where he was once again maneuvering them between trees at breakneck speed.

"What do we know?" he asked, aware now that a plan was in fact necessary to save his girl.

"They're about a mile up ahead," Steel explained. "In a spot where a small logging road once met up with the river."

"Think they're on a boat?" he asked.

"Lion said he sees a houseboat and a truck," Steel replied. "We're going to pull over half a mile out, go the rest of the way on foot. We don't know how many of them there are, but we know they're prepared for the possibility of us showing up. This was what they wanted after all, to use her as bait to lure us in."

"We're not going to give them what they want," he growled.

"Damn right," Blade agreed.

"We're getting your girl back," Lion said fiercely. "No one else is losing the woman they love."

It was only now that Voodoo had fallen for a woman himself that he fully understood the sacrifice Lion had made in walking away from the woman he loved. And the daily restraint it must take the man not to track her down and drag her back to their mansion, convince her to forgive him.

When Thunder pulled their vehicle over, they all jumped out, moving as one, as the bonded-for-life team that they were. There were no words exchanged, they all knew what they had to do and were prepared to do it.

As they approached the location, Voodoo could see that the river was wider there, deeper, fiercer, roaring through the dark night, like it were angry that Indigo had been spared from its clutches.

"He's here," Dragon said, nostrils flaring. "She is, too. Nineteen other scents."

"Nineteen to six, those odds are easy, that's like one on three," Blade said with a cocky grin.

"She's still alive?" he asked, needing to know before they went in that his girl was waiting for him. If she wasn't, then he had no reason not to allow the fury to take over, no reason not to give in and allow himself to become a monster.

"Alive," Dragon said the only word that mattered.

"Then let's do this," Voodoo said as they all started moving again.

The first layer of defense went down in a short burst of gunfire. Four bodies dropped, behind them others shouted, moving into positions they thought would afford them a measure of protection.

They wished.

Every single person there was going to die tonight.

"I knew you'd come," a voice called out. *His* voice. Dr. Gardner's. And as the guards began to fire back at him and his team, Voodoo spotted the man standing on a houseboat, watching them with a gleeful expression, like he truly believed he was going to get them back under his control.

"You're going to die for what you did to her," Voodoo roared into the night.

They all had reason to want this man dead. For what he'd done to them personally. For the way he'd tortured Rose from childhood. For putting a contract out on Cassandra just for being unwittingly dragged into this. For taking Whitney's drug, created with goals of saving lives, and twisting it into something dark and dirty. For misleading, imprisoning, and forever altering innocent people like Indigo. For every man and woman who hadn't survived the drugs.

But right now, Voodoo knew that he had to be the one to end it.

To steal Dr. Gardner's life like the man had stolen so much from so many people.

Knowing his team would have his back, would take out the remaining threats, and protect his girl, Voodoo headed for the houseboat. Scaling a tree close to the river, he got the first good look he'd had at Dr. Gardner since he and his team had escaped the facility seven years ago. The man looked smaller, older than he remembered. Or maybe it was the flash of fear on the scientist's previously cocky face as he realized one of his creations was heading right to him, and he didn't have the means to protect himself.

"Go!" Dr. Gardner shouted, and the houseboat began to move.

"Not this time," Voodoo vowed as he jumped, lifting his weapon as he flew through the air, firing at the man who had destroyed so many lives.

~

January 25th
2:56 A.M.

A constant war raged inside her.

Give up and let the inevitable happen, accept her fate, don't ask for more, don't want more, and don't wish for more. Wait to die, however long that took.

Or cling to the hope that Voodoo had planted and nurtured inside her, and keep fighting, find a way to make something happen.

At any given second, Indigo had no idea which side was going to win.

But she knew what was going to happen next when two of the men strolled down the walkway outside her cage.

She knew that look.

While technically speaking, she'd been a test subject kept in a lab, everything done to her was to measure and gauge her ability to withstand it, that was really just a cover for saying she'd been tortured. Didn't matter that the guards hadn't been allowed to touch her, because the scientists who worked for Dr. Gardner were every bit as sadistic as the doctor himself.

"Getting settled into your new home, little one?" one of them drawled as he pressed his palm to a panel outside the door to her cage. It was the man who had carried her earlier. From the hungry way he'd looked at her, she shouldn't be surprised that he'd found his way to her cage this quickly.

Since she knew they weren't really after an answer, she didn't bother to offer one. Just sat on her bed and watched them. No one had given her any clothes, and there had been none in the room, so she was still naked. When she'd been kept at the lab these last several months, she'd at least been given underwear, but that didn't look like it was going to be the case anymore.

Maybe she should be used to being mostly undressed in front of strangers by now, but she hadn't learned to completely let go of modesty. Something she was going to have to rectify pretty quickly because this was her new reality.

"You play real nice, and maybe we can scrounge up a nice meal for you," he said as he opened the door to her cage and stepped inside.

As he did, her gaze dropped to the ground, praying he wouldn't notice what she'd left on the floor right by the door.

In one of her bouts of determination, she'd tried to set up a way to escape. Chances were, it wasn't going to work, but maybe for once luck would be on her side.

Please be on my side.

You owe me after a lifetime of bad, I deserve one good.

Thankfully, neither of the men seemed to notice, too focused on whatever they had planned for her, and she let out a little breath as they stepped toward her. Whatever they were going to do would be awful, she knew that, but she would happily endure it if her little plan actually managed to work.

"You're like a real carnival show, aren't you, little one?" the man who had carried her in here earlier drawled. "Too bad freak shows are a thing of the past because you could have had a real career there."

"Still got an audience here though," the other man piped up. He looked young, way too young to be working a job like this, but there was no denying the sadistic glint in his eyes. Young or not, he was quite happy where he was and with what he was going to do to her.

"Sure do, little one. Pretty thing like you can probably learn real quick how to use that to her advantage. You're going to be the only girl, with six monsters living side by side with you, and a whole team of men watching over you. Don't think it takes a whole lot of imagination to figure out how to make the most of this situation."

Was that what they were planning for her?

If they were going to rape her, they'd only been doing what so many men before them had done. She could take it. She'd hate every second of it, but she could endure it. Would endure it. And this time, she couldn't make a play to bite anything that was put near her. Couldn't scratch it, or yank on it, or anything else either.

Because she wanted to see if what she'd done worked.

So she sat there, watched as they stalked toward her, waiting because there wasn't anything else for her to do.

Expecting things to take a sexual turn after what they'd implied, Indigo was a little surprised when the younger of the two grabbed her, sitting on the bed behind her and yanking her up so her back was pressed against his chest. He flung one of his legs over one of hers, pinning it in place, and with his arm keeping her arms pinned at her sides, there wouldn't have been anything she could have done to fight them off, even if she'd been going to try.

The older of the men, the one who carried her, was grinning at her like an idiot as he pulled out a knife. It glinted in the overly bright white light of her prison cell, and she didn't need a vivid imagination to guess what they were going to do.

"I didn't think this would be as cool as it is to hurt you and know you don't feel any pain," he told her as if she actually cared what he thought. She wasn't a game, wasn't entertainment, wasn't a toy to be played with and broken.

She was a human being, and that meant she was worthy of respect and basic human kindness.

For the first time in her life, Indigo actually believed those words, that sentiment. She *was* a human being, and that *did* mean she was worthy of respect and basic human kindness. It wasn't her fault that her parents were horrible people, nor was it her fault that some people signed up for the foster program because they wanted to get their hands on vulnerable children. It wasn't her fault that her first boyfriend had been a sadistic psychopath, or that he'd taken her need for love and affection and used it against her. It wasn't her fault that her ex-husband had decided to play with her because, apparently, dating a woman he saw as a loser, as less than him made him feel better about himself.

Nothing that had happened to her was her fault.

So she didn't shy away from meeting the man's gaze as he plunged the knife into her leg. She supposed it was a good thing that he had targeted her already broken leg, if she got a chance to run, this new injury wouldn't impede that ability any more than it already was.

"Look, she really isn't in pain," the younger guy who was holding her said in wonder, like this was a simple and fun kids' science experiment, making a baking soda volcano or something.

It was getting old.

Okay, she didn't feel pain, but that didn't make it fun to inflict wounds on her just to prove that.

"Dig it around a little," the younger guy said, his voice all heady with excitement.

Which the older guy seemed only too happy to do.

Indigo could feel the knife moving inside her, but felt no pain, just a weird and uncomfortable feeling that came from a foreign object invading her body.

"What about if you—"

Whatever the younger man was going to say was cut off when gunfire sounded outside the truck.

Both men immediately straightened, all traces of amusement and playfulness gone from their expressions as they realized that playtime was over. The knife was removed from her leg, the man behind her jumped up, and they both went running out of her cell, letting the door fall closed behind them.

But they never looked back.

Never noticed her drag herself off the bed and crawl over to the door.

Never saw that the tiny scrap of material she'd ripped off the blanket and placed right at the opening of the door, hoping that when opened, it might flutter into place and prevent the door from fully closing.

Never even thought to check that she was secure, as she grabbed hold of the tiny piece of material, now wedged between the door and the doorjamb, and managed to open the door.

Elation filled her, strengthened her, and Indigo couldn't believe that for once something had gone her way. This plan of hers, she would have given a less than one percent chance of working, and yet it had.

Now she stepped out of her cell and stumbled down the walkway to the back of the truck. She had to assume that it was Voodoo and the guys out there, but she couldn't place all her faith in that.

So the second her feet hit the ground she ran as fast as she could with a ruined leg, hoping that if it was Voodoo's team they'd be able to track her easily enough with their enhanced skills, and if it wasn't, that she was able to find a place to hide until she was strong enough to find her own way to safety.

January 25th
3:03 A.M.

Almost the second Voodoo hit the water, bullets followed him in.

Slicing through the water all around him, almost close enough to slice right through him.

Or maybe they did hit him.

Honestly, he was so hyped up on adrenaline right now that he was pretty sure he'd absorbed Indigo's ability to not feel pain.

Pain was nothing when both the man he'd focused all his energy on for the last decade, and the woman who had torpedoed her way into his life were both so close he could feel it.

Before him the houseboat was moving, taking Dr. Gardner away with it. He had no idea if he'd hit his target, or if he'd delivered a kill shot. While usually Voodoo would be confident that he hit what he aimed at, this was different. He'd been moving, flying through the air, and the scientist had moved, too, realizing he'd made a tactical error by remaining out in the open on the top of the houseboat.

Just because he'd bet he had at least winged the doctor, it wasn't enough.

Dead. The man had to die for every horrific thing he'd ever done.

A quick death wouldn't really be enough to repay the man for every evil deed he'd committed, but it would at least prevent him from committing more sins in the future. Torturing Dr. Gardner would feel amazing for him and the rest of his team, for every other victim, but it wasn't worth risking Indigo's life, keeping her in danger longer than she had to be.

So he'd settle for any sort of death so long as the scientist was no longer breathing.

As he came back up to the surface, he saw that the houseboat was trudging along slowly, maybe close enough for him to get to if he pushed himself.

Wishing for Thunder's speed, Voodoo dove deep, kept well below the surface, using the water and the dark to his advantage to make it harder for anyone to know where he was and get off a shot. It felt like chasing a puff of smoke. Every time you reached out for it there was nothing to grab hold of. It was there, you could see it, but it wasn't something you could hold onto.

But he had to keep trying. He was closest to the houseboat, and his team was laying down cover fire for him, taking out the rest of the threats, hopefully finding Indigo and keeping her safe until he could get to her.

When his hand brushed against the side of the medium-sized houseboat, elation flared through him. He'd done it. Reached the boat before it could get away.

Realistically speaking, that shouldn't have happened. The houseboat could move faster than a person, that was just a fact. And he wasn't Thunder with superhuman speed. But here it was, within his grasp, and Voodoo had to assume that one of his teammates had managed to take out the boat's driver, and it was no longer moving.

Coming up to the surface, he quickly located a ladder on the side of the houseboat and climbed up the side.

"I'm coming for you, Gardner," he yelled out as he reached the first deck. There were two more, but he had no way of knowing whether the man was still up there or if he'd run to hide down in one of the rooms.

If he was lucky, he'd find the man's dead body lying up there.

There was no answer, not that he'd really expected one. Just because Dr. Gardner had delusions of grandeur and seemed to see himself as a god of some sort, didn't mean that he wasn't a coward at heart.

The scientist just always set things up to give himself the upper hand. Take away that upper hand, and the man folded like a deck of cards.

"You wanted us back, didn't you, Gardner?" Voodoo roared as he climbed up the ladder, heading for the top deck. If the man wasn't up there, then he'd search every room, every hiding place, on this houseboat until he found him. He'd kill anyone who dared to cross him, and if he could get the doctor alive, then he would absolutely still go with their original plan of prolonging the man's death for as long as he could.

Suffering wouldn't change what he and his team and so many others had gone through, but it would go a long way toward easing that pain, that anger. Make it easier to move forward.

"Change your mind now that your monsters are right here?" he yelled. No one knew better than Dr. Gardner just what they could do, and while the man might be prepared to sacrifice the lives of others to try to get them back under his control, he didn't want to sacrifice his own.

Behind him on the bank, gunshots were still being fired, but he trusted his team to handle it. Trusted his team not just with his own life, but with Indigo's. His job right now was to find Dr. Gardner. Nothing more, nothing less. Kill him outright if he had to, incapacitate and capture him if he could.

As he reached the top, Voodoo scanned the area, finding no one but seeing a puddle of blood that told him he had hit what he'd shot at. Satisfaction rolled through him. Dr. Gardner was there, on this boat, finally within his grasp, injured to boot.

For so long he had dreamed of this moment, dreamed of how he'd feel when he was face to face with the man responsible for stealing a decade of his life from him, dreamed about what he'd do to the man. Even worried about whether he'd want to participate in the torture of their creator. While usually he hated inflicting unnecessary pain on another human being, he was pretty sure he'd be able to make an exception for the man who had kept him locked in a cage for three years while he experimented on him and sent him out on kill missions.

Now, as that prospect was tantalizingly close, Voodoo found he didn't feel a hint of remorse or apprehension for what he'd do to this man, and it had nothing to do with his own torture.

It was all Indigo.

Dr. Gardner had to suffer, had to scream, had to bleed, for every mark on Indigo's skin. Every stain on her soul that had been caused by the sick individual he was hunting.

"Come out, come out, wherever you are," he taunted, slinking across the deck, searching for the stairs that would lead him down. "You wanted to play, well now I'm here, come out and do your worst, Gardner."

Predictably, the man didn't make a peep, nor did he show his cowardly face.

But as he found the stairs, and was about to descend, the world suddenly went eerily silent.

Quiet enough that he froze, looked over at the bank, and saw a couple of shadowy figures moving.

"Might want to rethink that plan," someone yelled from the shore. "Wouldn't want anything to happen to the pretty little woman now, would we?"

"Don't stop, Voodoo," Indigo shouted. "Find him. Kill him. Saving me isn't worth letting Dr. Gardner go free."

Damn.

She'd been caught. If one of his teammates hadn't already taken out whoever had her, it was because they didn't think they had a clear shot that wouldn't endanger her life. No matter how badly they all wanted Dr. Gardner dead, not a single one of them would risk Indigo's life to achieve that goal.

If they did, they'd be proving they were the monsters Dr. Gardner wanted to create. The monsters they thought they were for the last ten years. It had taken Steel falling for Rose, Dragon for Cassandra, and Blade for Whitney to help them all see that while their emotions other than anger had been dulled, those emotions were still there. They had consciences, they could fall in love, they could experience the whole gamut of emotions, same as everybody else could.

They weren't monsters, and they had proved it over and over again.

Would prove it once again right now.

"Get off the boat if you don't want me to blow her pretty brains out," the man ordered.

"You kill me, then they kill you," Indigo said, and he loved the fire in her voice. The determination. His crazy girl was going to get herself killed, but she was finding her voice, her power, taking control of her life.

"Not going to kill you until I'm out of the line of fire," the man shot back, and Indigo laughed.

Hell, she was actually laughing at the man who was threatening to keep her as a hostage and use her to escape.

"You really have no idea what they can do, do you? There is no escaping them. They'll find you, and they'll make you wish they had given you the same death you have planned for me. I can assure you a bullet to the brain will be a blessing you'll be praying for, but they'll never give you," Indigo continued to taunt the man.

"Shut up," the man snarled. "Get off that boat now, and let it leave, or I'll start putting bullet holes in her. Maybe she doesn't feel pain, but I can still cause some damage. Damage she won't survive."

Knowing only one move he could make would keep his girl safe, Voodoo was about to concede temporary defeat, when suddenly, he heard Indigo's panicked voice shouting a warning.

"Voodoo, look out," she screamed.

Trusting his girl as deeply as he trusted his team, Voodoo didn't hesitate to fling himself sideways a split second before a bullet plowed into the spot where he'd just been standing.

~

January 25th
3:08 A.M.

· · ·

Her grand escape plan didn't work out the way she'd hoped.

Pretty much the opposite. Indigo had made it no more than a dozen or so yards from the back of the truck when she was caught.

Of course, it had to be the man who had carried her into the truck in the first place, the one who had thought it was fun to stick a knife in her leg and twist it around just to see once again that she wasn't going to scream in agony, that was the one to catch her.

As soon as she was yanked up against that big body, Indigo knew she was in trouble. She just hadn't realized she was going to be used as bait until she was dragged down to the river's edge, the cold metal of the gun pressed against her temple, making her already icy cold naked body that much colder.

But one thing she was certain of was that she wasn't going to go passively toward whatever fate awaited her. Didn't matter if that fate was death, capture, or freedom, whatever it was, she was embracing it and running toward it rather than cowering in fear, hanging back, being passive.

Voodoo had come.

The whole team had come.

For her.

They'd held off on going after their revenge, something that had been the focus of their lives for the last decade, all because they decided she was worth more than that.

Nobody had ever thought she was worth anything, so knowing what these men were willing to give up for her when they didn't even know her made her feel like she was worth a billion dollars.

It was all because of Voodoo, so when she saw a glint, off in the trees on the other side of the river, she knew.

Something was wrong.

Someone was going to try to shoot him.

They'd used her as a distraction, because as soon as Voodoo's teammates caught sight of her being dragged along, they'd all stopped shooting. She had no idea how many, if any, were still alive other than the one holding her and whoever was aiming a weapon at Voodoo, but it didn't matter.

No way was she going to be used to garner everyone's attention, keep them all on edge, looking for a way to get her out without getting her killed in the process, and then get them all captured.

They weren't spending the rest of their lives in the back of that truck.

Not so long as she could do something about it.

As soon as she screamed her warning to Voodoo, he acted. He didn't bother wasting time looking, trying to figure out if she knew what she was saying, he just trusted her. That meant the world to her. It made her feel valued, like maybe she was a part of this team in some small way.

Voodoo's shadowy form disappeared from view, at the same moment that five other shadowy forms appeared from amongst the trees. They surrounded her, only it didn't feel like they were boxing her in, it felt protective, because Indigo knew without a shadow of a doubt that they were there to do whatever it took to save her life. Save all their lives.

"You're not getting away," a cold voice spoke. She was pretty sure it was Steel's. Or maybe she just assumed it was because she knew that Steel was Delta Team's leader, so she thought he was likely the one who did all the talking.

"Stay back," the man behind her yelled, jamming the barrel of the gun into her temple. It probably would have hurt if she were capable of feeling pain like a normal person.

"If you think we're letting you walk away from here, you're stupider than I gave you credit for," Steel continued. The hard edge to his voice sounded almost bored, like this was all just a bothersome distraction before reaching the foregone conclusion.

"You won't risk her," her captor yelled, but there was a quiver in his voice as he said the words. He knew how dangerous the men surrounding him were, and he wasn't at all sure that he could get himself out of this alive.

A single shot was fired, and the houseboat that Voodoo had previously been on took off down the river as fast as a boat could move.

Where was Voodoo?

Had he moved in time? Had she issued her warning too late?

Had he been injured? Killed?

"Hear that shot?" another of the men surrounding her asked, this time she knew it was Dragon. That guy was one scary-looking man. Something about his unusual violet eyes told you he was not a person to be messed with. Since he was on her side, she didn't have to worry about him, but it didn't mean the man clutching her to him as a shield felt the same way. You couldn't be in Dragon's presence and not fear him.

"That was your buddy who just tried to shoot my friend meeting his maker," Dragon continued. "Know what that means?"

Her captor didn't say anything, but because he was holding her pressed up against his body, she could feel the shiver that rocketed through him. Seemed like the man knew exactly what Dragon was trying to say, even if she was having a bit of trouble getting her cloudy mind to put the pieces together.

"Let me help you out," one of the other guys said, Thunder this time. "Your buddy is dead. They're all dead. The only ones left alive are you and whoever is hiding out on that boat with your boss. Your boss is a coward, but he's going to get what's coming to him sooner or later. Right now, though, all our attention is focused on you."

"You know what we can do right?" another of the guys piped up. She was pretty sure it was Blade. "I'm sure you didn't take this job without knowing all the details. So you know that besides being able to hear each beat of your hammering heart, I love to play with my knife. Dragon can smell the fear leaching off you. Lion spotted your little friend before Indigo here called out a warning. Steel could quite literally rip you to pieces, and I don't think Voodoo is going to be very willing to help put you back together again since you're holding a gun to his girl's head like you really think we're going to let you blow her brains out."

"His girl?" her captor stuttered. "You're lying. She's not involved with any of you."

"I beg to differ," Voodoo said as he walked out of the river, water streaming down him, his weapon in his hands, looking strong, and whole, and real.

Alive.

Relief almost had her legs giving out. Or maybe that was exhaustion.

Now that Voodoo was there, she couldn't help but feel like everything was okay. She might trust Voodoo's team, but that was because she trusted him.

Actually trusted him. Her. The woman who didn't trust anyone because every single person in her life had let her down before.

Voodoo had never let her down, and she was beginning to believe he never would.

"You touch my girl, you're going to pay the price. Don't worry, your boss isn't going to get away even if he thinks he is. I tagged the boat, so as soon as we finish up here with you, we're going to go visit him. We have unfinished business," Voodoo continued, and Indigo smiled despite there being a weapon held to her head.

This was almost over. Really almost over.

She hardly dared to hope it might be. Just because her nightmare hadn't been anywhere near as long as Voodoo's didn't mean she didn't wish Dr. Gardner dead just as badly.

The man gripping her tightly enough that he'd leave behind bruises was panicking. She could feel it flowing off him. He didn't know what his next move was going to be, but she knew he was trying to figure out how he was going to do the impossible and get away from six highly trained killing machines.

There might be a whole lot more to these guys, but they knew how to kill, quickly and efficiently if they wanted to, slowly and messily if they chose.

Somehow, she knew what he was going to do before he did it.

Her captor was going to try to shoot his way out of this, only he wasn't going to start with her. He was going to try to shoot the Delta Team guys.

For some reason, she thought he was going to start with Voodoo.

No way in hell was she allowing that to happen.

Everything seemed to slow down, becoming almost unnaturally drawn out. The man behind her screamed, the sound much too loud for her ears, as he moved the gun, aiming it at Voodoo.

Indigo screamed, too, then she reached out, grabbed his hand, and yanked it down until the weapon was now aimed at her, at him. Her fingers fought with those of the man holding her hostage.

When she won, she pulled the trigger.

Sending a bullet plowing through both of them.

January 25th
3:14 A.M.

What the hell had she been thinking?

Didn't she know there were six expert marksmen standing around her, any one of whom could have taken out the man holding her hostage before he could get off a shot?

Voodoo bolted toward Indigo as both she and the hostage taker fell to the ground in a tangle of limbs.

Damn woman had to go and try to save him, always thinking that she was worth less than him, less than anyone, less than everyone.

Skidding to a stop on his knees beside the two bodies, he didn't even spare a glance for the man who had tried to steal Indigo from him. Regardless of how this would have played out, the man would have wound up dead.

Sure, Voodoo would have enjoyed torturing him a little, drawing it out, but in the end, he only cared that a threat to Indigo had been eliminated.

"She shouldn't have done it," he mumbled to no one in particular as

Steel and Lion grabbed hold of the man and pulled him out of the way, leaving Indigo lying before him.

"She cares about you," Blade said softly as the other man helped him lie Indigo out so he could get a proper look at her.

"Still shouldn't have done it. We would have handled it."

"Maybe she didn't know that," Dragon reminded him. "Maybe she thought she should do her part. After all, she's one of us, isn't she?"

"Always," he replied as Thunder switched on a bright light that allowed him to remove the NVGs and see her condition more clearly.

There was no denying the fact that Indigo would always be part of them. Even if nothing romantic ever developed between the two of them, his team had already adopted her as one of their own, a little sister of sorts. Voodoo knew that Rose, Cassandra, and Whitney would all immediately take to Indigo as well. She just had a sweetness to her that drew you in, and it wasn't because you felt sorry for her because of her tragic life, it was because despite that tragic life, she was still standing.

Now that he could see her properly, his heart dropped. There was a wound on her leg that looked deep. It hadn't been there when they'd been with her in the forest before she fell into the river, so it had to have happened once she was recaptured. The burns he'd noticed on her when she was brought out of the first building and bundled into the car she crashed looked much worse now that he was up close to them.

But it was the gaping hole in her stomach that had panic seizing his lungs.

"Indy, why?" he whispered as he ripped off his shirt, needing something to press to the wound to try to stem the flow of blood.

"You know why, brother," Steel reminded him, voice soft and gentle, so un-Steel like. "Because the thought of anything happening to you meant she was willing to go to any lengths, put anything on the line, so long as you walked away alive."

"I'd rather she walked away alive," he muttered. If only one of them was leaving this forest still breathing, then it should be her. Sacrificing his life for hers would be easy, Indigo deserved a chance to live a happy life, to have people in her corner, to be anything she wanted to be.

Now that chance was slipping through his fingers.

Literally.

Already, his fingers, holding his balled-up shirt to her abdomen, were stained red with her blood. It was soaking through the shirt. Coming too quickly.

Fear that he wouldn't be able to save her thrummed through his system.

"What about him? Is he still alive?" Voodoo asked, not bothering to look away from Indigo's still form as he asked about the fate of the man who had held a gun to her head, threatening to hurt her as well as kill her.

"Your girl is a warrior at heart," Lion replied. "He's dead."

"Good," he muttered. While he wouldn't have wasted any of his energy trying to save the man's life, the only life he was interested in saving was Indy's, he liked knowing that his girl had fought for herself as well as for him, even as he would ream her out for it as soon as she opened her eyes.

"What do you need us to do?" Blade asked, and part of him hated that everyone else was managing to keep their cool while he felt like his world was spinning faster out of control with each beat of his heart.

"I ... don't know," he said, pressing the shirt harder against Indigo's wound, wishing for the first time since he'd met her that she could feel pain. Pain was often a great stimulus in rousing an unconscious patient, but Indigo wouldn't feel the agony caused by touching anything to a gaping hole in her stomach, let alone pressing it firmly in a desperate attempt to keep some of her blood inside her system.

"Yeah you do, man," Thunder assured him. "You know what to do. You've always known what to do. Saving people is what you do. Has nothing to do with what Dr. Gardner did to us. Whitney even told you that what you can do, who you can save, shouldn't even be possible. But you do it. Because you're a healer."

"Not with her, I can't seem to make it work with her," he whispered. Yes, he'd been able to pull her back from the brink after infection almost stole her from him. He'd also been able to pull her back from the brink after hypothermia almost dragged her too far away for him to reach.

But in the end, he was pretty sure he hadn't been the deciding factor in either of those instances.

She had been.

Almost losing her had been because Indigo was giving in to the voices inside her head whispering that she was better off dead. That voice was loud because she'd already spent a lifetime thinking she was unworthy, unloved, that no one would miss her if she was gone.

Saving her had also been because she realized, instinctually, since they hadn't had a chance to properly discuss his growing feelings for her, that he would miss her, that he saw her worth, that he valued her as a human being. So she'd decided to fight.

It terrified him to think that the only thing that might save her now was herself.

What if she didn't realize that he needed her?

What if she thought now that she'd met people who wanted her, she could let go?

What if she didn't have enough cognizance left to know she had to fight?

"All she needs is you," Lion said with such confidence that he refocused his gaze on Indigo's face.

It was so pale in the harsh light of the torch, her skin almost translucent. Her eyes were closed, lashes fanned out on her bony cheeks. She needed some more meat on her bones, and he knew from personal experience that the food Dr. Gardner provided while they were kept in his lab was nutritionally balanced, but it wasn't enough to sustain them long term. Plus, Indigo had been living on the streets before that, so he doubted she'd been eating enough.

Now she looked too thin. All he wanted was to take her home, shower her with love and affection, and try to make up for all she'd never had.

Dirt and blood covered her face, her arms and chest, her legs. Voodoo didn't even need to look at her bare feet to know they'd be shredded from running through the forest as she escaped the wrecked car.

It was hard to look at her and look past the injuries, to see her dispassionately as he would look at any patient laid out before him.

Indigo wasn't just anyone.

She was his.

And he wasn't sure he could save her.

That was all he could focus on. But he had to try to push through it. Keeping one hand pressed against her stomach, his other reached out to sweep across her pale cheek. Her skin was still warm to the touch, shock not settling in enough yet to drop it dangerously low. She was alive, breathing, her heart still beating.

Settling his fingertips on her neck, he allowed each bump of her pulse to seep inside him, to reassure him that he hadn't lost her yet. As long as she was still alive, he had a chance to bring her back. This wasn't an injury he would normally think someone could survive, even immediate surgery in a hospital likely wouldn't be enough. But this wasn't anyone. Indigo had the same enhanced healing ability as he and his team.

Losing her wasn't a given.

Forcing himself to pull it together, he'd never forgive himself if it was his own panic that caused him to lose Indigo.

Leaning down he touched his lips to her forehead. "I'm not giving up on you, honey, so don't you dare give up on me."

~

January 25th
3:19 A.M.

I'm not giving up on you, honey, so don't you dare give up on me.

The words floated into her mind like pretty, colorful ribbons wafting on a breeze.

While of course Indigo felt no pain, she felt ... wrong somehow.

It was hard to put into words. It was just a deep knowledge, settled into her very bones, that she knew what was happening to her, and she knew there wasn't going to be anything she could do to stop it.

"Can you hear me, Indy?"

If it were anyone else other than Voodoo asking her that question, she probably would have allowed those words to flutter right on past her hazy mind and sink into the enticing quiet that was lapping at the edges of her consciousness.

Drifting off into it was almost too appealing to fight against.

But just like she knew what was going to happen to her, she also knew what it was going to do to Voodoo.

He was a healer, saving people was what he did, what he thought he had to do, the only thing he thought gave him any value. Indigo wanted him to know that he was more than that, that his value was simply because he was a human being with a good heart, who cared about others, who wanted to do what he could to help them.

The last thing she wanted for him was for her death to send him spiraling.

How she knew he was teetering on the edge of spiraling Indigo wasn't really sure, she just knew it, felt it. Maybe the rest of his team knew it, too, or maybe they didn't. She did know that when she was gone, they would still be there, and she wanted them all to know that they had to be there for Voodoo, to support him, to help him, and stop treating him as though his ability to heal was all that mattered.

So, because she cared more about Voodoo than she did the lure of peace and quiet in the dark place slowly surrounding her, Indigo summoned strength she wasn't sure she had left, and managed to jerk her head in a single nod. Not much, but it was all she could manage.

"There you go, honey, there's my brave fighter," Voodoo praised, and his words were like a rush of warmth flooding her system.

It wasn't until that warmth touched her that she even realized she'd been freezing cold. Now that had registered, her entire body began to shake in what she knew would have been painful shudders if she were capable of feeling pain.

"It's going to be okay, honey, I'm going to fix you right up," Voodoo said. His tone was meant to be soothing, comforting, reassuring, and maybe it would be if she were anyone else.

But she wasn't anyone else, and she could feel his fear as though it was her own.

More than that, she could feel his insecurities, his terror at failing, his deep-seated belief that if he didn't save her, then nobody would love him, nobody would care about him, nobody would be interested in having him around. After all, if his own parents didn't care about him no matter how hard he fought to gain their love and attention, then why should anybody else ever care about him?

"We need to get her off the cold ground," Voodoo said, only the cold slowly consuming her from the outside in, was no longer the reason she was shaking. Now it was him, his emotions, her own emotions over what her impending death was going to do to him.

"You sure we should move her?" someone else asked. Maybe she'd know who if she could concentrate on anything other than Voodoo, but he was all Indigo cared about right now, all she could focus on.

"She's in shock, we need to warm her up," Voodoo said, his voice so strong and confident, so many years of practicing not letting anyone get a glimpse at what lay beneath his surface serving him well.

Forcing her eyes open, Indigo reached out before Voodoo could gather her into his arms. She wasn't surviving this. She'd just shot herself through the stomach, the blood loss on top of the burns littering her body, the broken leg, the infection that had already weakened her, there was no way she was surviving. Attempting to live wasn't even her goal right now. She had accepted the inevitable, her only driving need was to assure Voodoo that he didn't need to blame himself, convince him somehow that he was just him and he was good enough like that, he was all he had to be.

"No," she said, annoyed that her voice was weak and insubstantial, nothing like the raging fire inside her. Voodoo had given her everything she always wanted in the short time since she'd met him. He'd made her feel seen, valued, like she mattered. He was nothing like her ex-husband, who even when she thought their relationship was everything she'd ever wanted, was always putting her down, issuing vague insults that she'd learned to brush off.

"Yes, honey," he contradicted, and she saw the tender affection on his face as he looked down at her. Or maybe she felt it rather than saw it.

"It's okay," she said, not sure how long she had left, but understanding she needed to use that time wisely.

"It will be," Voodoo promised her, his fingers gently caressing her cheek. "I'm not going to let you die."

There was no doubt he meant that with every fiber of his soul.

Only it wasn't up to him.

He wasn't responsible for her life, or anyone else's. His ability to save was miraculous, no doubt about that, but he was more than that. It wasn't what made him valuable. What she respected most about him, what she was even coming to love about him, was that he cared. Truly cared. For someone like her who had never been given an ounce of kindness from anyone in her life, that meant more than the fact that he could save the lives of people who should have died.

"Voodoo," she whispered, lifting heavy arms to press her hand over his, needing him to feel what she was saying, not just hear it. "You don't need to save me."

"Of course I do," he growled, like what she'd just said was personally offensive to him.

"No, you don't. It's not your job to save everyone, it's not what makes you special," she assured him, imploring him to believe her, to understand what she was trying to say so that her death didn't destroy him.

"It is," he argued, and she knew he believed that, had been conditioned to expect it was the only thing of value he could possibly offer the world.

"You've already given me more than I could ever have hoped for," she told him. "That's what matters. Not if you can save my life, I knew what I was risking when I shot us. I want you to live, I want you to soar, I want you to know that you deserve all the good things in the world, because you've given me only good things. I'm grateful that you healed me, saved me several times over already, but I'm more grateful that you cared, that you showed me what it meant to have someone care. You saw me, you never made me feel dirty, never made me feel that I was only the product of a terrible childhood, that I would only ever be a victim. You made me feel ... special."

That didn't seem like a strong enough word to convey all he'd given her, but it was the best she could come up with as her strength bled away with each drop of blood that oozed from the hole in her stomach.

"You're killing me, honey," Voodoo's agonized voice whispered. He lowered his head, touched his forehead to hers, and his breath, so very warm and soft against her skin, was the gentlest of caresses.

"You're more than your ability to save lives, you always have been," she told him. "I hate that your parents didn't make you understand that, but that's their fault, their loss. You're the best person I've ever met in my entire life. You made me believe in humanity, believe in goodness, in happiness. For the first time ever, I've felt what it was like to matter. You gave me that, and it means everything to me."

"It's not over yet, honey," Voodoo said, voice urgent as he lifted his head. "I ... can't save you on my own. Your injuries are too severe, you've lost too much blood, you're too weak. But I'll get a surgeon flown here ASAP—"

"On it," someone interjected, but Indigo didn't lift her gaze from Voodoo's.

"I can keep you alive until help gets here. Then we'll get you fixed up. I'll bring you home, and you can have everything you deserve, all the happiness, all the peace, all the opportunities, it's all yours, honey. All you have to do is hold on a little bit longer."

He was so desperate, so pure in his desire to save, that she smiled, despite the distance that seemed to be growing between them.

"Already too late," she whispered. "But it doesn't matter. I'm not scared. You've given me so much, and I'm okay with how this turned out. As long as you live, then I'm happy. Almost."

His brows arched in question, and her shaking hands shifted to frame his face.

"Kiss me. One last time. Please."

"Don't ever have to beg me for that, honey."

Lips feathered across hers, and Indigo felt the last of her strength waft away. If she was going to die, she couldn't think of a better last moment. The promise of what could have been infused in the kiss, Indigo was true to her promise that she was going to die happy, as consciousness filtered out of her mind.

CHAPTER

Twenty

January 28th
5:55 A.M.

She looked so peaceful.

Like she was just sleeping.

His beautiful fairytale princess, if only a kiss was all it took to wake her up.

If that was all Indigo needed, then Voodoo would do it in a heartbeat. In fact, he had kissed her several times over the last three days just in case that was all she needed to open those big, beautiful eyes of hers.

One thing he was certain of was that when Indigo had asked for that kiss when she'd been lying out there, naked on the forest floor, was that she believed it would be the last thing she ever did. She'd thought she was going to die, and she'd wanted his lips on hers as she took that first step into whatever lay beyond this world.

He didn't take her lack of faith in his ability to keep her alive until help arrived as an insult, if anything, he loved that she saw him as more than a miraculous healer. She was right in everything she'd said to him that night. When he looked at himself, all he ever saw was a man who had always wanted to save lives. It had been his entire identity for as long as he could remember, born from a desire to try to gain his parents' love and approval, over time, it had become all he was.

But it wasn't how Indigo saw him.

She saw him as the man who had saved her in a different way. She didn't care about her body, it had been used and abused so many times by so many different people that she no longer cared about what happened to it.

What she cared about was her soul, and that was what she was crediting him with breathing new life into. It was the most amazing compliment anyone had ever given him, and there was no way in hell he was going to let her die before he got a chance to tell her that.

After she'd passed out, they'd moved her into the back of a nearby vehicle and covered her with blankets. Thunder had called Eagle and asked their boss to find the nearest trauma surgeon they could trust, and on the drive there, he'd sat in the backseat, his girl cradled on his lap, swaddled in blankets, his hands pressed against her wound, willing life into her with a desperation he'd never felt before.

By some miracle, her heart had still been beating, her lungs still filling with air, by the time they reached the small clinic Eagle had given them directions to. It had taken the surgeon nearly four hours to patch Indigo back up, and it was clear the entire time that the woman was shocked that Indigo was even alive, much less that she made it through surgery and out the other side.

While the woman had insisted that she keep Indigo close throughout her recovery, Voodoo knew they needed to get her back home. He'd shot Dr. Gardner, the blood on the houseboat confirmed it, but he didn't know how badly he'd injured the man. There was a chance the scientist was dead, that they were all safe now, but there was an equal chance he was still out there, still hunting them, still desperate to get them back.

No way would he take any chances when it came to Indigo and her safety.

So they'd kept her with the surgeon for the first twenty-four hours only, before loading her onto a plane and flying her back to their place.

The entire time, he'd sat there, monitoring her vitals, refusing to leave her side even though he hadn't slept in days, was still filthy from the days spent traipsing through the forest, expecting at any second to find her flatlining.

It wasn't that Indigo didn't want to live, he knew she did. She was battling those voices in her head with every ounce of strength she had to give, but he also knew she was somewhat indifferent to living or dying. She was on the cusp of a brand-new life, he knew she understood that. That he wasn't just offering her a place to stay and a support system to get her life on the track that she wanted. He was offering her everything, a home, a family, a job, and himself.

Every lacking part of his unloved soul would be laid at her feet if she would just open her eyes and wake up.

Each hour that passed, her body grew stronger, her condition more stable. There was no sign of infection in her wounds, a miracle in and of itself, and her vitals were all stable and improving. Nothing indicated that she shouldn't make a full recovery, her body's enhanced ability to heal doing its job perfectly.

Yet she didn't wake.

No matter how many times he begged her, no matter how many times he pleaded with her, no matter what he promised her, or how hard he worked to convince her how amazing her life was going to be going forward.

None of it made any difference.

Indigo just lay there, in his bed, tucked under his covers, an IV delivering the fluids her body needed along with antibiotics and painkillers. In theory, Indigo shouldn't need any pain medication thanks to what Dr. Gardner had done to her, but he wasn't taking any chances. She was weak and had already been through so much. He wasn't going to risk her being in any pain if her system had been thrown into chaos.

While she was under, the surgeon had also taken a look at her broken leg. The woman had been in shock when she'd seen the damage done, and seemed unable to comprehend the fact that Indigo had been able to use her leg without passing out from agonizing pain, even though he'd explained briefly without much detail, that she didn't feel pain like a normal person.

Now there was a metal plate in there, holding her bones together,

her leg in a cast to protect it while it healed. The burns on her body had mostly already healed, although they'd left behind puckered scars that would likely mean the skin beneath would never feel normal sensation.

But she was alive, healing, and should be waking up.

"Come on," he urged, brushing his thumb across the knuckles of the hand he held in his own.

It was so much smaller than his, her fingers so thin and delicate, so easily snapped and broken, and he almost hated her ability not to be able to feel physical pain while still being forced to endure every drop of emotional and psychological pain inflicted on her by the people in her life who had never deserved her sweet heart.

"It's time to wake up, honey," he coaxed for the millionth time.

Hard as he was trying to believe in what she'd told him, that he was more than his ability to heal, it wasn't easy. Voodoo knew his teammates saw him as family, as one of them, regardless of the fact that he'd never been as angry and bitter as the rest of them about what had been done to them, even though he'd never had that same drive to destroy that fueled them.

They accepted him, but he'd never accepted himself.

Always examined himself and found himself lacking.

Never more so than in these last few days.

Saving Indigo was everything he wanted, but it was the one thing he couldn't seem to do. In the forest, he hadn't been able to save her until she was ready to be saved, and now he had no idea if the only thing preventing her from opening her eyes was his lack of ability to save her or her own lack of ability to believe that her future was going to be nothing like her past.

They were quite a pair. Neither of them found themselves worthy. Their parents had set them on paths that had led them to self-doubt, insecurity, and an inability to see themselves as others saw them.

But those paths had also led them to each other.

There was no way he could accept anything less than getting a shot at building something with Indigo. Something where they could both find what they'd spent decades searching for.

If his girl needed a reason to fight, to live, to come back to him and embrace this chance life had thrown their way, he would keep giving her one until she had no choice but to wake up.

Shifting on the bed so he was no longer perched on the edge, gripping Indigo's hand like it was a lifeline, Voodoo stretched out beside her. Exhaustion weighed heavily upon him. He hadn't done more than catnap in over a week now, he'd eaten only because Rose, Cassandra, and Whitney had hounded him into it, and he didn't want to disappoint the women he saw as little sisters. He had taken a single shower when he got home, only because he hadn't wanted to risk getting dirt in any of Indigo's wounds.

Now he shifted her gently, so she was wrapped in his arms, then he buried his face against her long, dark locks, and held her, whispering in her ear all the ways he would make up to her what life had denied her so far, and praying.

Praying for one more miracle.

~

February 1st
    1:01 P.M.

Indigo stretched as she woke.

That was the best sleep she'd had in … forever.

Her body and mind both felt well rested, so well rested in fact that it took her a moment to remember that the last thing she could recall was kissing Voodoo and then passing out convinced that she was close to taking her final breath.

Not only was she still breathing, but she'd obviously been out long enough to be moved from the forest. No longer was it hard, rough ground beneath her body, now she was lying on something soft and cozy. Her leg felt a little heavy, and there was a tightness to her stomach when she shifted position, so she must have been moved and patched up.

"You awake, honey?" Voodoo's rough voice asked, and knowing he was still right there beside her, had her smiling as she opened her eyes.

That smile faded as she got a look at him. He was sprawled out beside her in the huge bed they were tucked into. He wasn't wearing a shirt, but because his body was tucked against hers, she could feel he had on a pair of sweatpants. His eyes were red, and there was shaggy scruff on his face that hadn't been there the last time she'd seen him.

"Thought I was never going to look into these beautiful eyes of yours again," Voodoo told her as he reached out and smoothed a lock of hair off her forehead, and nuzzling into the touch was the easiest thing in the world to do. Didn't even take any conscious thought, it was just instinct to move toward this man for affection, even though she'd been denied tenderness her entire life.

"How long?" she asked, only the words came out as a croak and not much else. Her mouth didn't just feel dry, it felt like all the deserts of the world had gathered up their sands and used them to coat the inside of her throat.

"Let me get you some water."

When Voodoo shifted, sitting up and removing the warmth of his body from beside hers, Indigo whimpered before she even realized it. Embarrassed, she was turning her head, trying to think about what she could pretend had caused the whimper if asked, and knowing it couldn't be pain, when she caught the soft look on Voodoo's face.

From his expression, he knew exactly why she'd whimpered, and he liked it.

A lot, if the slow smile curving up his lips was any indication.

"Not going far," he assured her as he reached over to grab a glass of water that must have been sitting on the nightstand. "Let me help." Balancing the glass in one hand, he slipped his arm behind her shoulders and lifted her slightly. "Don't drink too much too fast, your system hasn't had anything other than IV fluids in a week, and we don't want to overdo it."

Almost choking on the water he guided into her mouth, Indigo's eyes widened as she got the answer to the question she'd been trying to ask.

A week.

Was that how long since that night in the forest she'd been positive she was going to die? No wonder her throat was so dry, and she felt like she'd been sleeping for so long. No wonder Voodoo looked like he'd been through the wringer.

Had he been lying beside her all this time?

"Yeah, honey, you've been unconscious for a week now," Voodoo said as he helped her lie back against the pillows.

"You stayed the whole time? With me?" she asked, still not quite sure that she was drawing the right conclusions and not wanting to make herself look like an idiot if she'd gotten things majorly wrong.

The look he shot her was a cross between offended and incredulous. "Of course, where else would I be?"

Since she didn't have an answer to that, Indigo merely shrugged. The obvious answer was, of course, anywhere else, but she didn't think he'd like hearing that. In her mind, it was more of a why on earth would he waste his time hanging around at her side, especially if she was unconscious. Wasn't like she'd be good company.

"I see nothing I said to you when we were out there has sunk in yet." Voodoo settled back down at her side, carefully tucking the blankets up and around her with such carefulness that it made her eyes sting.

No one ever bothered to be careful with her.

The opposite usually.

They treated her like she was nothing and that her body existed for their amusement.

"You did it," she whispered, her voice still rough, her throat dry but useable. "You saved me."

"Not alone. I had a little help," he admitted, although he didn't sound as upset about that as she would have guessed.

"That's okay, we all need a little help every now and then." Not that she'd ever had anyone around who cared enough to help her before now, but she still knew it was true.

"Yeah, maybe we do," Voodoo agreed, sounding almost like he was surprised by the admission, and he'd truly believed that asking for help or admitting you couldn't accomplish something on your own was a weakness to be ignored.

"Where are we?" Looking around the room, she could see it was stylish, although minimally, decorated. It didn't quite look like a hospital room, but she wasn't sure what else it could be. Maybe it was some sort of fancy, private hospital. From what she knew, Prey Security was owned by wealthy siblings, and if they thought Delta Team was family, then by extension, she could be considered part of them, too, even though she'd never met any of the Oswald siblings.

"Home," Voodoo answered simply.

"Home? The house where you and your team live?" Even though he'd said he was bringing her home when they got out of the forest, somehow, she hadn't truly believed he would actually do that.

As far as she was concerned, home was a sacred place, one you shared only with the people you truly cared about. Maybe her view was tainted by the fact she'd always longed for a home and never had a real one, but it was an almost magical idea in her mind. When she'd been married, she'd done her best to create the perfect home, make it every-thing she'd always dreamed of, but her ex had criticized every little thing she did, always telling her she never measured up.

"Where else would I bring you?"

"Is this room going to be mine?" It was almost too much to hope for that she might have her very own room in Voodoo's home, maybe even one she could decorate however she wanted without fear of being criticized this time around.

"I hope so." There was a slight hesitation in his words, and she turned from surveying the large space to find him watching her with a weird expression. "It's my room, Indy. Ours, I hope, from here on out."

"You want me to stay in your room with you?" The idea seemed crazy. Sure, they'd danced around the idea that something was brewing between them, but they barely knew each other, and what time they'd spent together had been running for their lives and him trying to keep her alive.

Why would he take such a big step so quickly?

What if things didn't work out between them?

How long could it realistically take before Voodoo realized what everybody else already knew, that she was worthless and—

"Better stop thinking thoughts like that before I have to take matters into my own hands and distract you myself," he warned, as his thumb dragged across her bottom lip. "Whatever worries you're coming up with let them go. Everything is going to be okay. Everything is going to work out the way it's supposed to."

"How can you know that?" Indigo whispered, desperate for an answer that would soothe every one of her anxieties. Surviving the gunshot wound hadn't been something she thought was going to happen, not even with her enhanced healing ability, so she'd never thought she'd get the chance to explore this thing between herself and Voodoo.

Now that she had the chance, it was overwhelming. Exciting but terrifying. Voodoo was perfect, but she'd also thought both her exes were perfect at one point, too, and she'd been majorly wrong. Not that she thought Voodoo would ever abuse her, but surely he'd grow tired of her at some point.

"Easy." Voodoo shifted, moving his large body so it was above hers, lightly pinning her down onto the mattress without adding any weight that might aggravate her injuries. "Because you're mine."

"Yours?"

"You know it, too, feel it, someplace deep down inside. It doesn't make sense, and I wouldn't believe it if I weren't experiencing it myself, but I knew from the second I saw you that you're mine."

"Yours," she said again, but not a question this time around, more like trying the idea out loud.

"Mine," Voodoo reiterated, brushing his lips across hers.

"And you're mine." Voodoo was right, it was weird, and it didn't make sense. If she didn't feel that same knowledge deep inside her, she wouldn't have believed you could meet someone, know them for such a small amount of time, and yet understand on some soul-deep level that she'd met the person who would complete her, give her everything she'd always dreamed of but never dared to hope for.

Twenty-One

February 4th
10:57 A.M.

"How much longer are we planning on hiding out in here?"

"I'm not hiding out," Indigo immediately protested, her cheeks flushed at the lie, and she was damn adorable looking all offended, pretending that she didn't know exactly what he was talking about.

"Okay," Voodoo agreed, leaning back against the headboard. If she wasn't ready to leave his room and face the outside world yet, she didn't have to. Wasn't like he was complaining about keeping her all to himself.

"I'm not," she insisted, jutting out her bottom lip, daring him to disagree.

He could, because she was hiding out in there, but he wouldn't, because he got it. Indigo hadn't just been through a trauma lasting the several months she'd been held hostage by Dr. Gardner and experimented on, she had been through a lifelong trauma, and meeting new people right now seemed to be more than she could handle.

Even though in reality she had nothing to worry about. She'd already met his team, and Rose, Cassandra, and Whitney were all wonderful people who were all dying to meet the newest member of their unconventional little family.

"Really, I'm not." Indigo huffed, and Voodoo couldn't help but chuckle.

Reaching out, he tapped the tip of her nose. "You are, but it's okay."

"You're supposed to be on my side here," she said with a pout.

"Always on your side," he assured her. They'd spent most of the time these last three days since she'd woken up talking when she wasn't sleeping. There'd been some making out too, and as much as he loved touching and kissing Indigo, he'd enjoyed getting to know her better just as much.

"I'm just ... it's ... I don't ..." Indigo didn't even seem to know what she was thinking or feeling, she just knew she was scared and was avoiding everything she thought was going to give her anxiety.

"It really is okay, honey." Leaning over, he pressed his lips to hers, infusing his growing feelings for her into the soft touch. What his girl needed was reassurance. He could tell her that everything was going to be okay, and she didn't have anything to worry about, but she wasn't going to believe it. Instead, he had to try to show her. Which was what he had been doing, interspersing stories about himself and his child-hood and adolescence, along with stories of his team and the three women who had recently become part of them.

For a second, she wouldn't meet his gaze, just picked at the edge of his sheets. "What if they don't like me?" she finally whispered, chancing a quick glance at him. "What if they think I'm ... you know ... pathetic or something?"

"Why would they think that? Why wouldn't they like you? What is there not to like about you?"

"Not like I've had people lining up to like me, and my ex, he was always telling me I didn't deserve—"

"I think you'd better not finish that sentence if you don't want me to track down your ex-husband and kill him," he said mildly, even though the familiar burn of anger was spreading through him.

Indigo smiled. "It's not just him, it's everyone. I've never really had friends. The other kids never wanted to play with me, I was dirty and always covered in bruises, then both my exes isolated me. I'm not good at interacting with people."

"Then this is the perfect family for you," he assured her. "Are you sure you're not worried about anything else?" While he didn't want to push her, and he wouldn't blame her if she had reservations about some of the people living there, he had to know if she was as afraid of Rose and Whitney as she was of what they would think of her.

"What else would I worry about?" she asked, brows knitting together.

"Rose is Dr. Gardner's sister, and Whitney is the one who created the drug." Just because he'd gotten to know both of them and knew they were good people didn't mean Indigo would agree. At least not yet. Not until she got to know them and saw for herself.

"But you said Dr. Gardner tortured Rose as he was raising her, and she's nothing like him. You also said Whitney didn't mean for the drug to do what it did, and she was just a kid. I don't blame her if that's what you're asking me, and I don't think Rose is like her brother. It's just they're important to you, they're your family, your real family, even if they're not technically related to you, and I don't want them to not like me."

"They're going to like you."

For a long moment, she just stared into his eyes as though she was trying to see all the way down into his mind to ascertain if he was telling the truth. Voodoo tried to keep his gaze open and honest, allowing her to see the truth of his words. In reality, the longer she held off on meeting the others, hiding out in his room, the more she was going to build this up in her head, making it much bigger and scarier than it needed to be, and the harder it would be to walk out there and meet everyone.

They couldn't stay there forever, but they could stay there as long as she needed.

"You're sure?" Indigo asked in a small voice.

"Positive."

"Okay."

"Okay?"

"You're right, we can't stay in here forever."

"I didn't say that," he said, although he had been thinking it.

"I know, but you were thinking it."

"And you were reading my mind."

She chuckled, and he could tell she was doing her best to gather her reserves of strength and face her fears. Resisting the urge to tell her once again that everything would be fine, that she was a brave, strong, lovable woman who his family would quickly fall in love with, and had already accepted as one of them, he waited, giving her the time and space to come to the same conclusion.

"We could maybe have lunch with your team," she finally said, and he grinned, leaning in again to kiss her.

"Proud of you," he told her as he climbed out of the bed and gathered her into his arms.

"It's not much really," she said, clearly embarrassed, although he caught a hint of pleasure in her eyes as well.

"It is for you." Carrying her with him, he headed out into the hall. Indigo was healing better than he could have hoped for, and he wasn't sure if it was his healing ability or just her own enhanced healing ability, nor did it matter. The only thing that mattered was that she was getting better, stronger each day, and would soon be back to full health.

Even though she didn't say anything, he felt her tension growing as he moved through the house. She was yet to see any of it outside of his bedroom and the attached bathroom, but he didn't think she was taking in much of the Gothic mansion. The place was stunning. He'd lived there for the last six years, and Voodoo still sometimes looked at it in awe. He had no idea how Eagle had found this place, but he was glad their boss had. This had been the perfect home to recover in, to rebuild their lives in, and now it was the perfect place to start building a future.

For so long now, all he and his team had done was remain locked in the past. They couldn't let go of what had been done to them, and their focus had mostly been on revenge. Now he still wanted that revenge, but it wasn't all-consuming anymore.

Something else had taken over.

A desire to be normal, or at least as normal as a man whose DNA had been altered by experimental drugs could get. He wanted to fall in love and build a life with Indigo. Wanted to marry her one day, have kids, build a life that wasn't solely focused on destroying the people responsible for changing them.

Voodoo wanted to learn to find joy, to shrug off the responsibilities he'd placed on his own shoulders, and not think his only value was in saving others. He wanted to laugh and talk, to do simple things just for pleasure. He didn't just want that pleasure for himself, he wanted it for Indigo more than anything else. She deserved happiness, deserved love and affection, deserved all the things that made her smile.

It started here.

With one small step for him and one huge step for her.

While he could give her everything she deserved, she had to be the one to reach out and take it. Was it possible for a woman who had been taught time and time again that life only wanted to kick you down, to learn to embrace the chance that this time things might be different?

~

February 4th
11:14 A.M.

It made her feel stupid, but Indigo was genuinely scared about meeting the rest of Voodoo's family. It would actually be easier to meet his parents, because she knew that while he'd spent most of his life trying to be good enough to earn their love and respect, he didn't really value them or think of them as family.

But these five men and three women?

They were the family he'd always longed for, even if he struggled to cut the final ties binding him to his old life. If they didn't like her, then Indigo wasn't sure what that meant for her budding romance with Voodoo.

Just because his teammates seemed to have accepted her, she wouldn't be there if they hadn't, and they wouldn't have postponed their revenge to try to save her, that didn't automatically mean that the three women would. After all, things were different with the guys, they had all been altered, and that gave them a common ground, made her one of them. She didn't have that same connection to fall back on when it came to Rose, Cassandra, and Whitney.

As Voodoo carried her through the house, she could hear chattering voices getting louder. They all seemed so happy, so at ease with one another, like they truly were one big family. She, on the other hand, had exactly zero experience with happy families. She didn't even really have any experience with friends, although there had been a couple of people she'd been friendly with while she was at college and then working.

Only that wasn't the same. Being friendly was really just being polite, and what she had to do with the people in there ran so much deeper than simply polite exteriors.

At the last second, Indigo very nearly told Voodoo to stop and take her back to his room, positive she couldn't do this. Somehow, she held the words in, although she had to bite down hard on her tongue to do it, and then he was opening the kitchen door and walking through it.

All eyes turned on her, and Indigo instinctively shrank into Voodoo's hold, so sure she was going to be judged and found lacking.

Except there didn't appear to be judgment in any of the eight sets of eyes watching her.

No pity either.

Judgment was preferable to pity if it came down to making a choice.

There was concern in each gaze, definitely some curiosity, but there was more than that. Indigo would have sworn there was also acceptance.

Which was crazy because they couldn't accept her this easily, they didn't even know her. If she was going to be accepted, she was going to have to prove herself worthy, and the thing was that she was pretty sure she wasn't worthy of any good thing.

"You hungry?" a pretty redhead asked, and Indigo knew the woman had to be Rose because she shared a lot of similar traits to her brother.

Before she could answer, her stomach chose that moment to growl loudly, and while Indigo's cheeks flamed in embarrassment, everybody chuckled, and the tension in the room seemed to bleed right on out.

Or maybe it was only she who was tense.

Everybody else seemed perfectly at ease, and like they were happy that she'd finally stopped hiding and come to join them.

"I'm hungry," she replied, even though it was a moot point by now, since her stomach had already given her away, but she felt like she had to say something. Scared or not, these people were important to Voodoo, and since Voodoo was important to her, it made them important to her, too, and she desperately wanted them to like her.

"Perfect, because we made way too much food, even with these guys' huge appetites," a brunette piped up, and Indigo was pretty sure that she must be Cassandra Charleston. Voodoo had given her a detailed rundown on who everybody was, how they fit into the group, and some of what had brought them here.

"Polyphagia," a blonde piped up.

"What?" Indigo asked, not sure what that word meant.

"Oh, it's the medical term for someone who has a huge appetite," the blonde, who could only be Whitney Daley, said as she blushed.

"You'll get used to her blurting out things when she's nervous," Blade piped up, and Indigo got the feeling he was letting her know she wasn't the only one scared about this meeting. Which made sense given the man had super hearing and had likely heard every single word of her conversation with Voodoo before leaving his room.

"Why would she be nervous?" Indigo asked. It was weird meeting the person responsible for everything that had been done to her, but she wasn't stupid, she understood Whitney hadn't been given a choice, and she didn't hold it against the younger woman.

"Because it's my fault," Whitney said softly, recrimination heavy in her tone.

"How?" Indigo asked as Voodoo carried her over to the table and sat down, settling her on his lap even though there were plenty of empty chairs left. Not that she was complaining, she definitely needed his support right now. She was challenging herself, but now that she was there, it wasn't quite as hard as she'd been expecting to face Voodoo's family.

"Because I created the drug," Whitney replied like it was obvious.

"From what Voodoo told me, you created *a* drug, but not *this* drug," Indigo corrected gently. Maybe it helped to know she wasn't the only one nervous about this meeting, but she also didn't want Whitney to blame herself for something she'd been forced to do as a ten-year-old child.

"Still, I was—"

"Was just as much a victim of Dr. Gardner as the rest of us," Indigo finished for her.

For a moment, Whitney just stared, her blue eyes full of confusion, then relief, and finally joy. "Thank you. For accepting me. I offered to leave if you weren't okay with me being here, even though Blade about had a heart attack when I suggested it."

"Oh, I can leave if you want me to," Indigo quickly offered. She was the newest one there, which made her the lowest person on the totem pole. If anyone had to go it was her.

"You're not going anywhere," Voodoo growled in her ear, his arms tightening possessively around her.

"No one is going anywhere," Steel said firmly, like he was refereeing a childish argument.

"Especially not when we already made all this food," Rose piped up.

"And not when Dragon didn't try to kill Indigo or advocate for her death upon meeting her," Cassandra piped up, grinning and poking the huge man with the unusual violet eyes, which he rolled even as he reached out and grabbed her arm, tugging her off-balance so she stumbled and landed up against his broad chest.

"You should definitely feel special about that one," Rose teased Dragon, who shot her an eye roll as well.

"No need to want her dead, she's one of us," Dragon said, looking over to her, and she understood what he was telling her. She wasn't just one of them because she'd also been experimented on and survived, she was one of them because of Voodoo, and that made her family.

Thinking about the crazed scientist put a dampener on her improving mood. So far, there had been no word on the man. According to Voodoo, he'd shot the doctor, but then things had gotten derailed when someone shot at him, then she was held hostage, and almost died. For the last several days, Delta Team had been trying to get a location on him, but so far had been unsuccessful. Voodoo had tagged the boat with a tracker, but by the time Prey had sent a team to locate it, they'd found it abandoned.

"Has anything changed?" she asked as the others began to bring food over to the table. "Do we know where he is?" While she wanted to build a new life, one where she belonged, where she could be happy, safe, and free, one where she could be loved and love in return, that could never really happen so long as Dr. Gardner was out there.

As long as he was out there, none of them could ever truly be free.

"Nothing yet," Thunder told her as he took the seat beside the one she shared with Voodoo.

"But we'll get him," Lion added with a confidence she wished she could emulate.

"Nothing less is an option," Voodoo said as he nuzzled her neck, touching soft kisses there that soothed her a little. "I won't allow anyone to hurt you ever again. You deserve to be free, to have a chance at living a real life."

Looking around at the people at the table, Indigo knew that it was all of them who deserved the freedom they sought. "We all do," she said softly.

There had to be a way to figure out where Dr. Gardner was hiding and finally destroy him and everything he'd built. It was the only way for all of them to move on, and she couldn't think of a group of people who had earned their freedom more than these men and women.

Maybe she had even earned hers, too.

CHAPTER
Twenty-Two

"Busy?" Voodoo asked as he strolled into the living room, where Indigo was curled up in a chair, reading a book.

"Umm, no, not really," she replied, glancing up. "Working on my Welsh before we do our next lesson."

When their eyes met, there was that same weird mix of warmth that seemed to seep into his heart, and heat that flooded a little further south. He didn't just want to claim every inch of her delectable body, he wanted to claim her heart as well. Wanted all of her, her heart, her body, her trust, her love, he didn't care if it was being greedy, the more time he spent with Indigo, the deeper that craving ran.

But they wouldn't take another step toward a physical relationship until she was ready.

And by ready, he meant giving him express permission, with her words, explicitly, that she wanted him as badly as he wanted her.

Until then, he was more than content to share kisses, hold her in his arms as they slept in his bed, get to know her better, spend his days with her, and help her with her physical therapy, basically soaking up every second with her he could get.

"Perfect," he said as he crossed the room, ready to scoop her into his arms.

"I can walk," Indigo protested before he could pick her up.

"Your leg is still healing," he reminded her. Yes, she was healing faster than a normal person would, faster even than he could have hoped for, but that didn't mean it wasn't still two weeks since she'd almost died.

"Only in your mind," she said as she gifted him one of her soft smiles. "In reality, I've been able to walk on it for a couple of days now. You're just being overprotective."

"Better get used to that, because I don't see it changing any time soon."

The warning made her giggle, and she reached for him, grasping his shoulders so she could pull him down and kiss him. "I don't mind. It's kind of sweet, makes me feel like I matter."

"You do matter." More than he'd thought a person he'd known for less than a month could matter to him. Forming attachments had never been easy for him. How could it when his own parents didn't love him? Trusting his team had taken time, and he wasn't sure that without being locked in a cage together for three years, forced to rely only on one another, it ever would have developed to the depths of trust that now bound them together.

There had never been anyone else he'd allowed into that inner circle. Even Rose, Cassandra, and Whitney weren't quite in that circle. They were close, and he loved them like little sisters, trusted them to love his teammates, the men he considered his brothers, and trusted them to be part of bringing down Dr. Gardner.

"I'm starting to believe that." She said the words as though they surprised her, but it was also clear that she liked them. A lot.

"If you're going to walk, you go slow, careful, and you tell me if you need a break," he listed his conditions, and she nodded her acceptance. Really, he'd prefer to carry her, but he also knew that Indigo was tough, strong, and determined. She'd survived a lot on her own, and he couldn't attempt to strip her of her independence. Especially since that same determination was one of the things that had attracted him to her in the first place.

Together they made their way through the mansion's winding passageways, up three flights of stairs to the top floor. This was where he and his teammates had their bedrooms, and some other personal spaces. With so many rooms and only the six of them, now ten of them, living there, there was plenty of space for them to spread out, having some rooms to themselves and others to share.

Leading her to one in particular, he paused before opening the closed door.

"Close your eyes," he ordered, and while Indigo arched her brows at him, she complied, and he took her hands.

The ease with which she curled her fingers around his filled him with more joy than he thought he could feel over something so small. Only he knew it wasn't really a small thing. Indigo wasn't just holding his hand, she was offering him her trust, and he knew that was a huge thing for her.

Opening the door, he guided her through it, then closed it behind them. Then he moved so he was at her back, guiding her to lean against his chest. Only then did he tell her she could open her eyes, realizing he was anxiously awaiting her reaction. It had taken a little while to get this set up, and he was pretty sure that Indigo was going to love it, but she wasn't the only one opening herself up to new possibilities, he was, too.

All his life, he'd worked to earn people's love and respect and never gotten it from the two people he previously wanted it from the most.

Only he no longer cared about those two people.

His parents were dead to him, even if they wouldn't care even if they knew. Now all he cared about was making this woman happy.

Her gasp told him she'd opened her eyes, but was it a shocked gasp, a happy one, or a disappointed one? Voodoo had no idea.

Unfortunately, Indigo didn't say anything else. Just stood there, her body going stiff in his arms, and the familiar sinking feeling in his gut returned. He'd tried to do something special for her, prove to her that she was never going to regret putting her trust in him, that he was worthy of her trust, but once again he'd fallen short.

Letting his arms drop, he was about to take a step back, apologize for dropping the ball, and promise her he'd do better next time, when her hands flew up to grip his forearms with a strength that shouldn't have surprised him but did.

"Voodoo," she whispered, with so much emotion in that one word, and when she wriggled in his hold to turn so she was facing him, he could see her cheeks were wet with tears.

Crying was the last thing he'd wanted to make her do.

Smiling had been what he was going for. Laughter. Anything that indicated she knew he was trying to show her how much she meant to him, and how he wanted to spend the rest of his life trying to make it up to her for all the suffering she'd endured.

"I thought this—"

"Was the most amazing, sweet, thoughtful, caring, considerate, loving thing anyone has ever done for me," she gushed, grinning so wide that he was surprised it wasn't hurting her cheeks. Maybe it was, and she just hadn't noticed.

"Amazing? Thoughtful? Loving?" he echoed. All of those things were exactly what he'd been feeling when he planned this, what he'd hoped to show her, but he'd been so certain he'd failed.

"Of course. No one had *ever* done anything like this for me. It's beautiful, magical, and you remembered what I told you, about the bubbles." Her eyes still shimmered with unshed tears, but now he was beginning to understand they weren't sad tears, they were happy ones.

"I remember every single thing you say to me, honey," he told her, and it was completely true. No one had ever cared enough about Indigo to listen to her, until now anyway.

"How did you manage all of this?" Remaining in his arms, she tilted her head back to stare in wonder at the thousands of bubbles filling the room.

"With a little help from the guys. We installed bubble machines in all four corners of the room, and on the floor and ceiling, built them in so you can't see them. There's a switch by the light switch to turn them on. I thought this could be your special space. You can furnish it however you want, you just tell me, and I'll get you whatever you want, anything."

"This is the absolute nicest thing anyone has ever done for me, and there isn't even a close runner-up." Turning back to face him, she lifted her hands and curled them around the back of his neck, guiding his face down to hers so she could press her lips to his. "Thank you, Voodoo. For saving my life and not leaving me behind. For listening to me, for caring, and bringing me to your home. For sharing your family with me, for making me feel like I matter for the first time ever."

Between her words, she dotted kisses to his mouth, and he could feel the heat simmering between them begin to boil over.

"I love you, Voodoo, I don't care if it's too soon, or if you don't feel it back yet. I'm falling in love with you, and I want you to know."

A growl ripped from his throat before he even realized it. Grabbing her hips, he lifted her and ground her center against the bulge in his pants. "Not falling, already fallen."

The smile she gave him was everything. "Make love to me, Voodoo."

And just like that, the thin leash he had on his control snapped.

～

February 14th
3:21 P.M.

If she was expecting any hesitation, Indigo didn't get any.

Voodoo's grip on her hips tightened, and he abruptly spun around and headed for the door.

"No, wait!" she cried out, wrapping her legs around his waist as she grabbed his shoulders to steady herself.

"What?" For a second, panic flittered through his gaze, and she could all but feel the recrimination flooding through him and out into the room. Like he thought he had somehow misread her blatantly clear request, although how he could have done that she had no idea, she'd asked for exactly what she wanted.

"In here," she said, her hands kneading his shoulders, not wanting any negative emotion, even in passing, into this special room Voodoo had created for her.

Glancing over her shoulder, she saw his gaze roam the room. "There's no bed."

"Don't care." As if a bed could make this any more special than being here with bubbles floating through the air, a constant—and magically beautiful—reminder of the most thoughtful and loving thing anyone had ever done for her.

There was nowhere else in the world she would rather take this step with Voodoo than in this amazing little cozy cocoon he'd created for her.

"You're injured," he reminded her, even though she could feel the thick bulge in his pants, pressed oh so close and yet not quite close enough to where she ached for him, and knew he wanted this as badly as she did. Only protective instincts wouldn't let him just jump all in without ensuring she was okay.

"I'm eighty to ninety percent healed," she corrected. A miracle, sure. Part her own body's enhanced ability to heal, part Voodoo's ability to heal others, but the truth was, it might only be a couple of weeks since she'd almost died, but she was almost completely back to normal.

"I want this to be perfect for you. From here on out, I want everything to be perfect for you."

His admission was so sweet that tears once again filled her eyes. Resting her forehead against his, she gave him the truth and prayed he believed her. "Voodoo, *this* is perfect, *you* are perfect. But perfect isn't what I need. You've already given me everything I need with your support, your dedication, your thoughtfulness, and your care. You brought me here, you've shared your family with me, you haven't held back anything I've asked for and given me things I didn't even know I needed. Don't you get it? All I need is you."

"You have me," he vowed, and then his lips crashed against hers and he was backing her up until she was caught between the wall and his huge body.

Safe.

That's exactly how she felt when she was caged in Voodoo's embrace like this.

It seemed like his mouth never stopped worshiping hers as he stripped her of her clothes, only Indigo knew he must have broken away briefly to get her T-shirt—which was really one of his—over her head. The clothes were discarded somewhere along the way, and it was only when Voodoo began to trail a line of kisses down the column of her neck that she realized he was now naked too.

And immediately, insecurity settled in. Her body was a literal roadmap of evidence for the study of her enhanced ability. Older scars layered with newer scars, and the freshly healed wounds that had been open and infected when Voodoo and his team found her.

She wasn't a beautiful woman.

Indigo knew Voodoo had seen her scars. She'd been mostly naked when he found her in the lab and completely naked when he found her in the forest. But it was one thing to see her when she was basically his patient, and quite another when she was supposed to be his lover.

A quick burst of pain stole her attention, and even though it faded almost immediately, she saw the specks of blood left behind from where Voodoo had just sunk his teeth into her chest, between her collarbone and her breast.

"Do I have your attention now?" he demanded, then his tongue began to lap at the small drops of blood.

All Indigo could do was stare and nod.

"What happened?"

As much as she didn't want to answer, didn't want to draw attention to the fact that he was gorgeous and she looked like a piece of mangled trash, Indigo found part of her did want to admit it. Because Voodoo would make it better somehow. He might not be able to take away her scars, make her skin clear and smooth again, but she believed he could soothe away her mental and psychological scars.

Chancing a glance at his face, she quickly looked away, afraid to see the truth in his eyes if it wasn't what she was hoping for. "Do you think I'm ugly?" she whispered the question she dreaded hearing the answer to.

A loud growl, like one that would come from a wounded animal, filled the room, making all the bubbles around them pop. Then his mouth was on her again, kissing her until she was breathless.

Without stopping, those same lips began to roam her body. Licking, sucking, and nipping their way across scars and fresher wounds. Each time they caressed her damaged skin, a little of her insecurity faded away.

"You are without a doubt the most gorgeously stunning creature I have ever had the pleasure of laying eyes on," Voodoo growled against her skin. "Every single one of these scars marks you as a warrior. *My* warrior. *Mine.*"

When his lips moved to capture her ruined nipples, seared by the burning man and his cigarette, she almost pushed him away. There was no way she would have feeling left in them, and she didn't want to be reminded of that particular failure when she was starting to feel better about her body.

"Voodoo, no," she murmured. "I can't ... the burns ... there's no sensation left there."

With impossible gentleness, he ignored her as his head dipped and his lips closed around her now useless nipple, sucking it into his mouth. His tongue lapped at her pebbled bud, and miracle of miracles, she could actually feel it.

It didn't feel normal, not how she expected it was supposed to, although she'd never had a man lavish this much attention on her body, but she could feel it, dull as it was, and that was a win as far as she was concerned.

Moving on to her other nipple, Voodoo lavished the same attention on her other breast, and then he began to kiss his way down her stomach. It wasn't until he hiked her up so her knees landed on his shoulders, her legs hanging down his back, that she realized what he was going to do.

The problem was, she'd been burned down there, too.

Not on the most important part, her bud and her entrance had been left alone, although she suspected, given enough time, the burning man might have moved on to burning her there too, but he'd worked his way around the area, and she wasn't expecting the same miracle down there as she'd just gotten for her breasts.

"Don't," she whispered frantically, pushing at his head.

But Voodoo ignored her.

Leaned in and with the same gentleness, captured her bundle of nerves between his lips, and flicked gently against it with the tip of his tongue. She could feel that, but it was only when he shifted slightly so his tongue could glide along every inch of her that she realized she could feel it all. It was distant, almost unnoticeable if she wasn't paying such close attention, but she felt it, each stroke of his tongue, each suck of his mouth, and soon she was lost in the building sensations.

Even though she was expecting it, the orgasm caught her by surprise.

Maybe it was the intensity of it. She'd had orgasms before, but her ex-husband was always annoyed about it, said she was trying to take all the attention, and that when she came, he never did as hard as he liked. She'd come to hold herself back, fight against her pleasure, her body's natural release.

Voodoo didn't let her do that, though.

He continued his delicious assault of her most intimate area, licking, nipping, sucking, not letting up until he'd dragged out every last drop of pleasure from her he could get.

Not even then did he stop.

He merely let her back slide down the wall until he had her lined up with the thick erection that seemed to be straining to get closer to her. In one smooth thrust, he was buried deep inside her. Indigo cried out at the intrusion, the quick sting as her body stretched to accommodate his more than impressive size.

That sting quickly morphed into pleasure, and she clung to Voodoo's shoulders as he began to thrust into her, hard and fast, not giving her time to think.

All she could do was feel.

Once again, his lips found hers, and he kissed her like she was the center of his entire universe. The second orgasm hit more powerfully than the first, exploding inside her with the same shimmery beauty that the bubbles floating all around her possessed.

"Happy Valentine's Day," Voodoo murmured as he rested his forehead against hers.

"Happy Valentine's Day," she whispered back. "Thank you for ... all of this, for everything."

For the first time in her life, she wasn't all alone. She had Voodoo, she had Delta Team, she had a family, connections, a place to belong, people who wanted to help her, not hurt her. She literally had everything her heart had ever desired, all her dreams had come true, and they were even better than she could have hoped for.

February 19th
5:50 A.M.

"If we keep doing this without protection, we're going to wind up with a little baby Voodoo," Indigo said, her words turning into a moan as he grabbed her hips and lifted them off his bed to change the angle as he thrust into her hard and fast.

She was right about that, and yet Voodoo didn't have it in him to care.

Wasn't like he'd been sitting around desperate to have kids, but then again, he'd never thought he'd be able to open himself up to someone the way he had with Indigo, which meant he'd sort of thought becoming a dad was off the table.

Indigo made opening up easy. Natural. And one day, he'd love to have a half-Indy half-Voodoo little one running around.

"Why do I get the feeling you don't mind that?" she asked, watching him through heavy-lidded eyes, her breathing rough, cheeks flushed, hair mussed, stunning in the middle of sex.

"I don't if you don't. But if you're not ready, we can start using condoms, or we can get you some birth control, whatever you want, honey." That was absolutely true, just because for the first time he was actually excited about the idea of welcoming a child into the world didn't mean he needed to do it this second. He could wait until Indigo was ready, and if she didn't want kids, he'd make his peace with that, too.

All he wanted was her happiness.

"I'm ... not as against the idea as I thought I would be," Indigo admitted. "Because I wouldn't be doing it alone."

"Never alone," he agreed, keeping his pace as he thrust deep, hitting a different spot inside her at this angle and making her moan all over again as her fingers clawed at the bedsheets.

Taking her that first time on Valentine's Day in the bubble room he'd created for her without using protection hadn't been a conscious decision. He hadn't walked in there expecting things to take the turn they had, and once she told him she was ready to make love, his control had snapped, and that had been all he could think about.

Their gazes locked as he felt her internal muscles begin to quiver around him, telling him she was seconds away from coming. There was no way he was riding his release without her, so he held back his own pleasure and focused on his girl's. Maintaining his hold on her hips with one hand, his other reached to touch her where their bodies were joined, taking her bundle of nerves between his thumb and fore-finger, rolling it, and then tweaking it, and sending her flying over the edge.

Her screams filled the room as she came hard, clenching around him and setting off his own orgasm, which tore through him like a tornado, leaving no parts of his body, his mind, or his soul untouched.

After riding out that high for as long as he could, Voodoo collapsed down against her, pinning her to the bed, but making sure his much larger body didn't crush hers. She gave a contented sigh and nuzzled her face against his neck, her lips dropping soft kisses to his skin, and he drank them in, relishing every one of them.

Over the last couple of weeks, his girl had changed a lot. Her confi-dence grew as she began to accept her place there, and she was forging bonds with all of his teammates and their partners. She smiled more often, laughed, contributed to conversations when they were all together, and helped cook meals now that she was up and about.

More than that, she was beginning to assimilate into the Prey family as a whole. Youngest sibling Dove was beginning to spend more time with her husband, helping run Prey Security's K9 unit, making her job as chief financial officer harder for her to do. With Indigo's background in accounting, Eagle had reached out and asked if she would be interested in doing some more training and then helping to take over some of Dove's workload.

She'd burst into tears when he asked her, but since he was getting much better at telling when she was crying sad tears or happy tears, he'd known immediately that they were the good kind. Maybe he was starting to work on his own insecurities as well. Not be constantly on guard against failure.

So now she'd been spending a couple of hours each day studying, and he loved the spark of joy and excitement that it put in her eyes. Everything was going better than he could have hoped for in their budding relationship.

Almost.

Dr. Gardner was still out there, wounded or dead, but until they had a body, they would have to assume alive. So long as the man lived, there was no way any of them could completely move on.

Would the scientist's death mean they suddenly started living normal lives?

No.

They were still different, still battled anger, even if for most of them that had diluted now they'd found love, but it still existed, and they still had enhanced skills that meant they needed to be careful, to protect themselves.

So logistically speaking, nothing would change. All of them wanted to stay there, where they felt safe, but knowing that they'd gotten their revenge, that the man who had played God with their lives without telling them the truth about his plans was no longer living would give them peace of mind. It would free them, leaving them to focus on the future instead of the past. Revenge might not be as all-consuming as it had been a few months ago when they started on this plan, but he still burned with a need to punish Dr. Gardner for what the man had done to Indigo. That drove him now more than wanting to punish the scientist for his own pain and suffering.

"Ready for breakfast?" he asked. He and his team should already be up and have already started on a morning training session, but things had changed, and even though they still worked out every day, four of them now started their day with sex rather than running and weights.

"Mmhmm," Indigo said with a nod. "I like my mornings just like this."

As he climbed off her and took her hand, tugging her up with him, he didn't have to ask to know why. He knew how her days had started as a child, no breakfast, dirty clothes yanked on to cover her bruised body, and a long walk to school regardless of the weather. He knew how her days had started when she was married, too. Up early to put herself together with full makeup and hair done, the house scrubbed top to bottom, and a full breakfast she wasn't allowed to eat laid out on the table.

Now her days started however the hell she wanted them to, but food and pampering were always part of it.

When Indigo reached for one of his T-shirts and pulled it on, Voodoo couldn't help but feel a swell of pride and possessiveness. Something about seeing your girl dressed in your clothes was a real turn on. If he couldn't keep her naked twenty-four-seven, and really, he didn't want to with so many other people in the house, then this was the next best thing.

Hand in hand, they headed downstairs, and he wasn't surprised when he heard voices coming from the kitchen. They weren't the only couple in the house to start their day working up an appetite, nor were they the only ones usually up early. Old habits die hard, and even if the workout wasn't the first thing they did each morning, he and his teammates still woke early. They just stayed in bed a little longer.

"Ugh, I can't wait for summer to come back," Rose's voice filtered through from the kitchen as they approached.

"Me too," Cassandra quickly agreed. "It's gorgeous out here in the summer, and this year I'm going to go swimming in the river."

"It's been a long time since I've enjoyed the sun," Whitney added, a little hesitantly. While she was settling in, accepting that they accepted her, they all knew she was still struggling with the knowledge that even though it wasn't what she'd intended, she was responsible for the beginnings of the drug that had changed all their lives.

"You'll get as much sun as you want," Blade growled in response.

Whitney giggled. "Too bad we don't get year-round sunshine out here."

Beside him, Indigo suddenly stiffened, her entire body going tense, and since he wasn't expecting it, anxiety hit him hard and fast.

"What's wrong?" he demanded, obviously louder than he'd intended because the hall suddenly filled with people, all attention focused on Indigo, who had gone pale.

"I remembered something ... the comment about sunshine ... I'm sorry, I didn't think of it before ..." she stammered.

"It's okay, honey," he soothed, clasping her shoulders and kneading gently. "What did you remember?"

"The first time he came to visit the lab after I was taken there," she explained. "Dr. Gardner was there for hours, days maybe, it was hard to tell time without windows. He directed everything that was done to me. I remember he was surprised but excited that I wasn't dead yet. Then, when he was ready to leave, I saw a glimpse of sunshine and tried to look behind him to the doors to see it. He noticed and laughed. Told me to enjoy my time indoors while he was going home to enjoy year-round island sunshine. I know it's not a huge amount to go on, but Dr. Gardner lives on some island where it's almost always sunny."

Thunder is unprepared for what he finds when he and his team raid Dr. Gardner's house in the fifth book in the action packed and emotionally charged Prey Security: Delta Team series!

Obsessive Revenge (Prey Security: Delta Team #5)

Also by Jane Blythe

Detective Parker Bell Series

A SECRET TO THE GRAVE
WINTER WONDERLAND
DEAD OR ALIVE
LITTLE GIRL LOST
FORGOTTEN

Count to Ten Series

ONE
TWO
THREE
FOUR
FIVE
SIX
BURNING SECRETS
SEVEN
EIGHT
NINE
TEN

Broken Gems Series

CRACKED SAPPHIRE

CRUSHED RUBY

FRACTURED DIAMOND

SHATTERED AMETHYST

SPLINTERED EMERALD

SALVAGING MARIGOLD

River's End Rescues Series

SOME SAVIORS CAN BREAK YOU

SOME REGRETS ARE FOREVER

SOME FEARS CAN CONTROL YOU

SOME LIES WILL HAUNT YOU

SOME QUESTIONS HAVE NO ANSWERS

SOME TRUTH CAN BE DISTORTED

SOME TRUST CAN BE REBUILT

SOME MISTAKES ARE UNFORGIVABLE

Candella Sisters' Heroes Series

LITTLE DOLLS

LITTLE HEARTS

LITTLE BALLERINA

Storybook Murders Series

NURSERY RHYME KILLER

FAIRYTALE KILLER

FABLE KILLER

Saving SEALs Series

SAVING RYDER
SAVING ERIC
SAVING OWEN
SAVING LOGAN
SAVING GRAYSON
SAVING CHARLIE

Prey Security Series

PROTECTING EAGLE
PROTECTING RAVEN
PROTECTING FALCON
PROTECTING SPARROW
PROTECTING HAWK
PROTECTING DOVE

Prey Security: Alpha Team Series

DEADLY RISK
LETHAL RISK
EXTREME RISK
FATAL RISK
COVERT RISK
SAVAGE RISK

Prey Security: Artemis Team Series

IVORY'S FIGHT
PEARL'S FIGHT
LACEY'S FIGHT
OPAL'S FIGHT

Prey Security: Bravo Team Series

VICIOUS SCARS
RUTHLESS SCARS
BRUTAL SCARS
CRUEL SCARS
BURIED SCARS
WICKED SCARS

Prey Security: Athena Team Series

FIGHTING FOR SCARLETT
FIGHTING FOR LUCY
FIGHTING FOR CASSIDY
FIGHTING FOR ELLA

Prey Security: Charlie Team Series

DECEPTIVE LIES
SHADOWED LIES
TACTICAL LIES
VENGEFUL LIES
CORRUPTED LIES
TRAITOROUS LIES

Prey Security: Cyber Team Series

RESCUING NATHANIEL

RESCUING TOBIAS

RESCUING MICAH

RESCUING JOSIAH

Prey Security: Delta Team Series

PERFECT REVENGE

FATEFUL REVENGE

SINFUL REVENGE

CUNNING REVENGE

OBSESSIVE REVENGE

Prey Security: Undercover Team Series

DEFENDING NATHAN

Christmas Romantic Suspense Series

THE DIAMOND STAR

CHRISTMAS HOSTAGE

CHRISTMAS CAPTIVE

CHRISTMAS VICTIM

YULETIDE PROTECTOR

YULETIDE GUARD

YULETIDE HERO

HOLIDAY GRIEF

HOLIDAY LOSS

HOLIDAY SORROW

Conquering Fear Series (Co-written with Amanda Siegrist)

DROWNING IN YOU
OUT OF THE DARKNESS
CLOSING IN

About the Author

USA Today bestselling author Jane Blythe writes action-packed romantic suspense and military romance featuring protective heroes and heroines who are survivors. One of Jane's most popular series includes Prey Security, part of Susan Stoker's OPERATION ALPHA world! Writing in that world alongside authors such as Janie Crouch and Riley Edwards has been a blast, and she looks forward to bringing more books to this genre, both within and outside of Stoker's world. When Jane isn't binge-reading she's counting down to Christmas and adding to her 200+ teddy bear collection!

To connect and keep up to date please visit any of the following